Beautiful Masterpiece

Book one in the Thin Red Lines series

GEN RYAN

HOT TREE
PUBLISHING

Beautiful Masterpiece © 2016 by Gen Ryan

Beautiful Masterpiece is a work of fiction. All names, characters, events and places found therein are either from the author's imagination or used fictitiously. Any similarity to persons alive or dead, actual events, locations, or organizations is entirely coincidental and not intended by the author.

For information, contact the publisher, Hot Tree Publishing.
www.hottreepublishing.com

Editing: Hot Tree Editing
Formatting: RMGraphX
Cover Designer: Claire Smith
ISBN-10: 1-925448-05-3
ISBN-13: 978-1-925448-05-4

10 9 8 7 6 5 4 3 2

WARNING:

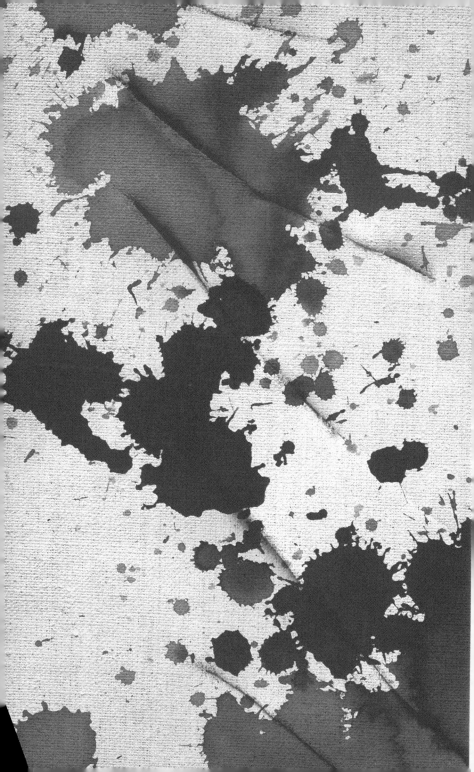

Part I: The Battle of Love

"We must not fear daylight just because it almost always illuminates a miserable world."

-RENE MAGRITTE

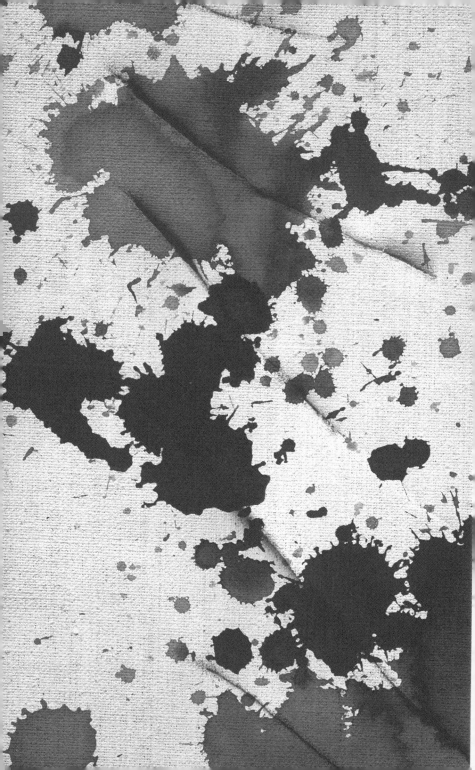

Chapter One

MADISON

My doll was gone. I cried silently as I sang "Songbird" by Fleetwood Mac, trying to comfort myself as I cowered in the corner. Mommy had told me to let Dolly go—that she was gone forever—but I couldn't. I knew where she was. I had seen Daddy take her with him into the basement. She had hung from his hand like a dead thing, useless and broken. Dolly was downstairs in his room waiting for me to save her. She was beautiful and delicate, and her porcelain skin looked just like Mommy's. What I liked best about her were her eyes. Dolly's eyes were the same bright blue as the boy's next door. Her pink cheeks and ruby-red smile made me happy, even if for a moment, and she reminded me of that boy, which made me feel safe and loved.

I had to be brave. I had to save her. I moved from the corner, my legs shaking wearily underneath me. I opened the basement door; it was heavy in my little hands. I shut it behind me and tiptoed down the stairs, quietly, like a mouse. I held my breath and didn't make a sound. Then I *saw her. Not Dolly, but a little girl not much bigger than me. Her wrists were tied with ropes from the ceiling, and blood pooled from her tiny frame onto the concrete floor. Oh, God, what had my daddy done to her? My next thought was of Dolly. I looked around madly.* Please let her be okay, I thought. *I saw Dolly sitting on the bench across the way, and I jumped over the puddles of blood, holding my breath and fighting back the vomit. The smell.... Oh, it smelled so bad. I made it safely to the other side, and swept Dolly into my arms. She didn't look the same. I touched her poor, battered face.*

I heard Daddy's feet and Mommy's petrified voice calling frantically for me. Furniture came crashing to the ground above me. Shutting my eyes briefly, I then ran upstairs with Dolly in my hands. Be quiet like a mouse. Be quiet like a mouse, *I chanted to myself as I tiptoed up the staircase and away from the bleeding body of the little girl. I opened the basement door and peered into the house. I had made it. My heart thumped loudly in my little chest. My daddy turned the corner, and his eyes filled with murderous rage. Quivering in fear, I held Dolly close. He wouldn't take her again. I wouldn't let him. Daddy had Mommy by the hair and blood was trickling from her mouth. He dragged us both up the stairs and into my room. Our bodies hit each step and the pain threatened to break me.*

He dropped us in the middle of the room, and I scurried into the corner—my corner, where I often sat and hid. He had his knife in his hand, and I saw him cut into Mommy, inch by inch, flesh wound by flesh wound. He made me sit and watch, but when he unbuttoned his pants, I shut my eyes tightly. I opened my eyes when I heard her whisper my name. Aimee. We stared at each other, and her eyes were filled with such love. Daddy put his hands around Mommy's neck and squeezed. She didn't fight him. She just looked at me as tears streamed down her face. I smiled at her, waving my small hand. She smiled one last time before she drifted off to sleep, eyes still open. He rolled off her, and stormed down the stairs and out the front door. I crawled to her.

My small voice croaked as I called out, "Mommy... Mommy... wake up...."

She was motionless on my sunflower-covered double bed, and blood flowed from her mouth like a leaky faucet. Her once dancing, smiling eyes were now wide, emotionless, and empty. Sometimes this happened when daddy hit her, but I could always wake her up. Today seemed different. I was so scared.

"Mommy! Wake up, Mommy!" I screamed over and over again. Grabbing her arm, I tried to drag her to her feet, but she just lay there. Why wouldn't she get up?

I heard the click of the front door and the familiar creak of the stairs, and I knew Daddy was coming back. I clutched Dolly and ran to the closet. I had to hide, just like Mommy told me to do when he got into his moods. "He loves you, Aimee," she'd say as she gently tucked me into bed, "but Daddy is really sick." She'd read me a story, sing "Songbird," and kiss me good night, trying to give me some normalcy. But no matter what she said, I knew he didn't love me. He only loved Mommy and those girls in the basement.

It was all my fault Mommy wouldn't wake up. It was all my fault. It was all my fault. It was all my fault. I held my legs, rocked back and forth, and hummed quietly to myself.

I heard Daddy open the door. The familiar sound caused me to scurry further into the closet.

My bedroom door crashed open.

I saw through the slats of the closet door that he was trying to get Mommy up. She lay there, unresponsive to his touch. He whirled toward the closet.

"You little shit! Since the day you were born, you took your mother away from me. She was willing to do anything to protect you. Now, you made me kill her! She's dead, Aimee, and it's all your fault," he yelled as he stormed toward the closet and began unbuttoning his pants.

"You had to go into the basement. Now I'll show you what I did to all those girls."

I whimpered, trying to stifle my sobs. I held my doll tighter, wishing she could save me and make me disappear. His shadow appeared in front of the closet and I closed my eyes tightly, tears pouring down my brown cheeks. Daddy swung open the doors and grabbed me, dragging me to the middle of the room. I fought him, and when he lay me on the ground and got on top of me, I tried to push him off, but it didn't work. I was too small, and he was too big.

"Mommy, wake up. Please, wake up," I cried. Her hand lay limply off the bed. I reached out and grabbed it, holding it tightly. It felt heavy, cold, and lifeless in my own.

As Daddy moaned and finished unbuttoning his pants, I knew there was no one there to save me.

I woke up sweating like crazy and feeling sick to my stomach. The darkness danced around my room like the devil himself. Immediately, I turned on the light. I hated the dark. I never knew what was lurking there; I couldn't see what was going on, and my imagination always got the better of me.

I swung my legs over the side of my bed and headed toward the bathroom. I turned on every light as I made my way.

When I made it to the bathroom, I looked at the clock: 4:20 in the morning. Typical. Wide awake, I decided to get dressed and go for a run. At that point, there was no going back to sleep. I quickly stepped on the scale to check my weight. I was obsessed. In order to get into the FBI, I had to lose those last four pounds. I constantly watched what I put in my mouth. I was two steps away from measuring and weighing my bowel movements. I'd been overweight my whole life. My dream, though, was to catch the bad guys, and that meant passing the FBI PT test and making weight. 150 lit up across the screen. Triumphantly, I put on my bright pink Reebok running shorts, my "Fat Bottomed Girls" T-shirt and my running shoes. I was going to kick ass on my run.

Wrapping up my doctorate in Forensic Psychology with straight As came easily to me. My dissertation was done, and my application was already in for the FBI. I loved being smart, but I also wanted to fight crime and catch criminals. It sounded clichéd, but after what I had endured in the first seven years of my life, I felt like I owed the world—and myself. I needed to erase what my father had done.

Father. I had no idea why I still called him that. Yes, I thought about him. I thought about what he had done to my mom and what he had almost done to me. If it hadn't been for the little blue-eyed boy next door who had called the police, it would have ended a lot differently. Scott Reynolds had been my savior.

Chapter Two

LIAM

Ugh. The aftertaste of alcohol still lingered in my mouth. I rolled over and felt the dampness of the sheets. Great, I'd thrown up again. I heard a moan from beside me, and I pried open my eyes to see which whore had come home with me this time. I caught the outline of her breasts under the sheet, and her perky pink nipples peered through.

I quietly rolled out of bed and pulled on my shorts. I laced up my sneakers and headed out the door. A good run always cleared my head. I vowed again to quit drinking, but it didn't matter. I vowed to stop drinking daily. All the fucked-up things I'd seen made that vow impossible to keep.

As my feet hit the pavement, I instantly felt the headache and queasy stomach disappear. I began to feel like me again. I heard the clamor of feet behind me, and I tried to pick up speed. The agent in me kicked in.

I was being fucking followed. Goddammit! I should have brought my weapon. I was running at a good clip, sprinting even. The person was gaining on me, though. Instinctively, I waited for them to get close before I turned around and went for their throat.

"What the hell, dude?"

I stared into two big brown eyes, fit into a beautiful, dark face more mocha than my favorite drink: Jack Daniels. Her face swam before me, and I tried to focus. Were there two of her? Shit, I really needed to stop drinking.

"I thought you were fucking following me," I said, letting go of her. "Didn't anyone ever teach you not to try and race someone at 4:00 a.m.?"

Her brown skin couldn't hide the blush.

"I was just trying to beat you."

"Beat me? Seriously?" I replied, crossing my arms and smirking at her. Beautiful and funny? This girl had my attention.

"Yeah. I've seen you out here running, and I've tried to match your pace, but you're *really* good. I've got a PT test in two weeks, and I really need to step up my game." She shifted awkwardly, grabbing and twirling a stray curl nervously between her fingers, and I grinned. She was edgy. I loved edgy. All she needed was a nice, playful smack on her ass. I bet that would calm her down. My dick twitched in agreement against my running shorts.

"Well, next time, maybe give a guy a heads-up, okay? Otherwise, I'm likely to knock the hell out of you."

She looked hurt. Fuck, I sure knew how to win them over. She ducked her head, turned quickly on her heels, and started jogging away. She had pissed me off, sure, but

I had quickly gotten over that. I didn't want her to go. I needed at least to find out her name. I jogged to catch up to her. When I was finally next to her, I watched as her breasts strained against her "Fat Bottomed Girls" T-shirt. Her nipples poked through, and I couldn't help but think about all the naughty things I could do to them. I wondered how she'd feel about nipple clamps.

"What's your test for, anyway?" I asked as I tried to run in rhythm with her.

"FBI," she replied, rather winded.

"Well, you came to the right place. Special Agent Liam James O'Leary at your service," I said, puffing out my chest and extending my hand as we both slowed. I had some leverage, a reason for her to want to see me again, and it just so happened to be the second-best thing I was good at. We'd get to the first-best thing I was good at later.

She took my hand in hers and grinned. Stopping dead in her tracks, she looked directly at me, and it was a punch to the gut. Damn, but she was beautiful. Her eyes glinted with anticipation. "Oh, my God! Really? What do you do? Was the test hard? How long have you been an agent?" Her words came out fast and all at once. She blushed, and took a quick breath. Her stray curl found its way into her fingers once again, and she twirled it. Fuck, that was hot.

I couldn't help but laugh at her eagerness. She seemed so excited. I wondered briefly if she would be as overzealous in other, more physical areas of her life. My mind switched gears, imagining her in the field, and I cringed. She was way too sweet for the FBI. If she only knew the horrors I saw every day.

She composed herself for a moment, and said, "Ah, yeah. Anyway, my name's Madison. Madison Sky Harper."

"Nice to meet you, Madison." I had to make my move. "Maybe we can chat over coffee or something? I'll have to prepare myself and ask my lawyer for permission if you intend to interrogate me."

She giggled. "Sorry, I'm just so interested in what you do—the whole process, and I've only known a few agents. Sometimes you guys are a little standoffish, and it's nice to meet someone who's giving me the time of day—well, n-n-n-not like you are giving me the time of day... b-b-b-but I don't know—just... I've never spoken to an agent outside of the interviews and people I know. Family and friends want to keep you safe, you know? Th-th-that's all, A-a-agent O'Leary," she stuttered.

"No worries, Madison. And, it's Liam." I smiled to reassure her. "I'd be happy to share the *truth* about the FBI." I winked, and she blushed again. "Let's say tomorrow, 7:00 a.m.? The red coffee shop down the street? I'd say that's too early, but it seems you're an early riser like me." I gave her a big smile, and caressed her arm subtly.

"Yeah, sure. That works." She shivered, and her cheeks turned a deeper shade of red when I touched her arm. "You mean the Chipped Cup on Broadway?" she confirmed.

"That's the one. They have the best cortado."

"Sounds great! Thanks so much, Special Agent— I mean, Liam." She smiled bashfully.

We said our good-byes and she jogged away. I watched

her for a moment, studying the way she moved. Her ass, peeking out from beneath the pink Reebok shorts, was a nice view. Her legs were forceful with each glide, and her feet hit the pavement with ease. I wanted to wrap those legs around my neck and worship her. This was going to be fun. I needed a challenge. Something different. I couldn't wait until tomorrow, to see her again.

Feeling way better, I smiled, turned away, and continued my run. It was going to be a good day.

Chapter Three

Well, that had been an eventful run. I hoped to God I hadn't made a fool of myself staring at his chest while he talked to me. It was his fault. He'd been running with his shirt off. The sweat had beaded down his chest, trailing to his deliciously toned abs. I licked my lips thinking about it, getting hotter with each thought. I could still feel his eyes on me, admiring me. Moisture built between my thighs. Dammit, I needed to settle down.

I frowned and mentally replayed the exchange, cringing when I remembered my stuttering. My social skills were that of a five-year-old. I giggled and stuttered every time I was around a halfway decent-looking guy. Ah, hell, who was I kidding? I stuttered a lot, even if I was just nervous or overwhelmed. That was probably why I spent so much time in my books. My books never let me down. Drowning myself in the lives of vampires and serial killers just worked for me. I had no friends—well, not *no* friends, but only a few and I mostly stuck to myself. I preferred it that way. The less people knew about me, the better.

I jumped in the shower. I had a 9:00 a.m. meeting with the board to review my dissertation. I had picked a simple, yellow daisy sundress and a pair of brown sparkly high-heeled sandals to make my final presentation. The yellow accentuated my darker skin, and it made me feel happy and light. Light was important to me. Darkness had surrounded me early on in life, and I craved the light. On such an important day—a day I had worked so hard for—I deserved the light.

Everything I'd done for the past eight years had gotten me to this point. My professors questioned me about my desire to join the FBI, but they knew so little about me. They didn't know who I really was; they didn't know about my past. I had fought so hard to hide it, and I intended to keep it that way. I didn't want my past to define me. When my father had gone to prison, I had been swept up into the system. I got a new name and a new family. I was given a new identity, but it would never take away my past, nor would it erase who I was deep down. My *true* self always lingered there, scratching at the surface like a bug bite, persistent and annoying as hell.

I was the daughter of a serial killer, one who was still alive and rotting away in prison. I was the daughter of a mother who had protected her husband out of what? Fear? Love? Who knew? All I knew was she had protected me as well, or had tried to, and here I was. Alive. Or at least trying to live a somewhat normal life, to make my past honorable, and to gain an ounce of respect and dignity.

My father had attempted to take those things from me all those years ago. Some days, I wished I could forget. Other days, I knew my past had made me who I was.

As I fixed my hair—which literally meant I threw some styling cream on it and let the curls roam wild—I looked at myself in the mirror. My brown eyes were way too big for my face, and my pointy ears made me look like some sort of exotic dark elf. I smiled, trying to be somewhat happier about my appearance, but I couldn't help noticing every single flaw and imperfection. My long curls were one of the only features about myself I actually liked. At least I had that going for me, right?

Yeah. It didn't matter. I looked too much like him, like my father. Where my mother had been light as porcelain, I had inherited my father's features, including his ebony-toned complexion, although I was a shade lighter. I loved my darker skin. I *didn't* love that I got my dark skin from a rapist, from a child killer. I didn't want anything that was remotely reminiscent of him. Every time I looked in the mirror, I saw him staring back at me, taunting me, haunting me. My face was a constant reminder of the repulsive things he had done. It ate away at me, little by little, whittling away at my self-esteem for years and years. And my self-esteem was already shot because of society's ideals. I was seriously curvy, and not in a pin-up model kind of way. I was twenty-seven years old, and I had only been in one real relationship. I was okay-looking, but there just wasn't anything special there. My mocha skin gave me an alluring look that intrigued some men, but I knew it was my double-D chest and my more than sufficient ass that turned heads. Whatever. I was never going to settle down and have kids—it just wasn't in the cards for me—so what did it matter?

I grabbed my briefcase and headed out the door. This was it. The meeting would determine whether I became Dr. Harper. As I rode the subway to the campus at City College, I thought again about how I would present my dissertation. The committee had almost canned the topic for fear of controversial viewpoints and an apparent lack of empirical evidence. I had forced the topic, though, going over the committee's heads and speaking to the dean of the school. The dean couldn't argue with my ten-page synopsis, nor could he argue with the evidence I had already found. I was pretty sure the dissertation team had hated me since that day, but I got to write about what I wanted.

My topic: *The gruesome truth behind serial killers' spouses: Are they victims or are they also perpetrators? A mixed-methods approach.*

Okay, so the topic could be an Alfred Hitchcock movie, but it was legit. There wasn't a lot of research on the topic, so I had to do my own. I had dug up information on families who had lived with serial killers. I had contacted and interviewed them myself. I had used a multi-method research plan to prove my theory was correct. Most families had been unaware of their family members', usually husbands', serial killer alter life. Usually, the officials had caught the serial killer, or the spouse had thought he or she was cheating and snuck after their significant other and found out the truth. Ironically, though, spouses rarely turned the serial killer in. The idea that the spouses kept their husband or wife's serial-killer activities secret for as long as they could intrigued me. Why protect a monster? Was love so blind and strong willed it superseded the morals and values of the law? Was the need for a mother to protect her children more important than the law? My dissertation had brought about many more questions than answers, but it had definitely proven the "love" these families shared seemed to mask their need to do right by the law.

As I waited for the masses of people to get off the subway, I noticed a man staring at me from the corner of the car. He wasn't much older than me. Even sitting down, he seemed gigantic, easily over six-feet tall in comparison to my scant five foot four. His shoulders were broad and muscular, and his toned arms protruded from his white T-shirt. His hair was the color of a sandy beach, and covered his brow slightly. I ventured a glance at his face, trying to make out the rest of his features, and was stunned at how strikingly handsome he was. Two bright blue eyes gleamed back at me from behind black-rimmed glasses, and he studied me as inquisitively as I had him. He took off the glasses and placed them in his pocket as he continued to look at me with an intense stare. In his hands was a book, and I tried to make out the title, but I stopped when a flood of memories battered me.

"Daddy, please stop," I yelled. I frantically tried to push

him away. My little body was no match for his massive, overbearing one.

"Shut up! You did this to yourself, Aimee. It's been a long time coming," he said as he positioned himself above me. I didn't know what was coming, but I knew it would be bad. I knew it would hurt, so I tried to stare at the sunflowers that covered my wall. I loved them. They were so full of light, so full of beauty.

A loud crash startled Daddy, causing him to fall off me and to the ground. My bedroom door shattered into teeny, tiny pieces as it was broken down.

"POLICE. GET AWAY FROM THE GIRL!"

I glanced up from where I lay on the floor, and I saw three police officers with guns drawn, aimed right at my daddy. One ran over and swept me up, getting me out of Daddy's reach. The policeman's face was gentle, yet a hint of sadness lurked in his deep green eyes. His mouth was pressed together so tightly, it formed a straight line, causing his eyebrows to furrow. He was angry, but he wasn't angry at me. He was angry at Daddy. I remembered the policeman's voice most; it was soft, soothing, and kind. The words he uttered comforted me, warmed me, and allowed me to forget about what was going on around me. He was like my personal shield, my temporary shelter.

Even though the policeman's voice soothed me, I couldn't help but let my eyes wander. I wanted to see what was going on. I watched as the police tore apart my room and took my daddy. Daddy didn't struggle. He just laughed and laughed, mumbling something about how he couldn't be stopped.

A nice old lady came and wrapped my cold body in a blanket. When she picked me up, I could smell strawberries and watermelon on her. She made me smile. Daddy saw the lady take me away, and he began screaming. She hurried me out of the room as the police struggled to subdue him. I hugged the lady tighter as we walked away. I closed my eyes, willing myself to go to another place. I looked back, only once. His face lay smashed on the ground, and blood trickled from his mouth as he cursed my name.

"Aimee, I will find you, and I will kill you. You ruined my life. You ruined your mother. And I will ruin you." I shut my eyes and my tears fell onto the nice lady's sweater. I didn't feel safe anymore. I felt helpless and scared 'cause I knew he'd keep that promise. No matter what, somehow he would keep that promise.

As I was taken outside to the police car, I started to panic. Where was my dolly?

"Oh no! Help! Help me! She's still inside! We have to get her out!" I started kicking and screaming. I tried everything I could to get out of the nice lady's arms. She gently tried to subdue me, reassuring me that no one else was left in the house. I saw the little blue-eyed boy in the doorway of the house next to mine, though, and I instantly calmed. I watched as he held on to his mom's hand. I remembered all the fun times playing with him outside. We'd played while Daddy was at work or in the basement. The boy had been so nice. Mommy hadn't let the boy come into the house, though. I'd never known why until tonight

*when I had found out what Daddy hid in the basement.
What Daddy did. The little boy waved to me, and his mom
kissed his forehead. I heard her say, "You saved her life,
Scott. I'm so proud of you."*

*As the police car drove away, I plastered my face to
the window, and I frantically waved back to the little boy
who had saved my life. Scott. I never forgot his face or the
brightness of his blue eyes—they had been just like Dolly's
eyes.*

I sometimes dreamt about Scott Reynolds. We would be
running in his back yard, playing tag. His mom would call
us in for lunch, and he would take my hand. "Best friends
forever, Aimee," he'd say, and I'd smile. He had been my
solace away from the chaos I had called my life.

I looked at the stranger, and my stomach dropped. I
knew those eyes. My first reaction was to run up and hug
him, but then panic set in. Had Scott recognized me? Did
he know who I was? If so, my cover was blown and this
meant a new life, a new state, a new town, a new me. I
wasn't ready to give up my life, one I had fought so hard to
maintain and build.

Suddenly, my dissertation was the least of my worries.

Chapter Four

LIAM

I walked into the office feeling much better than I normally did. Meeting Madison had definitely put me in a good mood.

"O'Leary. In my office, NOW!"

Well, there went my good mood.

Getting called into Assistant Director Thomas Harper's office was never a good thing. It either meant trouble or a big promotion. I definitely *wasn't* on the list for a promotion.

I followed him in and sat down as he shut the door.

"Liam, do you know who Michael Walsh is?" The question shocked me. Fuck! Everyone knew who Michael Walsh was. What worried me was why he was asking.

"Yes, sir. He was the serial killer who kidnapped, raped, and murdered young girls. His MO was to make cuts all over their bodies in between raping them, and then finally bury them. He called them his masterpieces. He had some cabin where he'd do most of his work. The cabin of horrors, we used to call it at Quantico training. He used the basement in his home when he needed to as well. I saw the pictures as a rookie. He was a sick fuck."

"Right. Well, O'Leary, Walsh escaped prison last week. We were moving him to a different facility in Chicago, and he stabbed the guard with a toothbrush shiv. Damn son of a bitch is gone." Assistant Director Harper rubbed his dark bald head. He was nervous and pissed off.

I sat up straighter in my chair. Michael Walsh was a horror story. He often plagued my dreams, and the pictures I had been shown during profiler training at the Academy played like a slideshow in my mind at night, keeping me awake. I already had my own nightmares from a fucked-up life. Those pictures had only added to them, and now he was free. This wasn't going to be good.

"Let me cut to the chase. We went to his prison cell and unpacked the box of belongings he had with him. In there was part of a journal. Not sure where the rest of it is. Son of a bitch probably took it with him. Anyway, this journal—he wrote in it every day for the past twenty years. Recently, he kept writing about his daughter Aimee and how he longed to see her again. Walsh wants to find his daughter and kill her. It's clear he blames her for everything that happened to him and his wife."

I got up from my chair and walked to the window. Looking below, I saw the people scurrying along, living their lives without the knowledge that some crazy serial killer had just broken free. Walsh was evil and manipulative, and he was going to hurt a lot of people. That much I knew. Deep down, though, I couldn't help but notice the similarities between

Walsh and myself. The same desires, although he tended toward young girls. That wasn't my thing. I loved a grown woman. A woman who was comfortable with her sexuality and loved sex. A woman who loved it when I made her do whatever it was I wanted, even when it hurt. Pain was the trigger to my sanity and ironically, to my madness as well. Eerily, when I had read his profile, I'd felt connected to him, drawn to him. My own fucked-up past had made me more broken on the inside. I wanted to catch this guy and sever all feelings and commonalities I felt existed between us. I needed to do this for myself. I needed to catch him. I turned to the Assistant Director.

"Sir, let me catch this son of a bitch."

"O'Leary, I know how eager you are to catch him, but I need you to do something else for me. I need you to protect his daughter." He sat up straighter in his chair, shuffling awkwardly with some paperwork he had on his desk.

"With all due respect, sir, I'm not a babysitter. I didn't join the Bureau to sit and hold some girl's hand. Especially a girl with daddy iss—"

"O'Leary, that's enough," Harper said with a harsh voice that had me stopping midsentence. "Aimee's identity was changed when she was adopted. There is absolutely no trace of who she used to be. Her father was supposed to be in jail for the rest of his life. We thought she was safe. *I* thought she was safe. She needs us now, and we must protect her at all costs." His face was solemn.

"Fine," I said, walking over to his desk. "But I'm letting you know now that I think this is fucking bullshit."

I slammed my hands down to accentuate my point. The Assistant Director just raised an eyebrow.

"Understood. She is actually finishing school now. Ironically, she is joining the Bureau herself. She was slated to start with the class after the current one, but we are bumping up her training. She'll be joining the current class next week. I'm assigning you as an instructor. The class is already underway, but we've dealt with the reason for the changes. Obviously, the real reason for your presence will be to keep an eye on her and make sure she's safe. That is your top priority. She's a lot like you, O'Leary. She likes to take things into her own hands." He smiled. "I'm having the media sidetracked right now to keep this under wraps. Last thing I need is a goddamn vigilante on my hands trying to find and kill this son of a bitch," Assistant Director Harper said.

I slumped back down into the chair. "Fine. What do you owe this girl, anyway? This isn't protocol. Normally, we'd just sweep them into protective custody and call it a day." I crossed my arms and sulked. Yeah, I could be a big baby.

The Assistant Director got up from his chair and came up behind me, placing his hand on my shoulder.

"Son, she was my brother's adopted daughter. I promised him when he died I'd look after her and do my best to let her live a normal life. Don't let me down. She's family." He gave my shoulder a quick squeeze and headed back around to his desk.

"Oh, shit, sir. I'm sorry… I didn't mean—"

"Enough, Agent O'Leary. No harm done." He sat down

with a thump and rubbed his face, which was etched with exhaustion.

"What's her name, anyway?" I asked, getting up and heading toward the door.

"Madison," the Assistant Director said nonchalantly. "Madison Harper."

Chapter Five

MADISON

"Next stop: Fifth Street," came the booming voice of the subway announcer over the intercom. It startled me, and I jumped halfway out of my seat.

Crap! The doors were closing. I ran for the door to see if there was any possibility I could make it. Right when I thought they would close on me, Scott came up behind me and held them open. I guess those muscles were good for something other than being eye candy. I blushed and tried to smooth down my untamable curls. We exited the subway, trying to weave through the masses of people moving briskly toward their destinations.

Finally navigating our way through, we stopped on the platform and stood in front of each other, both unsure of what to do. Scott shifted his book from under one arm to the other and cleared his throat.

"Thanks for holding the door," I muttered.

"No problem," he said, and then paused. "I think...

Maybe we should go somewhere and talk, Aimee?" he asked, and his beautiful blue eyes met mine.

I froze. It had been years since anyone had called me Aimee. My hands got clammy, and I began to sweat. My heart felt as if it might burst right out of my chest. *Deep breaths, Madison. Deep breaths.*

"Um, sure. I guess." I stood there, unsure of what to do.

"Great. There's a coffee shop around the corner. Let's go."

Good, a local place. Granted, I was petrified as to how this was going to pan out. How had he found me, and what did he want? But I was also curious. Oddly, I felt safe with him. Comforted. Something I hadn't felt in a long time. I took a deep breath and followed.

We walked through the subway terminal and stepped out onto the busy streets of New York in silence. He seemed nervous, and he kept brushing his hair back. It didn't matter, though. Every time he brushed it away, a strand would make its way close to his eye again. I watched his hand go back to his side and noticed the book he was holding was titled *The Psychology of a Wounded Woman: How to Bring Her Back to Reality.* I couldn't help the laugh that came from me. Scott eyed me curiously. I smiled, trying to make light of my outburst. Immediately, though, I noticed his firearm and became fearful. Why did Scott have a gun? I had the urge to run, but I quickly squashed that feeling. I was joining the FBI. There was probably a good reason for his weapon, so I tried to pretend I didn't see it, and I walked on.

He must have noticed me nervously gnawing on my fingernails and studiously avoiding his gun, because he immediately apologized. "I'm sorry, Aimee. I should have told you I have to carry the gun at all times. Bureau policy."

I stopped in my tracks. "Wait. You work for the FBI?" I asked eagerly. "And please, don't call me Aimee," I soberly added. "It's Madison or Maddie."

"Okay then, Maddie," he said with a smirk, my name rolling off his tongue playfully. "And yes, I do. I have for a few years now. I got my Masters in Criminology, and they recruited me right out of college."

"Wow, that's awesome. I'm starting at the FBI soon, as well," I said, excited that I had met not one, but two agents in one day.

"That's fantastic, Maddie! I'm sure you have a lot of questions, and I will answer all of them. But first, let's get to the shop, and then we can talk."

"Whatever you say, Agent Reynolds." I saluted him. Wow. Smooth move, Madison.

He smiled nervously, and I wondered why he was so anxious to talk to me. I was the one with a serial killer father.

I smirked. Despite my curiosity and fear for the coming conversation, I was happy to see him. The boy who had saved my life wasn't a boy at all anymore.

Scott's cell phone went off, and he grabbed it out of his pocket and read the text quickly.

"Figures," he said, annoyed. "Change of plans. My boss wants to update you at the office."

"Your boss?" I asked, and then it clicked. "My uncle."

"Aimee… I mean Maddie. Sorry. This is important. I'll share as much as I can, but Assistant Director Harper is the best one to talk with."

I was having trouble breathing, but then I remembered: "I have my dissertation. That's where I was headed," I said, my voice distant. A nagging thought was pushing at the corners of my mind, but I wouldn't—I couldn't—let that thought intrude.

"Trust me. I'm sure your professors will understand. As soon as this briefing is over, I will personally escort you over there. Deal?" He held out his hand for me to shake. I ignored the nagging feeling in my mind.

"Okay, but this better be life or death." I stormed ahead, leaving his hand untouched.

He grabbed my arm to slow me down, and as he looked at me seriously, he said, "It is, Maddie."

I gulped loudly and shifted my weight around a bit. Had I known we would be hiking all of New York City, I would have worn more comfortable shoes. Scott noticed my discomfort. "It's only a block away. Sorry, I didn't bring my car with me." He looked down at my shoes. They were really more for looks than for comfort. God, I wished I had my boots on instead.

"No worries. I've been through a lot worse." I shrugged. Okay. *Bad joke, Madison. Bad joke.*

He gave me the most compassionate look, his tense body softening. He motioned for me to walk ahead and we headed off to the Bureau.

The one-block walk seemed like a mile. Scott and I walked in silence, and the tension became awkward. I didn't know what to say, what to ask. I guessed silence was best for now. Ten minutes later, we had made it to the FBI office. My feet were throbbing from the walk. We hadn't said a word to each other. I didn't quite know what to say. I had a thousand ideas and questions running through my head, and yet, I couldn't voice any of them. I wanted to just let it all out, let him share in it. What had happened to me? I didn't react to men this way. But a part of me—probably a remnant of my childhood—felt like Scott understood me in a way no one else could. As much as I wanted to turn to him, to pick up where we left off over twenty years ago, it was impossible. We were different people. So, the silence… yeah, the silence was best.

Scott held the door for me, and I smiled up at him, taking him in. Despite the awkwardness between us, I couldn't ignore his beauty. He had grown into a handsome man, and he seemed so strong and capable. And yet, he also seemed to have retained his natural kindness and gentleness. Just like the little boy who had saved me that day. No, he hadn't changed much. He was still the little boy who had protected me. Who had given me a second chance.

We entered the elevator and stood at opposite sides. He quickly stepped in front me, pressing floor number seven. He didn't go back to his corner, though, staying by my side. I kept glancing over at him, willing him to speak to me. He stared off, intently, which let me know he was preoccupied, transfixed in thought about something. Was he thinking about me? I couldn't help but wonder what awaited us. I shifted from leg to leg, adjusting my bag to my other shoulder and smoothing out my dress. I didn't know what to do with myself. Scott sensed my angst and quickly grabbed my hand in his for a reassuring squeeze. It was magnetic. Parts of me—memories, emotions, all of it—came rushing back in that one instance. He looked down at me, his electric-blue eyes piercing me to my core. I felt alive, lit up. I leaned in closer to him, wanting more, needing more.

Just then, the elevator doors opened and there was Liam glaring at me. He looked down at my hand, and I whipped it away from Scott.

"Liam, w-w-what are you d-d-doing here?" I asked, pretty sure my face was bright red, and go figure, I was stuttering again. He looked pissed. Although, why should he be?

"You," he said, pointing directly at me.

"Me? What do you mean, me?" I looked to the back of the elevator, thinking maybe someone else had crept up behind me. What did he mean? I had no idea what he was talking about.

"Wait. You two know each other?" Scott asked, with what sounded like annoyance in his voice.

"Yeah, I'm no stranger to Madison's sweaty, muscular legs," Liam said with a wink.

"You motherfucker!" Scott said through clenched teeth, positioning himself in front of Liam. "You have some nerve."

Chapter Six

MADISON

"Enough, you two. Bring Madison in here," a familiar voice called from the other room.

"Hello, Uncle Tom." What the hell was going on? I walked swiftly into the office, placing my bag on the chair.

"Hey, sweetie." He leaned in to greet me with a peck on my cheek and a hug.

While Uncle Tom was hugging me tightly, I looked over his shoulder as Liam and Scott sat down at opposite ends of the room. Chairs lined the walls, yet they chose to sit far apart. Their faces were full of disgust, and they both stared at the floor. Liam picked at his fingernails. I noticed one had started to bleed. He lifted it to his mouth. God, Liam's lips were full and so kissable.

Uncle Tom ended our embrace, but then he quickly walked away and over to the window. Uncle Tom's brisk movements snapped me out of my daydream about Liam's flawless mouth. *What is wrong with me today?* "Sweetie,

I'm supposed to be retiring at the end of the month, as you know, but, well… I'm going to cut to the chase for the second time today. You know there is only one thing that would make me delay my retirement."

I immediately panicked. The thought that had been forming in my mind earlier with Scott was coming back, and it wouldn't let go this time. Here I was, surrounded by three men who all seemed to know what was going on, and I was so confused. That only meant one thing… some way, somehow, that bastard—

"How long ago?" I asked, knowing that my father had found a way to get out of prison.

"Madison— Wait… I wanted to…," Uncle Tom tried to interject.

"How long?" I raised my voice. I wanted answers. Scott was the first to speak.

"A week ago."

"A week? A week, and I'm just finding out about this now?" I asked. "We just talked on the phone yesterday, Uncle Tom. Why didn't you tell me?" I was furious. My father had been free from prison for one *whole* week, and I was just now being told about it? What the hell?

"We thought it'd be best to see how it panned out. It seems as though he hacked into the adoption agency's records and unsealed your file with the FBI. Christ knows how in the hell he did that. I have a guy looking into it. He knows it all, Madison. Your new name, where you live, and what you've been doing all these years," said Uncle Tom. "He knows about your adoptive family, where you go to school… there isn't anything that he doesn't know at this point."

"Great. Well, I guess it's time for a change anyway." I started to gather my bag to storm off. The last place I wanted to be was surrounded by all of this testosterone. These men had thought they could hide things from me… keep me in the dark. I hated the dark.

"No. You will stay here," said Liam, grabbing my bag from my hands, throwing it on the desk, and pushing me down into a nearby chair. God, he was so aggressive.

I shook my head, laughing. "So you want me to pretend nothing is happening and go on with my life?"

"Exactly," agreed Liam. "What better way to catch him for good? Make him think you have no idea what's going on and just continue your life. Yeah, he'll probably catch on, but it will anger him and make him screw up somehow. And when he messes up, we'll be there to get him, once and for all."

I laughed again, jumped out of the chair, and started pacing, trying to make sense of that absurd plan. "Guys, that's crazy. I want to finish school, but there's no way I'll put all my friends in danger!"

"What friends, Maddie?" Scott asked. "I've been watching you this past week. You don't have many friends. Well, except apparently Liam—"

"What do you mean you've been watching me?" I fumed, ignoring Scott's jealous tone. "Uncle Tom, what is all of this? You don't tell me about my father, *and* you've got agents trailing me?"

"Madison, it was necessary. We had to make sure you weren't being followed by Walsh. We had to make sure you were safe. *I* had to make sure you were safe." He looked so tired, I didn't have it in me to fight him. I turned back to Scott.

"I'm sorry. I know it was intrusive. We just wanted you safe, like your uncle said." Scott had the decency to look ashamed, but I wasn't letting him off that easily.

"Whatever, Scott." I plopped back down in the chair and I crossed my legs, further accentuating my annoyance with the plan they had put together without my knowledge. "So, what's this big plan to keep me safe, then?"

"You're going to the FBI Academy early," Liam said eagerly. "It's your dream. And the Academy is the safest place for you. All those agents-in-training and seasoned instructors. You will be well protected—and don't worry, I get to be one of your instructors!" His lips curved into a sly smirk. Good God, he was sexy.

"I think we should both be instructors. Assistant Director Harper, I don't trust him with her life," Scott, who was close to Uncle Tom's desk, whispered his demands. But it was in vain. We all heard.

"Seriously, asshole? I've been an agent longer than you have and I've made far more arrests. All you are good for is sucking up to the boss and using that brain of yours." He tapped his head. "It's a shame. All those muscles, and you don't know how to use them." Liam moved toward Scott and puffed out his chest. Scott retaliated, puffing his chest out as well. It was comical really, like some sort of primal ritual. Which ape could puff out his chest more? I shook my head in disbelief. A pissing match over who was the better agent? Get real!

"Enough, you two. You act like I'm not here. I'm not a child, and I don't need babysitting. But if you insist, I want Scott there too, Uncle Tom. He and I have a lot of catching up to do, and it would be nice to do that despite all the death and mayhem surrounding me. Plus, we have history together. He knows more about what happened in my past than anyone." I sighed. Oh, what fun. Two men who clearly wanted to be in charge. Only one way to solve that—take control.

"Very well. Reynolds, you will go the Academy as an instructor as well. No one should know what either of you are there to do." Uncle Tom looked concerned, tired, and overworked. I felt bad he was putting his retirement on hold.

"Yes, sir," Scott and Liam confirmed in unison.

"Well, it's been fun, guys," I said with a wave, grabbing my bag from where Liam had dropped it, "but I have to get to class before these past three years of research and hard work were for nothing. If I die, I'd at least like to have *Dr. Madison Harper* written on my headstone," I joked.

"Not funny, Madison. Reynolds and O'Leary will be taking you home. Tomorrow, you will present your dissertation at 9:00 a.m. I've already spoken to the committee." Uncle Tom focused in on me with a deliberate stare, letting me know not to give him any grief. "Then, after your dissertation, you will be spending the weekend at a hotel near Quantico. That way, you can start first thing Monday morning." Fuck my life.

"Fine. Let's go, gentlemen." I waved them on. I kissed Uncle Tom on the cheek and gave him a big hug. He pulled out a large three-ring binder that had FBI Basic Training Manual printed across the front. I almost groaned at its size, but the thought of reading to keep my mind off the troubles at hand was comforting. I was good with books.

"Here you go, sweetie. This will keep you busy for the next couple of days." I flipped through the endless pages. He was always looking out for me. I felt bad for giving him such a hard time, but he was no stranger to my headstrong ways. He was all I had.

Chapter Seven

SCOTT

As we headed out of the office to the elevators, I let Maddie and O'Leary know my car was in the far lot. We weaved through the masses of desks lining the office and made our way to the hallway that held the elevators.

I couldn't help but stare at Maddie as we walked through the office. She had become a beautiful woman. Her curvaceous body had caught my attention this past week, and it had been difficult for me to focus on her routine and gather intel. I smiled, remembering how different she had looked in her ripped jeans and tight tank top, a black one that hugged her chest just right. But the edgy outfit had made her look broody and lost. Her face had seemed clouded, and the happiness that was once visible on her youthful face had been missing. Then she'd smiled, and I'd seen the sweetness in her. She was still the same girl I had known all those years ago.

Heading off on an assignment with Liam wasn't my idea

of a good time, but for Maddie, I'd do anything. I had felt like I was betraying her this past week as I'd watched over her and gotten a feel for her life and routine, but I'd have been lying if I didn't say that I had loved being close to her again. It had taken every ounce of discipline in me not to reveal myself and jeopardize the plan. I had to remind myself she wasn't mine. That even when I was watching her, she didn't even know I was there.

Just now, in the office, I had watched her with her uncle, and the moments they had shared reassured me. I was relieved that she'd had a loving family growing up, and people to care for her, guide her, and give her the life she deserved. It broke my heart that she was back here again, reliving her horrific childhood, but I was also grateful for the chance to spend time with her. I had lost her once, and I wasn't going to let her go again.

"So, are we still on for coffee tomorrow morning, sweet cheeks?" Liam asked as we waited for the elevator.

I scowled at him. I was being petty, but the guy was an asshole. Maddie didn't deserve to be called names like sweet cheeks. She wasn't just another notch in his bedpost. She didn't need a man like Liam. In fact, *we* didn't need Liam at all. He shouldn't have been put on this case, especially since her uncle knew about Liam's rough edges and proclivities. Liam always brought wickedness and anger wherever he went. Maddie had endured enough of that in her lifetime. She didn't need it in the man she fell in love with, too; and from what little I had seen, Maddie seemed interested in Liam. It left me bitter and confused.

She deserved better than him. She deserved everything good. I wondered if, deep down, Maddie was intrigued by Liam's bad-boy appeal. I hoped she would realize he wasn't right for her before she got hurt, because I also sensed that she really just wanted someone to love her. Liam would never be able to offer her love. Anyone could tell he was too damaged for that.

"Yeah. Sure," Maddie answered, blushing. Why was she blushing? Did she actually think that name was endearing? I frowned. She needed to be shown how a real man treated a woman. I wasn't sure if I was that man, but I somehow had to prove to Maddie that a life of standing in O'Leary's darkness was just going to bring her the same pain and heartache her father had brought. I had struggled with relationships. I had struggled with always being the good guy and never wanting to rush into anything too fast. I could count on one hand how many women I had been with. I was always searching for someone who could love even the nerdy side of me. Watching Maddie—although intrusive—had reminded me of the type of woman I wanted. She was everything I could ever want and I wanted to be everything she could dream of in a man, but now wasn't the time. We had bigger issues to deal with.

Her cell phone brought me out of my thoughts as it buzzed incessantly from her bag. Maddie crouched and practically emptied the contents of her bag on the floor in the hallway as we continued waiting for the elevator. Finally, she found the small phone and answered it on the fifth ring. The idea that she could fit so much in her bag made me smile.

"Hello. Madison speaking." She was happy, and I felt a tug of jealousy, knowing she was looking forward to her date with Liam.

"Wh-wh-who is th-th-this?" Her happiness quickly dissipated, her nerves and fright evident. I went on alert as the elevator dinged open and the people who were inside stared at the scene unfolding in front of them. I slammed the elevator button with my fist and watched the doors shut. We would catch the next one.

Maddie's eyes grew as big as saucers and she fell back against the wall. I immediately moved closer and stood before her, gently rubbing her arms and trying to calm her.

Madison stayed silent as she listened to the caller on the other end. She managed to move her lips just enough to let me know that it was her father. Fury flowed in the pit of my stomach. Walsh. He was tormenting her, and I felt so helpless against him, unable to shield her from the pain. I looked for Liam but when I couldn't immediately find him, I motioned to one of the agents walking by to get Assistant Director Harper and to start a trace. With my years of experience, I knew it wouldn't matter. We wouldn't have enough time to trace him, but I had to try.

Just as quickly as it had started, the call ended.

"It was my f-f-father," Maddie told her uncle when he came rushing out of his office. Assistant Director Harper swore under his breath, grabbing hold of the poor agent who had been trying to get the trace.

Walsh had been too quick. He'd stayed on the line just

long enough to scare the shit out of Maddie. She shook uncontrollably, and her teeth were chattering as if she were cold. I couldn't hold back. I took her in my arms and held her. I wished I could take the fear from her, draw it from her body, but all I could do was hold her. All I could do was let her know I wasn't going anywhere.

When I pulled her in to me, I was met with a full head of buoyant curls that wrapped themselves around my face. I breathed in, and she smelled exotic, tropical, like mangos and kiwi. I touched her curls. She stayed in my embrace longer than I expected. I didn't want to let her go, and she grasped at my shirt and pulled me in closer.

"I've got you, Maddie," I said as I held her, stroking her hair. "I've got you." Assistant Director Harper gave me a nod, rubbed Maddie's back, and whispered something in her ear before he went back to speaking with the agents around him.

I glanced at Liam, who still stood in the corner waiting for the elevator. His arms were crossed over his chest and he'd raked his fingers into his arms, leaving fiery red marks. I glanced at his face, not to torment him, but to see what was going through his head. His eyes startled me. They'd changed. They looked black, as though he were plagued with jealousy and hate. Liam was battling with something, and his look was so frighteningly familiar. I had seen the look before, the night I had looked through the small window on the outside of Maddie's house, frantically searching for her. Instead, I had seen her father. Walsh's eyes had been wild, murderous, jealous, and angry at the world. In that moment, as I looked into the window to Liam's fragmented soul, I knew I had to protect Maddie— not only from her father, but from Liam as well.

Chapter Eight

LIAM

I probably should have been more concerned about Madison's psychopathic serial-killer father, but I didn't care. I cared about what I wanted, and I wanted her. Of course, the only thing I wanted right *then* was to rip Madison out of Reynolds's arms.

I hated Reynolds. He had his Master's degree and he followed the damn rules. He was a favorite at the FBI, but he couldn't pull the trigger. That was where I came in. That's where I got my recognition.

Now, I had to spend God knew how long with Madison and Reynolds. I wasn't going to let him get in my way. Reynolds was *not* going to win. Madison and I clearly had a connection, and I intended to pursue it.

"Madison, we better get you back home." The words spewed like venom from my mouth. I moved closer to the elevator.

She let go of Reynolds and shot him a beautiful smile.

He put his hand on the small of her back and took the bag from her hands, pressing the button on the elevator again.

"Let's go," Reynolds said. "I'll grab the car and drive you home." Reynolds held the elevator door for her as it opened. He sure was laying it on thick.

"Correction," I reminded them. "We'll be driving you."

Assistant Director Harper looked like he was going to clock us both. I quickly made my way onto the elevator and into the corner, cutting Reynolds off in the process. The button for the lobby was already illuminated, but I pressed it three more times for good measure. I had to get out of there. No sense in getting on the boss's bad side any more than I already was.

As we walked to the car, Reynolds and Madison strode ahead, and I glared at their backs. Every few seconds, she would tilt her head back and laugh. God, she had an infectious smile, but I couldn't help but feel a *ping* of resentment every time Reynolds was the one to make her laugh.

Madison's dress hiked up as she entered the car, exposing way too much of her legs. I inhaled loudly, and she turned to smile shyly at me as she quickly smoothed it down. I imagined my hand roaming up her leg. I wouldn't stop there. No, I *couldn't* stop there. I wanted to feel every inch of her body. As if she knew what I was thinking, her complexion turned slightly red.

"Do you want the front seat?" she asked. "You're much taller than me."

"No, thanks," I replied with a touch to her arm as I got

in the back. "Hey, so how do you two know each other, anyway? From what I was told, you were whisked away and got adopted after the—the, um... incident." Fuck, I was an idiot. She looked like she was going to cry, but immediately straightened out her shoulders and appeared to harden up a bit. *Madison.* She was a trooper. She glanced over at Reynolds, and I studied the elongation of her neck and the muscles in her back that tightened with her movements. My heart beat faster, and I started to sweat. Her neck was so exquisite, so enticing. It looked so smooth and so soft, seemingly begging for a caress. I wanted to reach out and gently stroke her.

"Scott saved me," Madison said with a smile.

Fan-fucking-tastic. I shifted awkwardly, picking at my nails again.

"Yeah, we were neighbors when we were little," Reynolds said, looking longingly at Madison. "We used to play outside—hide and seek, soccer." Reynolds described their childhood together with a grin, and then he paused for a moment, as if thinking.

"We had some fun times. I always knew something was off, though. You always seemed so sad and damaged." He peered over at Madison, and she stared intently back.

"The night your mom got murdered, I heard you scream. My mom had fallen asleep on the couch, so I snuck out the front door to see what was going on. I wanted to be sure you were safe." Madison looked out the window and tears glistened in her eyes.

"I saw the basement light on, and I poked my head

through the window. I saw him. I saw him. He looked so angry. He was throwing shit around. Yelling. I saw so much blood and that girl hanging from the ceiling—" He gulped loudly and took a breath. "So, I ran home and told my mom. We called the cops. I was so terrified for you, Maddie. I can't even imagine what you went through." Reynolds grabbed her hand. He shook his head, fighting off his own emotions.

"The FBI came later and asked me questions and told me I was a hero," he said proudly. "After that day, I knew I wanted to join the FBI." He paused and looked directly at Madison. Their eyes locked, communicating without the need for words, but then he slowly drew his gaze back to the road. I tightened the seat belt around myself, allowing it to squeeze me hard. I wanted to feel something, anything. Pain was better than nothing at all.

"You were a hero," Madison replied, squeezing his hand in return.

"I never knew what happened to you until I was older and joined the FBI. I was told you were adopted and given a new identity. That you were happy. That you were well taken care of. That's all I ever cared about," Reynolds said lovingly.

Madison wept silently.

"Fucker," I said aggressively, sitting up and moving closer to the front seat. "You made her cry."

"No," Madison uttered, wiping away her tears. "No, it's okay. I never heard this from his perspective. I'm so sorry, Scott, that you had to see that," Madison said, finally letting go of Reynolds's hand.

"Sorry? Maddie, what your father did was *not* your fault. Your dad is an awful man, and he did horrible things. You are not like him, and you are by no means responsible for what he put you and your mom through. Do you hear me?" Reynolds reassured Madison, gently taking her hand in his again. "Look at me," he whispered.

Madison turned her head slowly and focused her big brown eyes on his. "Thanks, Scott."

I didn't know what to say. Her past was so tied to his. Even though her early years had been horrible and traumatizing, Reynolds and Madison had a history together, and I was just a fucked-up, self-absorbed agent who was willing to get the bad guy at any cost. Madison might have looked fragile and wounded, but she was determined to become a person who could fight her own battles despite her past. As I sat silently in the car, staring at Madison, I realized I had my work cut out for me.

Chapter Nine

SCOTT

We pulled up to her house and after I got out, I opened the door for Maddie.

"Thanks, Scott." She took my hand and smiled at me.

"Park along the side. I'll be right down," I told Liam when I poked my head into the car. He got out of the backseat and hopped into the driver side, where the keys were already in the ignition.

"Yes, master," Liam said. He chuckled. What an asshole.

I walked behind Maddie, watching her take each step on the stairs. Her curls bounced behind her, framing the curves of her body. She was striking, the curve of her back sleek and voluptuous. Every smooth rounding of her body spoke to the primal urges within me, urges that were begging to be set free. The dress she wore blew in the breeze, and her legs were exposed and bare. They looked soft, yet strong enough to take my large frame. I wanted her—all of her—so much it hurt.

"This is me." She grabbed her keys and stood expectantly

at the door.

I smoothed her hair away from her face so I could see her eyes. She hid those brown eyes behind the fullness of her hair, maybe for fear of what people might see. But what I saw was nothing that should be hidden. I desired and admired her, and I didn't want her hiding anything from me. She closed her eyes and leaned into my touch.

"It's going to be okay, Maddie. You know that, right?" I took her hand in mine, gently caressing it. "I won't let anything happen to you."

"Promise?" She looked at me again. I wanted to hold her, love her right then, but I didn't want to be like Liam. I didn't want to scare her away. She needed someone strong, caring, and supportive; she didn't need someone trying to get her into bed. I focused on my breathing, trying to suppress the intensity inside of me.

"*Always.*" I kissed her hand, and then released it gently. "Don't worry. The agents who will be keeping guard just checked the apartment. It's safe," I said as she opened the door to her apartment and walked inside.

"I'll see you tomorrow?" she questioned, once again looking for the promise that I wouldn't leave her.

"Eight o'clock. On the dot. And don't worry, someone will be monitoring the apartment all day and night. You'll be safe."

"I'd feel safer with you here." She shut the door, but I didn't miss a quick glimpse of her eyes, which had been filled with disappointment.

"Damn it," I said under my breath as I descended the

stairs. I should have stayed. I should have friggin' stayed with her. She'd all but asked me to. I just didn't want to come on too strong. I wanted her to trust me, to know with all certainty that I'd keep her safe. I didn't want to blur those lines by jumping into anything too fast with her, but I was drawn to her, like a paintbrush to canvas.

I made it to the car and opened the front door, getting in the passenger seat.

"Took you long enough," mumbled Liam.

"Yeah. Let's go back to the office. We have work to do." I reclined my seat, trying to relax for a moment. Sexual tension and longing streamed through me. If I didn't figure out what I wanted to do about my feelings for Maddie, this was going to be a long, long assignment. I sighed, closing my eyes, hoping for a dream that included her.

Chapter Ten

MADISON

I leaned up against the closed door. My breaths were coming fast and shallow. Anger and frustration clawed at me, leaving the illusion of open, potent wounds in its path. Tears stung at my eyes.

I knew my roommates, Missy and Jenna, were gone until tomorrow morning, but the thought of being alone in my apartment put me on edge. Agents were probably right outside, but the instant comfort I had felt with Scott was what I wanted. That comfort, that human contact, was what I needed. I don't know why I'd told him that I wished he would stay. He didn't owe me anything, especially with the twenty years of distance between us, but that didn't seem to matter.

Seeing him again had brought back the memories and feelings of my past, of my father, and of my mother. But it was more than that. Those dark memories, for the first time in forever, had seemed almost secondary to the time I spent with him. I couldn't help but focus on the rapid beating of my heart each time Scott came near me. My body ached to be closer to him, to have him touch me. I knew I'd dream of his body pressing against mine for weeks to come.

I fanned myself. I couldn't remember the last time I'd wanted a man so badly. I craved him. I had felt physically attracted to Liam, but there was something there, something scarred. Because of my schooling and my work with the local police, I knew when there was something more to a person, and with Liam, there was definitely something more peeking out from his intense eyes.

I shuffled around the apartment all day, packing and studying the big FBI manual Uncle Tom had given me. I tried to forget about my father and the fact that he was probably planning how to kill me—slowly. But those thoughts, coupled with thoughts of Scott, seeped into my brain more often than not. I exercised—inside, of course— and I managed to get in some squats and some push-ups to kill time.

When night fell, sleep came, but it was restless and sporadic. The nightmares flowed easily, waking me multiple times. Finally, the sweet sound of my mother's voice in my dreams soothed me, and I dozed off as she sang to me.

The loud beeping sound of my alarm clock pierced the peaceful sleep I had fallen into. Shit! I glanced at my clock, which read 7:45. Liam and Scott would arrive in just fifteen minutes. I'd cancelled my coffee date after receiving the call from my father. I jumped out of bed, desperately looking in my closet for something to wear. I chose my black dress and red pumps. That would have to do. I ran into the bathroom and brushed my teeth. I checked my phone. 7:55. Shit! Shit! Shit!

I grabbed my black super-lash mascara and gently brushed it on. My lashes became instantly fuller, accentuating the almond shape and brown hues of my eyes. After adding my favorite cherry-red lipstick, I was ready to go. For once, my hair looked amazing. Each curl was defined, and ringlets were forming around my face. I smiled. Today was going to be fantastic, well, as fantastic as can be under the circumstances.

Right at 8:00 a.m., the buzzer for my apartment sounded. I pressed the intercom button.

"Who is it?" I asked. I knew Walsh probably wouldn't buzz my intercom but hey, I couldn't be too careful.

"Scott," his husky voice replied.

"I'll be right down," I yelled into the speaker. I grabbed my brown leather bag that held my dissertation and an apple from the counter in the kitchen, and I sprinted out my apartment door.

Scott met me at the entrance, holding it open like the gentleman he was. A girl could get used to being treated so nicely. So much love radiated from him. His admiration was so uplifting, so unbelievably attractive. His blue eyes sparkled, flashing with what looked like appreciation, and I upgraded my 'maybe' fantastic day to a definite.

"You look beautiful, Maddie," he said, looking down at the ground.

"Thanks, Scott. You look pretty handsome yourself."
His white shirt and jeans had been replaced with a tailored

gray suit. The tie had hints of blue, which brought out the lightness in his eyes. He looked stunning with the sunlight highlighting his features. When we got to the car, Liam was in the driver's seat, black shades covering his eyes.

"Hey," I said, sitting in the back.

"Hey," Liam muttered, not bothering to look at me. What had crawled up his ass this morning? I sighed and put on my seat belt.

Traffic was horrible. We hit every red light on the way, and construction—well, apparently the powers that be decided to redo every street on the way to campus. Ugh!

The clock read 8:58 when we finally pulled up to City College. Oh, man. I had to be there at 9:00 a.m.; otherwise, I was screwed.

I ran as fast as I could in my pumps and with every ounce of energy I had left. Scott and Liam were jogging behind me, looking much less winded than I felt. My heart was pounding out of my chest, and my calves were cramping up. No one would have known I had been working out daily.

I was a mess, and as I plowed into the conference room, I tripped and dropped everything on the floor.

"Shit," I murmured.

The conference area was filled with PhDs and professors already judging and scrutinizing me. I quickly tried to compose myself. The boys entered behind me, and I felt a hand on the small of my back. Liam's hand. We locked eyes, and he smiled at me, sending shockwaves up my spine. My body tensed and relaxed all at the same time. Oh, that crooked smile. I was about to say something, but I was stopped by Scott clearing his throat behind us.

"Um, Maddie, you better get going." He handed me the books he had gathered from the floor.

Oh, yeah, the presentation. I got up and tried to shake off thoughts of Liam and Scott. I needed to focus on what I had come here to do. Grabbing the books, I shoved them in my bag. Scott shut the door, and I was left alone to face my destiny.

As a favor to the Assistant Director of the FBI, who had arranged for this extension, the committee advised I had thirty minutes to present. It was a lot less time than the normal two hours, but I'd take it. Uncle Tom had told the committee I was being used as a consultant on a special case. Gotta love Uncle Tom. He certainly came through in a pinch.

I started presenting, and before I knew it, forty-five minutes had passed. I apologized for going over. I knew my topic. It was personal. The committee looked intrigued, disgusted, and mortified all at the same time. On the projector were pictures of my father's victims: dead, mutilated girls. Their penetrating eyes were glossy and white, and seemed to look directly at everyone in the room. Their eyes begged for closure, begged for peace. One lady leaped from her chair and bounded out of the room. I could swear I heard vomiting from outside the door not long after her departure. I certainly knew how to wow a crowd.

I took a deep breath. The board glanced at each other and then asked me to step out for a moment. Well, I definitely hadn't been subtle. I gathered my things and slouched away, afraid I had gone too far.

Chapter Eleven

LIAM

I watched Madison come out of the room looking defeated. She had all of her things shoved under her arm, and she kept adjusting herself.

"Hey, how'd it go?" I asked.

"I'm not sure. They asked me to leave. I think they have to convene before they let me know whether I accomplished what I needed to." She looked down apprehensively and shook her head as if struggling with her thoughts.

"Well, I'm sure you did fine, Maddie," Reynolds said. He jumped up and embraced her.

"Thanks, Scott." She smiled as she hugged him back.

"Once this is over, we better get you back to your place and help you pack. After the weekend, you are no longer a free woman. You are property of the FBI." Reynolds finally let go of her and gave her a big smile.

Madison sighed. "This whole transferring thing *really* sucks. I want to get the full training, to get in on my own. I don't want to be pushed through. I swear it feels like

I'll never be rid of my father." She frowned and started organizing the contents of her bag.

"Don't worry. I can help you train the next few days. We'll try to keep things as normal for you as possible. Wouldn't want you missing out on any hazing," I said. "After all, you do owe me a coffee date." Madison looked between Reynolds and me nervously. She grabbed a stray curl and twirled it repeatedly while chewing on her bottom lip. Reynolds raised his eyebrows.

"I doubt that dates are on Maddie's mind right now. Just focus on the task, and stop trying to get into her pants, O'Leary. Maddie isn't that type of woman." He shoved my shoulder awkwardly, emphasizing his point. I clenched my fists, took a deep breath, and counted, trying to remember the tools to help stop me from knocking someone's lights out. *Anger Management 101*.

"Don't worry, Scott," she purred affectionately. "You'll always be my guy, but I did promise Liam a coffee date." She grinned up at me. Her eyes were bright with excitement. "I'd love to have coffee with you, Liam."

She placed her hand on mine briefly, as if she understood my struggle. I took another deep breath. Her hand was so delicate. The door opened, and the committee members asked her to come back in. I watched as Madison walked away, her ass swaying against the fabric of her dress. My dick twitched, threatening to break free, and I knew she was going to make me lose my shit.

Chapter Twelve

MADISON

I walked into the conference room with a newfound confidence. I was hesitant to accept a date with Liam with all that was going on, but I needed that moment. I had needed to feel normal. The last date I had been on was before grad school. He was nice enough, and we ended up dating for a few months. However, he wanted more, and I wasn't ready for that. I was so tired of living in the shadow of a murderer. For the first time, I wanted a normal relationship. I *needed* a normal relationship, and I almost believed I deserved it.

I walked to the head of the table and took my seat. I wasn't nervous anymore. I wasn't scared or shy. I was proud. Proud I had made it this far. Proud I had reached some semblance of normalcy after having lived through such a chaotic, messy childhood. I heard one of the board members clear her throat and I looked up.

"Madison, to be honest—at first, many of us were taken aback by the topic that you chose. It is difficult for many of us to see those poor innocent girls murdered and broken. But this is our field, and most of us in Forensic Psychology don't go into something *pretty*. It's a sad world, and the hope is we can leave it a little bit brighter. It is not our job to judge your career choices or even your topic, however. It is our job to judge how well you researched and presented," she stated firmly. "With that, we all agree you did a wonderful job."

I was in disbelief. They had actually liked it?

"There was a sense of ownership, responsibility, and personality reflected within your dissertation. It seemed as if you had lived through these brutal killings; it was so well researched. And it is with this thought that I would like to congratulate you, Dr. Harper," she said, smiling.

I was speechless. I had worked so hard over the years, and I was finally reaping the rewards. This was just the beginning for me, *if* I could leave my father behind. How could I do that, though? It seemed as if all my accomplishments were because of him. I was tied to him.

I tried to push those negative thoughts aside and graciously accept my success, but I couldn't help feeling no matter what I did in my life, I would owe it all to my father.

I thanked the committee and shook their hands, but I was unsure. Unsure of why I was entering the FBI. Unsure of my degree. Unsure of why I had fought so long and hard to find my place in this field. Had I really done all of that to save girls like those who had been on the projector during my presentation? Or was I *really* just fueled by my need for revenge?

Chapter Thirteen

LIAM

When she came out smiling and announced she was now a doctor, Reynolds and I both jumped up to hug her. She looked conflicted, but walked over and hugged Reynolds first. Only afterward did she accept my hug. Jealousy shot through me like a dagger, but when she planted a kiss on my cheek as well, it quickly fled. I couldn't help that every sway of her ass, every move of her lips, sent me into a tailspin. I craved her. She was the only remedy for my incurable disease. When Madison was around me, everything stopped. The urges, the feelings that I fought so hard to hide. To get into the FBI and to lead a normal life, I had to pretend that I wasn't a fucked-up mess. And when Madison ran into my life, she had become my cure.

Reynolds was many things, but he was also right. I slept with women. *Lots* of women. Women made it easier for me to cope with the job, the anger, and my past. I'd seen some shit. One memory always got me, luring me in like bait.

I couldn't help but remember that little girl's face; it still haunted me to this day. Her lifeless limbs plastered against my skin… I should have saved her… So yeah, I fucked my memories away. Reynolds held on to his screwed-up sense of righteousness and couldn't pull the trigger. A simple pull of that godforsaken trigger would have made it all end so differently with that little girl. But in the end, in this fucked-up, imperfect world filled with death and chaos, those parents had had to bury their little girl. What was worse?

A few women were on speed dial, but most of them I picked up at the bar during late nights. We'd have sloppy drunk sex, and I wouldn't remember much else. Just the way I liked it. But here was Madison, totally not my usual. I liked them bone thin with blonde hair and blue eyes. College girls. Ah, good ole college girls. There was something about Madison, though, that made me want to get to know her. She was magnificent, beautiful, a masterpiece. I wanted to worship every part of her. The way her breasts trembled when she laughed sent my entire body into a frenzy. I wanted to feel those heavy, full beauties. Not with my hands, but with my mouth. I wanted to feel them overflowing from my lips, and taste her mocha skin. And her ass… Yeah, I could most certainly give her ass some attention. My groin throbbed in anticipation.

These feelings were new, and they antagonized me. I was supposed to steer clear of those emotions and entanglements. Sex, sure—that was my life. But sex with lots and lots of women. All I could think about was

Madison. I craved everything about her. I needed to stay away, and instead seemed to be asking for it.

Madison sighed deeply, and drew me from my thoughts. "So guys, I guess let's head to my place, so I can finish packing and let my roommates know I won't be living there for a while." She looked trapped, uncertain, and I wanted nothing more than to help her forget those feelings. But this was Madison, and in this short time, I had already learned she could—and would—quickly pull herself together.

"I'll order pizza on the way. My treat!" She sounded a little more enthusiastic. "Let me just text my roommates and let them know I passed." She smiled again, becoming wrapped up in her phone.

We headed toward the car with Madison at the middle of our odd line. She tried to make conversation, but Reynolds and I just stared at each other, which made small talk nearly impossible. Her cell phone rang, interrupting the awkwardness. Without even looking at who it was, Madison answered cheerfully.

"Hello!" Her demeanor changed suddenly. She stopped dead in her tracks and slouched over as if trying to hide. She frantically looked around. Of course, Reynolds was there, right on cue, consoling her, holding her.

"How do you know this? What do you want from me?" At that point, she was trying to hold her emotions together. She clutched the phone tighter in her hands, and I heard a loud crack. She ripped her hand away from Reynolds and obsessively started pulling at her hair. She wasn't nervously playing with her curls like she usually did; she was yanking hard. I knew she was borderline hysterical. I couldn't take seeing her like that, losing all sense of tranquility and composure. It had to stop. I ripped the phone from her hands.

"Listen up, asshole. I know who you are, and you'd better know that Madison is being protected by two of the best-trained FBI agents. If you even try to lay a hand on her—"

"Oh. Which agent are you?" He laughed. "I love how Tom thought assigning two agents would protect Madison. Trust me when I say that I highly doubt you will be able to find me or protect her." I listened intently, trying to make out any background noises, but all I heard was Walsh's unsteady breathing, hoarse and cracked.

"I'm Agent Liam O'Leary and let me tell you how happy I will be to put a bullet through your head." He let out a low, threatening laugh. I could feel his malicious intent through the phone, and my body tensed, waiting for the danger.

"Well, O'Leary, you have definitely proven yourself to be the interesting one out of all of them. I see potential in you. So much anger. Goodbye, for now." The way he said 'for now' made the hair on the back of my neck stand on edge.

Madison was staring at me when I hung up the phone.

"Goddammit!" I yelled loudly, slamming her cell phone on the ground. Madison put a hand on my shoulder, and Reynolds did his usual flattening of the hair as he paced. Madison sighed, smoothed out her dress, and appeared to solidify her bearings.

Reynolds was talking on his phone. I caught bits and pieces of the conversation as he let Assistant Director Harper know what had happened.

"Well, at least we know he's watching everything we do. He already knew that my dissertation was approved. He has eyes everywhere. Seems he's been following me since he got out, too. He mentioned a few things."

"Same here. Your dad sure has some balls, man."

Reynolds shook his head as he put his cell phone in his pocket.

"What did he say?" I asked.

"That it can't be Walsh watching us. No one has seen him." I nodded my understanding.

Madison went over and picked up every piece of her phone that was shattered on the pavement. I should have helped her, but I enjoyed watching her bend over. Her ass was perfection. She tensed suddenly.

"Let's get something straight here, fellas," she said with an exaggerated tilt of her hips. "He isn't my f-father, okay. He is Michael Walsh. Some scumbag that we are going to c-catch. A-a-and—ugh!" She took a deep breath to stop her stuttering. I found her stuttering captivating. She seemed more vulnerable. "And, as far as I am concerned, he may have been a sperm donor, but he was not and never will be my father." She continued fuming as she walked toward the car. Something had changed. The past couple days, and her recent success, seemed to have strengthened her resolve.

"Okay, Madison," Reynolds reassured her as he opened

the car door. "Hop on in, and let's get you home. Oh, and don't forget to order that pizza you promised us. I like cheese." She smiled and seemed to relax a little. I hated Reynolds, but he sure knew how to handle Madison.

"Can I borrow your phone to order the pizza? My phone's done," Madison asked, holding the pieces of her phone in her hand.

I handed mine over, trying to focus on the road and not to become distracted by how gorgeous she looked sitting in the backseat. The dress brought out her beauty, lighting up pieces in me I didn't know existed. She'd smiled at me when I'd handed her the phone, and the smile had brightened her face. I didn't know what the hell to do with my feelings. I was conflicted. Part of me wanted to hike up her dress and fuck the shit out of her, but a new part of me struggled with the desire to protect her innocence and spirit, to help her keep that purity.

I went with what I knew best: women. "So, we've got packing, pizza, and roommates. Hey, any of those roommates hot, Madison?" She playfully punched my arm.

"Yes, smart-ass," she growled, her lips thinning. She continued looking down at my phone. The sound of a message coming through my phone caught my attention. Then her voice changed. "But none of them would be caught dead with the likes of you." I kept taking my eyes off the road, glancing in the backseat to catch glimpses of her. She crossed her legs and yet again, her dress hiked up. I held my breath. Just a few more inches... please. "Anyway, if you're interested, give it a whirl. Maybe they'll take you out for coffee because I sure as hell am not." She crossed her arms deliberately in the backseat. Fuck, she was pissed.

Reynolds chuckled.

"Hey. Hey, now, I'm just teasing," I shifted the mirror down so I could see her more closely. "I only want to have coffee with you." I shot her one of my sideways smiles. It worked like a charm every time.

Madison glared at me in the mirror, the red blush returning to her face, but not a blush of passion or sex. Her face was now flushed with annoyance and pure contempt. "I know you want to have coffee with me, O'Leary, but it's the other things that you want to do with other women I worry about. I guess it doesn't really matter. Let's face it; you aren't the dating type. We'll keep it professional."

"Whoa there, sweet cheeks. A couple hours ago, you were all for the coffee date. What gives?"

"What gives?" she asked with a furrowed brow. "Honestly, O'Leary. First, I am not your sweet cheeks. And second, I don't need to be a rocket scientist to realize what your type is. Blonde, tall, thin, fantastically gorgeous. That isn't me—at all. So instead of playing dumb next time you let me borrow your phone—after I'm done talking to my psychotic sperm donor—delete some pictures and text messages." She sat up in the seat, her head between mine and Reynolds's.

"Oh, and by the way," she said impassively. "Marcy can't wait to see you again. Hugs and kisses."

Again, Reynolds chuckled next to me. I wanted to smash his face against the window.

I had to speak up. I could save this. I could save how she felt about me. I didn't want to be that guy with her. The womanizing, alcoholic sadist. I wanted to be different when I was with her. I wanted to be different because of her.

"Listen, Madison, I can—"

"You can what? Explain? It's okay, O'Leary, I gotta hand it to you. Trying something different. Spreading your wings with someone like me. But I will not just be some loser's conquest, some way for you to let off steam. Forget it. You do your job, and I'll do mine. Understood?" Madison stated loudly.

"Understood, but—"

"Good. Now, shut up, so I can order the pizza."

Chapter Fourteen

MADISON

Checking to make sure I had enough cash, I ordered two pizzas for delivery.

"It'll be about an hour," I told the guys. *Perfect, just enough time to pack my stuff and get out of there.* I didn't know why Liam's text message had pissed me off so much, but part of me had liked the attention he had been giving. I should have listened to my gut. I should have trusted myself enough to know Liam's attention was something that would always be fleeting. I'd known there was something off about him, and there it was. *He sticks his dick in everything that moves.*

I had thought that maybe he was serious about a date with me. But why should he be? We didn't have a history, and he didn't feel any loyalty toward me, and let's face it, his rude, vulgar nature wasn't soothing. Hell, he was good to look at, but his personality left a lot to be desired. I tried to rationalize the situation, but I still felt a pinch of disappointment.

As we rounded the corner to my apartment, I noticed my roommates were home by the blaring rock music that was playing. Excellent. Liam would sure get an eyeful. Missy and Jenna were nice, but living with two strippers who were putting themselves through college was no walk in the park. My modest, shy personality contrasted heavily with their overt sexuality, and our relationship was challenging to say the least. Every night, there was a different guy. But they paid the rent on time and kept the place clean. That's all I cared about. I still had my childhood home in Connecticut, but I couldn't go back. Not now. Not ever.

As we were about to enter the apartment, I looked back at the guys, wanting to prepare them—and maybe prepare myself for their wandering eyes. "Hey, just to warn you. My roommates are interesting characters." I paused, trying to talk about them without saying outright what their day— uh—night job was. "They are very touchy-feely and will likely try to sleep with you." I twirled my hair. "So, uh, yeah, just a heads-up."

Liam spoke first.

"Sounds like my type of girls." He smirked.

"Don't worry. *Not* my type," Scott said, raising his eyebrows at Liam.

"I don't care what your type is. I just wanted to let you know." I paused, knowing I should probably tell them. "Look, they're strippers over at Center Stage. They're working to pay their way through college, so no snarky comments." I pointed at both of them.

"Huh, wonder if I know either of them," Liam said.

"I'm there a lot."

"Why doesn't that surprise me?" I asked with a roll of my eyes. Just another reason I'd never measure up.

I reached for the door again, but before I could grasp the handle, the door burst open. Jenna hugged me, screeched, and jumped up and down, forcing me into her boobs. I couldn't breathe. "Oh, my God! YAY! We knew you could do it, Madison. You're so smart!"

I mumbled, "Thanks." Then, because I was being smothered, "Can you let me go? I can barely breathe."

"Oh, sorry," Jenna said with a sly grin. She adjusted her boobs, seemingly proud of her assets. "Missy and I are just so happy for you. We're making you a cake! Well, trying to anyway." She pushed her bottom lip out, and a pout strategically formed on her lips. "Oh yum, who are these hunky guys?" She started touching Liam, feeling his toned arms. His muscles flexed under her touch. As she stroked Liam, she looked Scott up and down, taking in every inch of him. Scott crossed his arms, unamused by the attention. I grinned. At least I could count on Scott.

As if Missy could smell the men, she came waltzing to the door, joining us. Both Missy and Jenna were tall, model thin, with straight blonde hair and big doe eyes. The only difference was Jenna had blue eyes and Missy had green. They were every guy's dream. I looked frumpy and boring next to them. Not to mention short. They were all legs at just under six feet each.

"Missy, Jenna," I introduced them reluctantly. "Meet Special Agents Scott Reynolds and Liam O'Leary with the

FBI. They are helping me pack for the Academy and seeing that I make it there in one piece." I brought them inside the apartment. Missy and Jenna followed closely behind.

"That's so cool. Do you have a gun?" Missy asked Liam while twirling her gum between her fingers. Jenna reached out and touched Liam's arm again, squeezing. Her eyes lit up like a child's at Christmas.

"I sure do. It's really big. Do you want to see it?"

Both girls giggled. I snickered, annoyed by Liam's blatant flirtation.

"Anyway," I interrupted, "I am leaving for the Academy sooner than expected, so I won't be around for a few months."

"Aww, we'll miss you! You guys have to stay for cake, though. We worked *really* hard!" Jenna whined, placing her hands on her hips, pushing out her chest dramatically. Not that she needed to. My boobs were big, but holy hell, you could hide the kitchen sink between those things.

"Yes, please," Liam replied eagerly. "Let's stay for cake." Liam looked at Jenna and Missy, drinking them in. He propped himself dramatically against the wall, flexing his muscles. I rolled my eyes and looked over at Scott. He shrugged. Guess I had to make the decision. I blushed as Scott looked past Missy and Jenna, his eyes transfixed on me. I knew by the way he looked at me, how his body instinctively leaned in to mine, that he wanted me. But no matter what I felt, or he felt, Scott played by the rules, and he wouldn't say or do anything about those feelings. Hell, if he'd slammed me against the wall right then and ravished me, I wouldn't protest. My insides clenched with the thought.

"Whatever. I don't care. Pizza will be here in about forty-five minutes anyway. As long as we are on the road at a decent time. You guys have to drive all the way to Virginia, not me." I tried to calm the storm of tension that beat at me.

"Yay!" Jenna clapped. "Cake will be done in about twenty minutes! It's red velvet. Your favorite." Jenna smiled at me, looking proud that she remembered what my favorite cake was.

I walked into the living room, and Liam sat on my couch with Missy beside him. Jenna joined them and sat on the other side of Liam. I grabbed Scott and headed down the hallway. As I walked away, I heard them all laughing.

"Ugh." I couldn't help but make noises. Honestly, he was just so... "Ugh!"

"You okay?" Scott asked.

"Yeah, I'm okay. Just irritated."

"Why are you irritated? Because of O'Leary? Don't worry about him. He does this all the time."

"Great," I snapped. "It's just... never mind. It doesn't matter. Let's just get my shit together, please," I pleaded. I didn't want him to see how badly the scene with Liam hurt me. I walked over to my drawer, grabbed the extra cell phone, put in the SIM card, and threw the cell in my bag.

"No, Maddie," Scott said affectionately. "Please tell me. I want you to talk to me." He grabbed my hand.

"I just... I just never had that!" I flung my hands up. "I

was never the pretty one. No one has *ever* wanted me to the point of losing their shit. Hell, no one has ever wanted me at all. I guess I just thought when O'Leary showed me some attention that maybe, for once in my life, someone actually liked me." I looked away, taking one of my bags and filling it with shoes. They flew all over the room, more of them making their way onto the floor than into the bag. "Guess my naiveté is showing."

"Maddie, listen to me." He gently pulled me down next to him on the bed. His touch on my skin made the tornado return. It was swirling now, hovering, wanting to land. "You are beautiful, funny, and obviously wicked smart. Don't let some douche rocket like O'Leary cause you to second-guess that. Any guy would be lucky to have you by their side."

I burst out laughing, snorting in the process. I couldn't help myself. It had been so long since I'd seen Scott, and in the past couple days, I hadn't seen this side of him. He was so lighthearted and funny. It was refreshing and turning me on more than I had thought possible. The list of things that drew me to Scott kept getting longer and longer.

"Douche rocket? Since when do you say stuff like that?" I giggled again, and lay back on my bed.

"Had to get you to laugh somehow, Harper." He lay back and joined me. Our heads were right next to each other, and I turned to him.

"Scott?"

"Yeah?"

"Did you ever think about me?"

He turned and faced me. We were only inches apart. A little move on his part would cause our lips to collide. I wanted him to move closer to me. I wanted to feel—

He perched himself on his elbow and looked into my eyes. Being there, with Scott, felt so right. So perfect. *Damnit, Scott, kiss me!* I closed my eyes, willing it to happen.

"Maddie," he said, prompting me to open my eyes. "Not a day went by I didn't think about you. My mom, to this day, says she thought I was going to go crazy. I always talked about you, even at eight years old. I wrote you letters and everything. Even when I didn't get a response, I still wrote you. She seemed to think it was some phase; but when I joined the FBI, I think it finally clicked for her. She realized you were a part of me. Forever. You made me who I am today."

Silent tears dripped down my cheeks, a physical representation of how I truly felt. That this was where I was meant to be. Right here, right now. Not chasing dates with men who were more interested in the fake companionship they got from screwing random women.

"Oh, Maddie, I didn't mean to make you cry." He softly wiped a tear from my cheek. I leaned into his touch.

"It's okay, Scott. They're all good tears. I've never had anyone say anything like that to me before." I moved away, sitting at the edge of the bed, putting some space between us. "I never got any letters, by the way. You know I would have written back."

"I figured as much. Once I joined the FBI and I learned

you were adopted, it all kind of made sense. Why you never wrote back. Why you never tried to find me." His voice drifted off, as if he were remembering what it felt like.

"Scott." I reached out and briefly touched his arm. "I would have, if I could have. You meant so much to me. It was so hard not to get to say good-bye." I gave him a big hug. He tensed under my touch, hugging me back awkwardly, the geekiness I had noticed about him yesterday on the subway peeking through. I smiled.

"I meant a lot, huh?" He pulled away and lay back on the bed casually, all nervousness gone.

God, what did he want me to say. That I'd never stopped thinking about him? That I'd often wondered what had happened to that bright-eyed eight-year-old boy who had been a seven-year-old girl's savior? No, I couldn't say that. At least, not yet.

"Yeah. So how's your mom, anyway?" Time to switch topics.

"She's good." He paused, and sadness filled his eyes. "Dad died a few years ago, so it's just her and the dogs now. She still lives in the same house in Connecticut," he explained with a croak in his voice. He cleared his throat, sitting up.

"I'm sorry about your dad." My heart ached for him. I remembered my mom, and how hard it was at seven years old to know she was gone. I tried to imagine what it was like for him to grow up with his dad and have to say good-bye. It must have been devastating. I joined him, and we sat at the edge of the bed together.

"He was a good guy," I said, placing my hand on his leg. "Your whole family seemed so nice and loving. Your mom, especially. She always had an extra spot at the table for me, and she made me bags of food in case I got hungry." I smiled. His mom had been my savior, too.

"She did? Huh. I didn't know that. I knew you'd eat with us, but I didn't know she'd send you home with food." I drifted off, thinking of the chocolate chip cookies she used to make. They had been so gooey. My little hands would eagerly take the bag from her when she'd send me home, the smell permeating around me. It brought me back to some of the better times of my childhood. No surprise Scott was there. All my happy memories seemed to involve him. That had to mean something, right?

I grabbed one of my curls, nervous. "Oh, yeah. She'd pat my head and say, 'Honey, stay strong and be brave. One day you'll be free from all the hurt and pain.' I used to say that to myself when I would hide in my closet from my fa— from Walsh." I shuddered just thinking about it.

"Do you mind if I ask what happened to your house?"

I paused, and took in a breath.

"The house is mine now, but I haven't been back since that day. I just can't."

"You didn't sell it?" Scott questioned.

"I know it seems weird, but I just can't let it go. It seems so final. Like I'd lose the last bit of my mother that I have." I looked away, ashamed at how silly I sounded.

"I can only imagine," Scott said sympathetically, taking one of my curls in his large hand. "I always remembered your curls. Always so unruly." We laughed. "So very much like you."

"What do you mean? I am *not* unruly. If anything, I'm boring and dull. Just look at me." I looked away. Why had I said that? I sounded like a child, an insecure child, begging for attention.

"I am." He gently grabbed my face. I fell into his touch, following his lead and lifting my head. I looked into his eyes. The once bright blue was sensual, lustful—*all for me*. The tornado had faded. I was suffused with warmth, as though the sun were shining down on my body. His eyes devoured me.

"Scott." I was breathless, his name a need-filled whisper. *Kiss me, please kiss me,* I pleaded again silently. I shut my eyes, hoping, praying he felt what I felt.

Blazing passion filled me as our lips met for the first time. Silk enveloped my senses, and I was reeled into a feverish state of being. I was aflame. I was scorching heat. *The kiss.* Oh God, the kiss was thrilling. I opened my eyes and looked deep into his. They were filled with light, with passion, with pure, raw emotion. He wanted me. He craved me just as I craved him. I wanted him to take me, all of me, right there and then. I couldn't wait anymore. Before I knew what I was doing, I had straddled him and was kissing him intently.

My bedroom door creaked open.

"Oops! Sorry." Jenna giggled. "Didn't expect that. Cake's ready, lovebirds."

I blushed and jumped off Scott, tripping on my shoes

that were strewn all over and falling on the floor with a loud thud. Wow, I was graceful. Scott laughed and joined me on the floor.

"You okay?" he asked, crossing his legs.

"Y-Yeah. Umm… I-I'm f-fine," I stuttered. Shit, how embarrassing. I blushed.

"Maddie, you don't have to be nervous around me. I promise I won't hurt you."

"I kn-know. I-I j-just…" I kept stuttering. I couldn't even form a sentence at that point.

"Come on," he said, standing and extending his hand to me. "Let's go eat some cake. We'll talk about this later."

"Okay." I managed to get that out easily enough. I grabbed his hand and let him pull me off the floor. We walked out of the room hand in hand, and for a moment, I felt calm and secure.

Chapter Fifteen

LIAM

I watched as Jenna walked away with a dramatic sway of her ass. She wanted it bad, and she was certainly playing all her cards right. She had such a nice, tight body. She'd do just fine. A nice little distraction from Madison was greatly needed. Those feelings just had to go. Lord knew Madison had made it perfectly clear how she felt, or rather, didn't feel about me. I was a fuck up. That's all I'd gathered from our little exchange. But honestly, what else was new?

Jenna quickly came back, giggling. "What's up?" I asked casually, reclining back on the couch.

"Maddie's back there, and I just caught her practically dry-humping Scott. That totally isn't like her. I like it!" Her voice was childlike and ditzy. She started dancing around the room, carefree and wild.

Missy had been listening in, and when she heard, she yelled down the hall, "Whoa! Go Maddie! If you don't do him, I will!"

Missy and Jenna laughed, grabbing each other's hands

and dancing around the room. I should have been paying attention to their swaying hips and bouncing breasts, but a part of me just didn't care. Why the fuck was Madison kissing Reynolds?

I tried to contain my anger, but the clenched fists and jaw must have given it away.

"What's wrong? You don't have a thing for Maddie, do you?" They both laughed and walked toward the kitchen.

"Right," Missy laughed. "As if two smoking-hot guys would want *her*. She's nice and smart and all, but she dresses like she's straight from the fifties. And those damn glasses she wears? Hellooooo," Missy said, looking to Jenna. "What's that show she watches?" She paused, looking at the ceiling as if it held the answer to her question. "*Criminal Minds*! Yeah, that nerdy chick called. She wants them back." They both burst into laughter.

Madison walked into the room, and I was compelled to look at her. I wasn't focused on Missy and Jenna anymore; Madison was commanding my attention with just the simple motion of her inviting body. She was sexy as fuck. She gave me a subtle smile, the corners of her luscious lips turning up in irritation as she then looked at Jenna and Missy. Her lips were swollen, blood-filled from the kiss she had just shared with Reynolds, and my anger rose.

"Ahem." Madison cleared her throat. "If you two are done scrutinizing my wardrobe, I would really enjoy a piece of cake."

"Oh Maddie, we love you! You know that, right? If you'd just let us *please* take you shopping!" Jenna begged her.

Missy chimed in enthusiastically. "Yes! You've been working out so much, and you *so totally* need a makeover."

"Ladies, ladies," Reynolds said. "Leave Maddie alone. She's perfect how she is." Scott ducked his head, and his face turned red. *Dickhead.*

It was at that point I noticed they were holding hands. He raised her hand to his lips and kissed it.

Madison looked over at me, gave Reynolds a peck on the cheek, and slowly removed her hand from his. *This can't be happening,* I thought. I had left them alone for twenty minutes, and he was kissing her hand like some dashing knight? He needed to be knocked down a peg.

The intercom buzzing pierced the awkwardness.

"Saved by the bell," Madison murmured as she hurried away and let in the deliveryman.

She opened the door, and I heard her making small talk as she paid for the pizza. Reynolds came and grabbed a seat across from mine. The smile that was plastered on his face pissed me off even more. He was happy. I couldn't say I blamed him. If Madison had kissed me, I'd be pretty fucking happy, too.

"What the hell do you think you're doing?" I questioned. I sat up, so close to Reynolds I was almost in his face. He needed to know this shit had to stop.

"I'm not sure what you're referring to, O'Leary," he replied. A laugh vibrated in his throat. I wanted to rip out his larynx so he'd never be able to laugh again. I smiled. Ah, that would be perfection.

"You know damn well what the fuck I'm talking

about, Reynolds. Don't mess with her, man. It isn't good to get involved with someone you work with. Plus, she's complicated." I was just making shit up at that point. Anything to get him to back off.

"You don't think I know this, O'Leary? I'm the one who saw her being pulled from her home when I was eight years old. Eight goddamn years old." He placed his hands on the coffee table and leaned in closer to me. Grief, heartache, love, all covered his face. "Not a day went by I didn't think about her. Wonder about her. Now I have her back, and I will do anything to protect her. That includes protecting her from the likes of you." He shoved my shoulder, and I was knocked back into the chair. What was it with this fucker and shoving me? The shove wasn't like before, though. He had put some power into this one. I sat up straighter and positioned myself for a brawl. If he wanted to fucking fight, we'd do this. I clenched my fists in anticipation.

"I don't care what you think you feel for her—don't. She's innocent. Don't take that from her. Don't cross that line. It's thin, and you're teetering on the edge." Reynolds got up and went into the kitchen to help the girls set the table for lunch. I gritted my teeth and rubbed my face, hoping those actions would take away the complex emotions welling up inside me. He was right on so many levels, but I just didn't want to let her go. I *couldn't* let her go. She was different, and I *needed* different. It was my turn for rescuing, and she was my savior.

Chapter Sixteen

MADISON

During lunch, I sat between Scott and Liam. Two guys—both of whom I clearly found deliciously attractive—were ready to kill each other, and I was sandwiched between them. Fantastic. But Liam was proving to be a total asshole and Scott—well, Scott was proving to be everything I had ever dreamed of. Damn, that kiss had been fierce. I touched my lips, running my fingers gently across them, remembering the feelings that had overtaken me.

Jenna and Missy took care of most of the conversation, talking about their careers as dancers. I chuckled every time they said that. I'd watched them dance before and—well, let's just say their version of dancing was, basically, a lot of vagina in your face. Not so much arabesques and pliés. I reached for another slice of pizza, and of course spilled my water in the process.

"Jesus, I'm a mess," I commented. The water cascaded down Scott's pants, soaking the front of him. Automatically, I took a napkin and started dabbing at the wetness. I felt a sudden hardness underneath the scratchiness of the napkin and I blushed. What the hell was I thinking? Scott cleared his throat.

"I can do it, Maddie." He gently took the napkin from my hand and finished cleaning himself up. He was beet red, and he wouldn't look at me. I flopped down in the chair, feeling like a complete idiot. I shot a quick glance down at his pants as he was cleaning up. Sweet Jesus, he had a nice package. I shoved another piece of pizza in my mouth before I said something stupid, like how I wanted to take him for a ride. Yep. More pizza please!

Liam slammed his fists down, shaking the entire table.

"This is bullshit!" he yelled as he stormed out of the room. I got up to go see what was wrong, but Scott grabbed my arm.

"Leave him be, Maddie. It's best to let him just cool off." I nodded, sitting back down to finish my pizza.

The rest of the lunch went by quickly, and Scott and I went back into my room to finish packing up my stuff. Scott took off his suit jacket and dress shirt and stood in just his comfortable white T-shirt and suit pants. There was something so bewitching about Scott dressed so simply.

He was super helpful with the packing, and we listened to music as he told me more about his childhood. The soothing voice of Norah Jones played in the background, and a sense of contentment filled me. It was nice to hear he had grown up happy, loved, and normal. Whatever normal was. I was so comfortable with him. He was like that friend you hadn't seen in years, but nothing ever changed. We picked up the conversation like it had never ended. Well, except in this case, when Scott had hit puberty, he had become a Greek god. Actually, it was more like a Spartan warrior and a Greek goddess had a love child, which had resulted in a smart and *fine*-as-hell man.

With each lift of a box, his muscles strained. Sweat beaded on his forehead. He lifted his shirt, exposing his sculpted abs, and gently wiped away the sweat. I stared at him, my eyes never leaving the perfection that was his body. He caught my stare, smiling with all-knowing satisfaction, and a sheepishness that spoke to my own insecurities. I turned around, bending over to finish packing another box. I wanted him to have something to look at; after all, it was only fair. I couldn't help but laugh to myself as I continued, picturing Scott in full Spartan warrior attire, the tunic barely covering his manhood.

It wasn't until the music stopped that I heard the noises. Pandora had this way of just stopping whenever it pleased, and I was too cheap to pay for the premium membership.

Moaning and groaning came from somewhere in the apartment. Scott shook his head and went to turn the music back on.

I slammed my dresser drawer shut and stormed out of the room. My steps were so forceful, the lamps and the pictures in my room shook with my anger.

"Maddie, don't. Just leave it be." Scott reached out for me. I ripped my arm away.

"No, I won't, Scott. This is just rude and so, so, so—just so incredibly fucked-up. I mean, at my house? Hours after

he asked me out on a date? The nerve of this guy. I swear!"
I stormed across the hall on a mission. I was going to teach
Liam a lesson.

I opened Jenna's door and saw no one. Confused, I
walked down the long hallway and saw something I would
never be able to unsee. Jenna, Missy, and Liam on my
couch. My couch! And not just *on* my couch. *Fucking* on
my couch. It wasn't any fucking I had ever seen, though. In
fact, I was sure what they were doing was illegal in some
states.

Jenna and Missy must have not heard me because they
both continued like I wasn't even there. Liam, though,
locked eyes with me as he proceeded to hammer Jenna from
behind. He stopped for a moment, as if he were second-
guessing himself, but then continued his movements.

My mouth was wide open. I wasn't sure what I had
wanted to say, but I had to say something, right? Instead,
I just stood there looking at him like an idiot. When he
looked back at me, I couldn't help but feel sorrow for him.

This Liam wasn't the Liam I had met the first day on
our run. His eyes, the windows to his soul, were dark. Dark
like a barren wasteland no one could touch. He seemed
lost. Lost in the coldness that had overcome him. I wanted
to scream for him to snap out of it, but it was no use.

He grabbed Jenna's neck, squeezing it hard. I saw the
whites of his knuckles and Jenna gasped as she struggled
to breathe. Tears welled in my eyes, and I wanted to look
away. He didn't stop. Instead, I heard the wet slap as he
increased his tempo and rammed her harder and harder,

until they both were screaming loudly in ecstasy.

Missy was giving Jenna attention, *lots* of attention. She played with her breasts, molding them with her hands. Jenna's hard pink nipples were taken into Missy's mouth, and Jenna moaned through her gasping. Liam had let go of her neck and continued his pounding. It was a writhing of limbs, and I couldn't tear my gaze away from the scene.

Scott came up next to me and whispered something into my ear. I don't know what he said, but I allowed him to guide me back into my room.

"Maddie," Scott said, giving my hand a gentle squeeze, trying to snap me out of whatever trance I was in.

"Sorry. What?" I chewed on my bottom lip, thinking about Liam's eyes.

I was all flustered and bothered by what I had just seen. Why had he looked at me? Why hadn't he stopped? It had seemed like he couldn't. I was so confused, pissed off, and sad. I wanted to help Liam, but I didn't know how. I was so fucked-up myself. How was I going to help someone else?

"Are you okay? I told you not to go out there."

"Yeah. Yeah, I'm fine. I know what sex is, Scott." I folded my arms, plopping myself on my bed.

"I know that. It's just Liam can be rather in-your-face about it. In this case, literally." Scott sat down next to me.

"Go figure," I spat. "I just found him screwing my roommates on my couch, in broad daylight, when he knows we're down the hall. Real upstanding guy," I said sarcastically. I wanted to talk about what I had seen in his eyes, but I wasn't ready for that conversation with Scott.

Plus, the moment had felt like something between Liam and me. A shared darkness.

"Let's just finish packing so we can get out of here. The sooner, the better. I'm ready to be rid of all this." I went to stand up, and Scott grabbed me, keeping me on the bed.

"Maddie, Liam's hurting, big time. He doesn't know how to process his emotions."

I sighed. "I know he's hurting, Scott. That's what I'm afraid of, how far he's willing to go not to feel. That look in his eyes…" It seemed I was ready to talk about it. I brought my hand to my mouth. God, he had looked so scary. So dark. "It was alarming. I want to help him, Scott. I just don't know if I can. I don't want to sink into that darkness."

Scott took me in his arms, holding me. Just being with him in that moment was so comforting, so refreshing.

"I know. I know you want to help him, and that is what is so incredibly amazing about you. I know you. It may be years later, but I know you. You think you're broken." He shushed my protests. "You aren't. You are whole, and I'm going to find a way to prove that to you." He kissed me on the forehead then got up, extending his hand to me. I smiled at him, taking his hand in mine. I was relieved. Scott understood me. He understood what I needed.

We started packing and lugging boxes. The silence was comforting, clear, and exhilarating. Scott and I were content just as we were—together. We continued lugging boxes back and forth, until all I had left was one more box in my closet. Scott reached for it and I stopped him, letting him know I'd get it later. We sat down on the edge of the bed again. After a few moments of companionable silence, I heard a knock at the door.

"Maddie, it's Jenna. Just wondering if you needed any help." Jenna's voice sounded content and satisfied.

I forced myself to get up and open the door.

"Nope," I said, looking her in the eyes and studiously avoiding the red handprint on her neck.

"We're actually all done. Just going to lug these two boxes down to the car. The rest will just stay here."

"Cool. Hey, bring Bradshaw back anytime. He's amazing." She smiled.

"It's O'Leary," I said without malice. "And I have a feeling, after this assignment, he won't be back."

"Huh? What assignment?" She looked at me questioningly.

"Nothing. Never mind. Can you tell him that we are all done if he is?"

Jenna chewed her gum loudly, which annoyed the hell out of me, and adjusted her boobs. "Oh shit! Were we too loud? I'm sorry. I tried to be quiet but he was just so—" I cut her off. She had a smile plastered on her face and was no doubt about to share the events that led up to her very loud climax.

"Jenna, really. Please don't share details. I don't want to hear about it. It's fine. Just next time, not on my couch."

She smirked. "No problem, girlie. I'm going to miss you!" She grabbed me and hugged me. Again, I was unable to breathe, suffocated by boobs.

"I'll miss you, too. Be careful and focus on school, okay?"

"Okay, *mom*." She scrunched her face at me and walked away. Scott smiled, grabbed a box, and left. I sure knew how to clear a room.

I sighed, went to my closet, and grabbed the last box, placing it on my hip. As I closed my bedroom door, a nagging feeling hit me that I wouldn't be returning. I said my good-byes and shut the door, heading to the car.

I decided to sit in the back. I needed to sleep, and to clear my head. Too much had happened over the past two days. We pulled off my street, and I pressed my forehead against the glass and closed my eyes.

As I drifted off to sleep, I felt the familiar tug of my dreams. The same dream I always had after a stressful day.

Daddy, please. No...

Chapter Seventeen

As I merged onto the highway, I heard the faint sound of Madison's snoring. I smiled. I was glad she was getting some sleep. She'd definitely need it. The Academy wasn't easy, and I wished I could talk her out of this life. The one thing I did agree with Reynolds on was that she was an innocent. This life—it wasn't for her. She deserved better. Better than me, that was for sure.

"So, really? Her roommates?" Reynolds said, ridiculing me and interrupting my thoughts.

"Reynolds, I'm not having this conversation with you. I can fuck who I please." I gripped the steering wheel tighter, wishing it were Reynolds's neck.

"Yes, you can, but not when it affects Maddie. We're supposed to protect her."

"Since when are you her protector? She's a grown woman. She can tell me if something bothers her." I looked at him pointedly. He needed to stop treating her like a porcelain doll. She wouldn't shatter.

"O'Leary, enough. Don't screw with her, okay? She's got a lot going on. Just be more sensitive."

"Dude, seriously? Sensitive? I swear you have a vagina. Get real. I'm an FBI agent. Sensitive is not in my vocabulary." I chuckled.

"Whatever. Thought you cared. That's all." He smoothed his hair back.

"Not sure what gave you that impression, but I don't. I fuck women. No strings attached. It's much easier that way."

"Suit yourself, man. Just don't hurt her, okay?" Worry formed in Reynolds's eyes, but I shrugged off the encroaching guilt, little whispers that would only lead to me needing more sex.

"Hurt her? Fuck that. I don't care what the hell she feels," I snapped at him, the crudeness of my own words startling me. "Let's make that clear. So if you two want to go off and hold hands together, go for it. You won't make it past second base." I snorted. "You're too scared."

"Right. Okay, O'Leary." Reynolds folded his arms, sitting back.

"It's true. How many girlfriends have you had since we've known each other? That's right: *zero*. You can't pull the trigger in the field, and you can't pull the trigger in the bedroom." Reynolds cringed, reacting to the harshness of my words.

"Why do you have to bring that shit up? It's in the past. I fucked up, okay? Let it go," Reynolds said pointedly.

"Let it go? Oh sure, no problem, man." I rolled my eyes.

"That little girl that you let fucking die—yeah, sure. I'll let that shit go *real* quick. All you had to do was shoot the fucking son of a bitch, but you couldn't. Catching him alive was more important to you, asshole. You wanted to analyze him. Analyze *this*, you scared bastard: *you* let her die." I looked Reynolds right in the eyes when I said those last words, aware that my own eyes were probably turning obsidian. He hadn't had to hold that little girl as she'd died. He wasn't the one who'd promised the little girl's parents he would protect her. He hadn't had to let those same parents down. No way in hell he had to do that. Reynolds got to go into the office and work his profiling magic. He had no idea what it felt like.

Reynolds shook his head, and it gave me a sick sense of satisfaction that I'd shaken him.

"That was my *job*, Liam. To profile. To analyze. Not to kill. Human life is not for me to take. It is for me to protect."

I snorted. Seriously? A protector? Such a fucking joke.

"*Right.* Okay," I said sarcastically. And to piss him off further, "So, how many women, man? How many women have you been deep inside of? How many have you felt quiver at your touch?" Reynolds adjusted his groin slightly. *Yeah, squirm, you son of a bitch,* I thought.

"There've been women, okay? Just because I don't screw each of them doesn't make me less of a man than you. You're too damaged to realize when something is good. Maddie is good, and instead of protecting that goodness, you screw her roommates. You can't lose her, though, because you never had her. She may have been attracted to you, but you'll never have anything beyond sex with anyone. And it's too bad because Maddie—well, Maddie might have given you a chance." Reynolds looked back at Madison—his precious Maddie—and his eyes filled with adoration.

My heart beat faster at the thought of Madison wanting me, of me having her. Anger streamed through me because I knew I'd fucked up. Just like I fucked up everything else.

"What are you talking about? Because I wanted to have coffee with her? It was just a damn ploy to get in her pants. That's all. Nothing more. Anyway, look at her. She isn't exactly as hot as her roommates. Who wouldn't trade up?" I lied. I had to distance myself from the emotions I felt. I wanted her. I wanted her so bad. I remembered her dress hiking up, exposing parts of her leg to me. I wanted to look into her eyes as I fucked her. At first, I would be gentle, slow and methodical with my movements, teasing her, taunting her. I wanted her to feel the intensity I felt when I looked at her. I wanted her to scream my name, beg me to pleasure her. I'd rock into her faster and faster until she wouldn't have anyone else, until I owned her. My dick jumped in agreement. We *really* wanted to be buried deep inside her.

"Good to know." The aggressive words came from the backseat.

I looked in the rearview mirror and caught her stretching.

Rubbing the sleep out of her eyes, Madison said, "Looks like I dodged a bullet."

"Yeah." Reynolds shifted in his seat, moving closer to the door, away from me, and he glanced in my direction. The tension built in the car, and he looked like he'd jump out if he could. If *only* I could open the door and give him a nudge.

"Madison, you weren't meant to hear that." I looked in the mirror, trying to make eye contact.

Her eyes locked on mine, dusky and filled with fire. "I know I wasn't. But it's fine. I figured as much. I don't need you, Liam. I'm perfectly content with what I have." She looked at Reynolds, and their eyes met. The feelings that lingered between them made me grit my teeth. Motherfucker. In that moment, I knew I'd lost her.

She adjusted herself in the backseat, fixing the seat belt so it lay properly against her breasts. I was an idiot. I sure knew how to open my mouth. I wasn't sure what my deal was with her, but I knew it was probably better we didn't have anything between us. I was damaged. She was damaged. She was looking for someone to fix her, and I was looking for someone to break. We continued driving in silence for a good thirty minutes. No one talked. No one looked at each other. Reynolds and Madison stared out the window, lost in their own worlds. I focused on the road, but mostly I tried to focus on something other than my dick. The damn thing kept springing to life. *Stand down, buddy; she's on a rampage and we're her target.* I smiled.

"I have to use the bathroom," Madison stated, still looking out the window.

"No problem. There's a rest stop about two miles away,"

I said, looking at her in the mirror again. Her dark curls were even crazier than before, scattered around her sleepy face. I watched her take out a hair tie from her bag and lift her arms to pull back those beautiful dark curls. I adjusted the mirror again so I could only see the road behind me. Clearly, I couldn't even watch her tie her hair back without wanting to fuck her.

"Where are we going to be staying?" she asked.

"Well, you aren't due at the Academy until Monday morning, so your uncle booked a room nearby." I glanced back at her. "We'll be staying over the weekend, and you can get focused on the reality that you will be an FBI cadet in just a few days," I reminded her. "We'll be doing some running, calisthenics, and maybe some weapons training to keep you in shape."

"Cool." She yawned. "I hope there's a pool. I could go for a swim."

"Assistant Director Harper mentioned you'd say that," Reynolds said with a chuckle. "There's a pool *and* a Jacuzzi." He paused and smiled. "Your uncle said, 'you're welcome.'"

Madison smiled and relaxed a bit in the back. I kept fighting back my feelings for her. I was so screwed up. No matter how hard I tried to push her away, my body reacted to the smallest thing she did. The thick, impassable wall I had put up to protect myself was chipping, snapping and breaking beneath me; my feelings for her seeped through the cracks like dank mildew. I was afraid of letting those feelings show, because with them came a whole breed of fucked-up. All I knew was the sooner I was done with this assignment, the better.

Chapter Eighteen

MADISON

After stopping for a bathroom break, I settled into the backseat again and thought about what Liam had said about me earlier. It had been uncomfortable to listen to. I knew there was no way he could care about me, but I guess I had just wanted to feel desirable. For once, I wanted to have guys attracted to and fighting over me, vying for my affection. It was a foolish thought, and I had other things to focus on.

Then there was Scott. He was light and warmth; and I knew instinctively he would be all I needed him to be. I just didn't like needing anyone. I felt like I was constantly struggling with myself. Struggling between wanting to be independent and wanting someone so bad it hurt even to think about that bone-deep need. Up until now, I had been able to survive on my own. The past two days had sent my mind and body reeling. Scott and Liam had waltzed into my life, and now I felt like an uncontrollable mess.

I didn't remember the last time I had felt this way, and the thought of having a boyfriend terrified me. Hell, who was I kidding? Liam had shared his feelings, and it wasn't as if Scott was asking for my hand in marriage. Companionship, trust, and love were all terms that were lost on me. I had never felt those things for anyone but my adoptive family, and even then, sometimes I had felt a little outside their family growing up. I wasn't sure if I knew how to truly love, but the emotions rolling through me for Scott—those feelings were more than the physical attraction I felt for Liam. Those feelings for Scott were real. Those feelings were also intense, and they threatened to overtake me. *How can I think of loving someone else when I barely know how to love myself?*

Liam turned off the highway, and I broke away from my thoughts, looked at the Hilton where we had just stopped, and laughed to myself. Uncle Tom sure knew how to make me happy. I got out of the car and closed my eyes for a moment before taking in the moon. It was full and lit up the sky. The stars were bright, giving the illusion of shimmery sparkles. It was dazzling. I didn't like the dark, but this sky… The light illuminated my surroundings and made me feel comfortable and at ease. It was getting late, and despite having slept almost the entire way, I was exhausted. I moved to the trunk and started unpacking when Scott came up behind me and propped himself against the vehicle.

"Hey." That one simple word held so much seduction, I contemplated dropping my panties right there in the middle of the parking lot. Okay, not one of my finer moments, but he turned me on something wicked, and I wasn't opposed to having a little romp in the backseat of the car.

"Hey," I replied. I felt like I was going to stutter. Deep breaths. *In and out. In and out.*

"I've got to head over to Quantico and do some paperwork. Talk to some people and whatnot about the game plan. I'll have to do that over the next few days. I'm going to leave you with O'Leary, okay?"

"Sure," I said, not really sure how I felt about being left alone with a man who had just called me ugly. "Do I really have a choice? Anyway, I thought that just us and Uncle Tom were going to know what's going on?"

"Director Stone runs the Academy over at Quantico. He and your uncle are close, and your uncle wanted us to have a go-to person there. So unfortunately, it's necessary to ensure you're all set to start Monday." He smoothed back his hair—a nervous gesture, which gave me butterflies low in my stomach.

"No, I understand. I would just prefer not many people knowing. That's all. I don't want it to be going around that I received any special treatment or anything."

Scott laughed. "Don't worry about that. No special treatment will be given. If anything, I think they'll be harder on you since you're a newbie. That usually isn't allowed."

"Great! I'm already hated, and I haven't even started." I lugged my big duffel bag over my shoulder. Scott quickly grabbed it and proceeded toward the hotel entrance. The moonlight bounced off his face, making his eyes that much more blue. He was beautiful. My nipples got hard, and I felt the wetness soaking my panties. I clenched my thighs together, hoping that would stop the moistness forming there, and shook my head. I got crazy when I was horny, but crazy and I were apparently on a first-name basis these days.

"I can get that, you know?" I had to say something to interrupt my thoughts. Totally not PG.

"I know you can," Scott replied.

"I guess chivalry isn't dead," I teased, mock curtseying.

"Far from it." He opened the door for me, bowed, and said, "My lady."

I laughed loudly. We walked into the hotel, the cool air brushing against my face. It soothed me, easing the eagerness swarming inside me. I looked over at Scott as he carried my bag. He grinned, tenderness forming on his face. I ached for him. All of him.

I gulped loudly. It was now or never. I had to take what I wanted. "What's our room situation anyway?" I asked nervously.

"We had to get one room and share per FBI budget rules. Two double beds in one room and a pullout couch in the living room. I'll take the couch." He looked ahead, not once glancing in my direction.

"Oh," I said disappointedly as we walked into the elevator.

"Oh? Something wrong?" He gave me a questioning look, and pressed the button for floor five.

"No. It's just, I don't mind if you share with me. I figured you'd want to be comfortable." I played with my hair, mortified that I had just said that out loud. Oh hell, who cared? I just wanted him to say yes.

"Why, Miss Madison Sky Harper, are you asking me to sleep with you?" His eyes met mine and excitement played there.

"Scott!" I blushed, smacking him playfully on the arm.

"I'm just teasing. I should warn you, though. I hog the blankets!"

"I snore, so I think we're even." The tension left my shoulders. Well, he hadn't said no.

"Don't worry. O'Leary and I already found out about your snoring." He started imitating my snoring noises.

"Not funny!" I pouted.

"It really was. You are quite an interesting person to watch sleep."

The elevator door opened, and another couple squeezed in next to us. The couple in question was so into each other that—well, let's just say what they were doing didn't leave much for the bedroom.

Scott raised his eyebrows at me playfully, and I giggled.

The couple stopped and took a breath. Thank goodness, because I'd thought I'd have to practice my CPR skills any minute.

"I'm sorry," said the woman. "We just got married!" She flashed me her ring.

"Congratulations," Scott and I replied in unison.

"Thanks! I'm just so happy. I mean, I know we just met a few weeks ago, but it feels so right, you know?"

"Sure," I said. "I totally get it. Love at first sight and

all."

Jealousy surged through me. I wanted to *be* her. I wanted that ring on her finger to be *mine*. I looked down at my hand, imagining what it would look like. I glanced over at Scott, willing him to look at me. Mrs. Madison Sky Reynolds. I felt like a child writing her crush's name on her notebook over and over again. Okay, I was losing it. I put my hands behind my back and tried to shift my thoughts to something else.

"Yes, absolutely," the man chimed in. "Look at her. Who wouldn't love her?" He kissed her so affectionately on the lips, I sighed. Did I really want that for myself?

Who was I kidding? Yeah, I did. I wanted the comfort and the passion. I wanted it all. My pity party was interrupted by the sound of tangling tongues as they started making out again. Scott looked at me, a smile forming on his lips. I smiled back, my eyes twinkling with desire. He had to know how I felt, right?

"Finally," I said aloud as we reached the fifth floor.

We got off and headed to our room. Scott took out his phone and called Liam. "Hey… Yeah, we're outside the door. Can you let us in?"

The door opened, and there stood a disheveled-looking Liam. He greeted us in only a towel, and he must have just taken a quick shower because he had droplets of water skimming down his naked chest. His eyes looked me up and down, turning dark and sensual. I shifted from foot to foot, pulling my dress down apprehensively. I didn't like the way he looked at me. It made me feel exposed and a little dirty.

"Hey," he said to me. What was it with guys saying "hey" and me wanting to drop my panties? I didn't have the butterflies and emotional connection with Liam I had with Scott, but a guy fresh out of the shower was enough for any girl to get a little sexual buzz. At least that was what I was telling myself when my panties became wet—again. Plus, Liam was a manwhore—yeah, there was that.

"Hello. I see you made yourself comfortable. Feeling dirty?" I jabbed. Despite repeatedly saying I hadn't cared about his romp in the sheets with my roommates, I had. *A lot.* I wanted to make him feel as bad about it as possible. I nudged him as I made my way through the doorway. I entered into the hotel room, only to realize it was a two-bedroom suite. Awesome. Privacy.

"Scott and I will take this room." I ran into the room on the right and threw myself on the bed.

"Scott will take the couch, Madison," Liam scolded as he stepped into the room.

"No, he won't, Liam," I said, standing my ground. He would not throw his weight around, not this time. I still had some control over my life and over who slept in my bed. It certainly wouldn't be him. "He and I discussed it, and we'll share a bed. Contrary to your beliefs, not everyone who shares a bed must actually have sex."

"Reynolds, I need to speak with you."

Scott and Liam stepped outside the room, but they were still within earshot. I watched as they walked away, Liam's shirtless body still dripping. Small burn scars covered his back. They were sporadic, and there was neither rhyme nor reason to their design. I guessed that Liam had had a tough past. A past he buried much deeper than I had buried my own, but looking at him now—seeing the scars that riddled his otherwise perfect body—I knew. His struggles were much rawer than I even realized. It wasn't the time to ask him about his past, so I pushed the thoughts to the back of my mind as I lay on the bed listening intently to their conversation.

"Reynolds, this isn't the way we handle our assignments. It isn't professional. How can you protect her if you're sleeping with her?" His words were punctuated by what sounded an awful lot like jealousy.

"Relax. I know. We aren't sleeping together like that. We are sharing a bed. What better way to protect her than to be next to her?" Scott asked matter-of-factly.

"You can't stand there and tell me you don't want to sleep with her," Liam said, his words punctuated by what sounded like his foot tapping against the carpet.

"I didn't say that. Yes, I care about her. Yes, of course, I want to sleep with her, but I know this isn't the time nor the place to be doing that. Unlike you, I still hold some semblance of morals." The only sound I could hear beyond Scott's words was my heart beating against my chest. Hearing Scott actually say he wanted to sleep with me sent flutters through my body, and I couldn't help but think, *Damn Scott and his morals.*

"Fuck you, asshole." I heard Liam storm off, followed by a loud bang as his bedroom door slammed shut.

I'd been lying on the bed listening to them, and I didn't bother to move as Scott walked back into the room.

"Maddie, I've got to head out before it gets much later. Director Stone at Quantico is waiting on me. Please don't leave the hotel room without O'Leary, okay? We aren't sure yet of the comings and goings of Walsh, and we don't want to risk anything just yet."

"Roger that!" I signified my compliance with a salute. Scott laughed and gave me a peck on the cheek. His eyes wandered over my body, but I didn't feel exposed with him. I felt like he was discovering me, getting to know the many facets of my body. I lay there for a few moments, letting him look at me, staring at him as passion radiated from our bodies. That fierce passion collided, like waves in the sea, overtaking us. He moved quietly over the bed and placed his hand gently against the cheek he had just kissed. He lowered his mouth ever so slowly, and I felt on fire. His kiss made me feel as though my body was being torn at the seams. Every part of me craved him. Wanted him.

All too abruptly, he eased himself away.

"Maddie, we can't. Not yet." He looked away, and just as quickly as they had come, the waves subsided.

Scott stood and I lay on the bed quietly.

"Not yet," I whispered. I knew this was the start of something, and I was willing to wait. I kicked off my shoes, knelt on the bed, and drew Scott in to give him a light kiss.

"You've got to go," I said, giving him a small, knowing smile. "Plus, I've got to take a nice long shower."

Scott laughed. "A cold shower would do me good right

now."

"My shower would be better with you in it," I purred softly, then looked away, flustered. Scott barked out a laugh.

"I'll be back as soon as I can, Madison. Keep my spot warm for me."

"I'll be waiting for you." I watched him walk away, admiring his tight ass in those suit pants. Jesus, I couldn't wait to get my hands on him.

My feelings subsided as Liam propped himself against the doorframe. He cleared his throat, looking entirely unamused by whatever part of our exchange he had seen.

I went to close the door.

"Open," he demanded as he pushed the door open wider with his arm. His muscles flexed, temporarily distracting me from the fact that he was acting like a complete ass.

"Excuse me?" I asked, forcing myself to look away from his chiseled arms.

"The door stays open. I can't watch you if I can't see you."

"I don't need a babysitter, O'Leary," I said, folding my arms.

"It's my job." He opened the door wider, standing completely in the doorway now, preventing me from closing it.

"I know it's your job, but you don't have to watch me shower, do you? Pretty sure that isn't in the FBI handbook. I mean, I know I'm behind in my lessons, but—"

He laughed and dropped his towel. I screeched, covering

my eyes.

"Honestly? Come on!" I yelled.

"What? You act like you've never seen a man naked before," he teased.

I blushed and turned around, removing my hands from over my eyes. "That's none of your business, and beside the point. Most don't just pull it out in front of you. Can I please take a shower now?"

"Why, Madison, are you flustered? I can take care of that for you." I turned around and I stared at him, only looking at his face. The infuriated look in my eyes should have stopped him, but it was Liam. He started moving toward me, strutting and gyrating his hips. I held back a smile.

"Really? I wouldn't touch you with a ten-foot pole, especially after you just slept with both of my roommates—at the same time!" He really had some nerve coming on to me after that. The reminder put a dampener on my need to laugh at his antics.

"That was *hours* ago. I'm clean now. See?" He turned around, stepping further away so he could show off his nice round ass. There he stood, completely naked, and *all* of him was standing at attention. I immediately slammed the bedroom door, but I did allow myself a small, soft chuckle.

He laughed loudly. "You're no fun, Madison."

"I've been called worse. I'm taking a shower. Stay out." Liam was annoying, but I couldn't help but laugh. I smiled. He was crazy.

I entered the bathroom, saw the enormous tub, and decided a bath was much more appealing. My muscles ached from the car ride, and I needed a break.

I ran the water hot, very hot, and poured in some bubbles from one of the novelty samples. Yum. The now-frothing water smelled like lavender.

I took off my clothes and stared at myself in the mirror. Sighing loudly, I lowered myself into the water and untied my hair. The curls cascaded down my smooth back like a waterfall, thick and lush.

Lying back in the hot, comforting bath, I closed my eyes and sang. Avril Lavigne wasn't my favorite, but "Keep Holding On" had gotten me through some pretty rough times. The lyrics spoke to me, fueled me to keep moving forward.

This time, though, the song didn't fuel me. The song ate at me. Peeled away at me slowly, like layers of dead skin. I just hoped what was underneath all those dead layers was worth all the pain. Before I could make it to the next verse, the tears started streaming down my face.

Singing was the one thing I could do to let out my emotions. It allowed me to escape. My mom used to sing me Fleetwood Mac's "Songbird" when my dad would get into one of his moods. She'd come into my room, all battered and bruised, and she'd hold me. She'd brush my tears away, and she'd tell me we would be together forever. She'd tell me that together we could make it through anything, and I had believed her. But without my mom, I wasn't so sure anymore.

Walsh had loved her. In his own twisted way, he had loved her, and according to him, I'd taken her from him.

She'd loved me and protected me until the end. She would have done anything for me. My love for singing was all because of my mother. Music became my safety and to this day, it soothed the darkest parts of me. I couldn't stem the flow of my tears as I sat in the overly hot bath, alone. There was a faint knock at the bathroom door, and I sat up, brushing away the tears.

"Madison?" Liam asked, longing wavering in his voice.

"Yeah?" I answered, my voice cracking.

"You okay?"

"I'm fine." Mostly just insecure and emotional. *Yeah, sure, I'm fine.*

"Okay," Liam said, and then he paused. "It's just you stopped singing, and well—it sounded like you were crying."

"I'm okay," I sniffled, and grabbed a nearby hand towel to blow my nose. "Please, just go away," I asked in the nicest way possible.

"All right. Madison?"

"Yes?"

"You have a lovely voice." I paused. Liam's voice had seemed kind and lost, so unlike the tough exterior he often showed the world.

"Thanks," I said sincerely. My heart ached a little for Liam. He could be kindhearted when he wasn't tormented by whatever constantly ate away at him. As I heard his footsteps walk away from the door, I sank deeper into the tub and shut my eyes. I felt a little better. Sometimes, you just needed to cry a little.

Chapter Nineteen

MADISON

I stayed in the bath much longer than I expected, and my appendages had started to wrinkle. The warm water had exfoliated the layers of me that needed to be melted away, and the lull and the tug of sleep pulled me under. I pried myself out of the bath, not wanting to leave its comfort. I toweled dry, put on my white cotton underwear and my Rolling Stones T-shirt, and opened the door to the main suite. I crawled into bed and left a light on to illuminate the room and drive out the darkness. I couldn't deal with the dark. Not ever, really, but especially not tonight.

I snuggled into the cozy blankets and the cool sheets, and closed my eyes reluctantly, terrified of the dream I knew would meet me. But the nightmare never came. Instead, I dreamed of walking down an aisle surrounded by bright, lively yellow sunflowers. The sounds of a church organ played "Pachelbel's Canon" in the background, and my white dress clung tightly to my body. A veil covered my face, obscuring my view, but when I finally made it to the end, I saw him. *Scott.* There were no horrors, no bodies, no blood. Just us. Together and happy.

I slept soundly, enjoying the peaceful dream until the sun beamed through the curtains. I had slept through the night, and not once had I felt the normal tug of Walsh roping me into the dreams that had haunted me since childhood. I looked over at the clock, rubbing the sleep from my eyes: 7:15. The other side of the bed was empty. Scott must not have gotten any sleep, I thought worriedly. I placed my feet on the carpet, feeling the tiny shreds of fiber cushioning my toes. I padded into the living room. Scott was sprawled on the couch, his long legs draped oddly over the side.

I snuck over quietly, leaned in, and kissed him gently on the mouth.

"Hmmm," he moaned, waking slowly. "Good morning to you, too." His eyes remained closed, and his voice was still sleepy.

"Good morning. How'd you sleep?" I moved his legs from the end of the couch, sat down, and placed them in my lap.

"Eh, not so great. This couch is small." He opened his eyes, the blueness of them piercing my very essence.

"I said you could sleep with me." I frowned at him, disappointed he had felt the need to sleep on the couch instead of with me.

"I know. You just looked so peaceful sprawled out on that bed. I didn't want to disturb you." He sat up so we were sitting side by side.

"I see," I mumbled.

"Maddie." He placed his hand over mine. "We don't have to rush this, okay?" He grabbed my hand and gave me a reassuring squeeze. I wanted to jump his bones—right there and then—but I knew he was right. We had time. We could wait.

"I know." I kissed him quickly and got up from the couch. I stretched, my shirt hiking up and exposing my white cotton underwear to him, then blushed, realizing I had padded out of the room without thinking. I'd just wanted to find him. Now, I was standing in front of him in only my underwear and a long T-shirt.

He looked me up and down, desire lingering in his eyes. "Let's spend the day together before I have go back to Quantico tonight." He cleared his throat, looking away.

I smiled. "I'd love that, but first, I have some training to do with Liam. Running and weight lifting. Maybe I should put some clothes on, though." We both laughed, and he nodded. I wanted to spend the entire day with Scott, but I knew I had to train so I was ready for the Academy. I'd been reading the manual Uncle Tom had given me, but I hadn't worked out since a couple days before.

"No problem. You do that for a few hours, and I'll do some paperwork. I can connect to the database on my work laptop." He got up, sat down at the desk, and opened his laptop.

"Perfect!" I walked away to go change into my workout clothes. Glancing back, I caught Scott staring at my ass. I flushed, wanting to pull my shirt down and hide myself, but instead I lifted it as I entered the bedroom, pulling it over my head. My back was to him and I stood there in just my underwear. He was staring at me wide-eyed when I looked over my shoulder. He shook his head, looking away. I shut the door with my foot. Maybe with enough teasing, he'd do something about it.

Liam and I spent a few hours doing some training. I did squats and push-ups, and he had me practice my pull-ups. He also had me practice dead lifts because as he said, "You never know when you'll have to drag someone to safety."

I got 320 pounds off the ground. My legs were thick and strong, and Liam grunted at the number. I took it as a compliment. We ended with a three-mile run. I ran it in 26:37. My fastest yet—*and* I managed to keep up with Liam.

After the workout, my muscles ached and I was exhausted, so Scott and I spent the rest of the day by the pool swimming and lounging around. Once we were tired of the pool and the Jacuzzi, we broke out old movies to play on the hotel TV. I fell asleep to *The Breakfast Club*, wrapped in Scott's arms.

While we watched old films, Liam slouched around, complaining about how bored he was. We offered a place on the couch to watch movies, but he mumbled something about not wanting to be a third wheel. He spent most of his day at the hotel bar. Just him and his good pal, Jack Daniels.

When I awoke from our nap, the sun was going down, and Scott was gone. A note was lying on his side of the couch.

MADDIE,

I'LL BE BACK TONIGHT. SAVE MY SPOT THIS TIME. I'LL
MISS YOU.

SCOTT

My heart leapt in my chest. I got up and headed to the
shower reluctantly, not wanting to wash away the day.

Chapter Twenty

LIAM

Those two made me fucking sick, cuddling and spooning all day. *Oh, come join us, Liam. Come to lunch with us, Liam.* Fuck that. I'd rather be sent to the fiery pits of hell before I'd spend a day with those two. Seeing him with her made my blood boil. I didn't need an excuse to do something stupid.

I heard the shower turn on, and Madison's voice filled the suite, calming the rage building inside of me. She was so happy. Thoughts of her father were a distant memory. All because of Reynolds. A voice in my head whispered: *That should be you.*

My cell phone lit up as an incoming text message came through, interrupting my thoughts. I didn't recognize the number.

Meet me at the bar downstairs. Ten minutes. I have information you'll want regarding Walsh, the text read.

Who the fuck was this?

I texted back quickly. *Who is this?*

A friend. Leave the girl and meet me in ten.

"Fuck," I said out loud.

"Everything okay out there?" Madison asked from the bathroom.

"Yeah, I gotta—um… run downstairs real quick and get something from Reynolds. I'll be right back."

"Uh, okay. Do you want me to come with you? I'm getting out now." I heard the water turn off.

"No," I quickly replied. Fuck, I wasn't being too stealthy. "Just stay up here. It'll just take a minute."

"Okay, sheesh. No need to yell. I'll stay."

I grabbed my hotel key, my weapon, and put my wallet in my back pocket as I left my little room in the suite.

"Great! I'll be right back. Stay put."

I slammed the door to the main suite and rushed down the flights of stairs that led to the bar. I didn't know what I was walking into.

Within seconds, I arrived at the hotel bar. I chose to sit down at the table nearest the EXIT sign, and ordered a Jack Daniels. I surveyed the area. Nothing seemed odd or out of place, so I sat back and waited.

The waitress brought my drink right away, and even stopped to give me an extra glance, which wasn't unusual. I smiled. Never a dull moment. I was thinking about passing her my number when *she* entered the room.

Stunning and tall, the woman was curvy in all the right places. Her long, straight dark hair went down to her waist, and she had the most beautiful pale white skin. As she smiled in my direction, I noticed her eyes were a piercing green. She waved to the wait staff and the hostess, and then proceeded to walk toward me. She wore tight jeans and a pale pink tank top, which accentuated her large breasts and showed just the right amount of stomach. A silver shimmer gleamed from her belly button, further highlighting her toned body. When she reached my table, she sat herself across from me.

I sat back in my chair and adjusted my hardened cock. "Do I know you?"

"You don't know me yet, Special Agent O'Leary, but you will." She smirked.

"How do you know who I am?" She had my attention now. Well, okay—let's be honest, she'd had my attention since she walked into the room.

"I know you're here with Aimee and Special Agent Reynolds. You're protecting her from Walsh, or should I say *trying* to." She sat back, enjoying the torment.

"All of that is classified." I sat up in my booth. Who the fuck was this chick?

She laughed. "Classified. Right. I know Walsh escaped prison about a week ago and he happens to be staying here in Virginia as well. He knows what you are all doing even before you do. You know that, right?"

"How do you know all of this?" My dick was soft now. What a fucking buzzkill.

"Somebody reached out to me with information a few days ago. She gave me all the information I needed."

"And you didn't think to call the police?" Who did this woman think she was? "Why do you even care?"

"Let's just say we have a mutual interest in the apprehension of Walsh. I follow him. He follows you. I know stuff. Now, you know stuff." A martini was placed on the table with extra olives. She slowly took one out of the glass and proceeded to place it in her mouth. Her pearly white teeth, behind juicy red lips, sank into the olive. She didn't once take her eyes off me as she ate. It was strangely erotic. My dick sprang to life again. What I wouldn't give to put something else in that mouth. Okay. Back on track, here. Walsh… Aimee…

Shaking my head, as if to drown out the sexual thoughts, I asked, "Okay, so how do you know where to find Walsh?"

She looked angry, and she placed the toothpick that contained her olives aggressively back into her glass. "I *did* know where to find Walsh, but I think he finally got tired of me following him. Some woman named Alice gave me information. She didn't say much. Just where I could find him. I should have questioned her motives behind giving me the information, but I had him right where I wanted him." She frowned. "She seemed so scared." She shook her head as if trying to forget about the woman. "But now, he lost me. I'm surprised he let me follow him this long."

"Yeah, me too. That's a guy who knows what he's doing."

"I know. Which is why I sought you out. I'm not sure why he allowed me to follow him. I'm convinced he knew I was there the entire time and didn't care. Until now. He's planning something big, Liam."

"What's he planning?" I asked eagerly.

"Not so fast. I need something in return."

"Of course you do," I snipped. "What is it?"

"I need to see him when you catch him. I need to see him. Please," she begged, grabbing the edge of the table in a panic. She was waiting for my response like it could answer her prayers. I didn't know this chick, but what she was asking seemed to mean a lot to her. Walsh was the scum of the earth—a serial killer who fed off the pain of girls who were unable to help themselves. Why did she need this? Because that's what it looked like: *need.*

"Why would you want to see him? He's nothing. He's scum. I'm sure you know what he did to all of those girls." I was fuming. She had no idea what Walsh was capable of. What did she think this was, some sort of joke? *I bet she's one of those serial killer fangirls,* I thought disgusted.

"Oh, I know firsthand what he did to those girls." She lifted up her shirt and showed me a stomach full of scars. Big, red, fiery scars. Her seemingly flawless body was not so flawless. She looked like she had been cut over and over again, and never allowed to heal. Her face showed so much pain that it seemed as if she were reliving the moment she had first been given those scars. Scars that still looked like they had been freshly inflicted.

I sat back in the booth, confused, but oddly intrigued.

She sighed, the pain on her face slowly being replaced with sadness and remembrance.

"I was 'lucky' they said. Lucky?" she said with disgust. "Look at me…! He would call me his beautiful masterpiece while he took the knife and carved my skin. Sick son of a bitch." She slammed her fist on the table, causing it to shake. My Jack Daniels spilled, the syrup-colored liquid pooling on the table. I left it there, watching it collect and fuse together.

"Just when I thought I was healing, and started to feel better, he would reopen the wounds." She took the knife out of its neatly wrapped napkin and placed it to her skin. I sat up, ready to place my hand on hers, to snatch the knife away. She pretended she was cutting herself, carefully tracing the faint thin red lines that scarred her skin. She didn't break the skin, but that look in her eyes—dark and needy—let me know she had done this more than once. She put the knife down, shifting her focus back to me. "He'd cut me over and over again. This continued for a few months until they found me in his basement. They thought I was dead."

"Oh, shit." I sat up in the booth again. I was close to her, our faces almost touching. "There was a survivor... just one... his last victim... You're Macey Winslow," I whispered, a secret only we could share. She nodded, a single tear streaming down her cheek. There was no sound, but this wordless moment held so much emotion, it tugged at me, pulling me in. It wasn't fair. This woman had so much life left to live, yet she was plagued by the scars Walsh had left. I reached out to touch her hand, to comfort her. She ripped it away, holding it close to her body, protecting herself. She was clearly uncomfortable with a man's touch. I sighed, knowing the torment she must have endured was endless and had forever left its mark on her—in more ways than one.

She squared her shoulders and placed her hands in her lap. She didn't want to feel. I was sure the only feeling she had was the reopening of those wounds. I frowned, thinking about this beautiful woman harming herself just for the hope of feeling again. Her voice was strong when she continued with her story.

"I felt bad for the woman he dragged along with him, though. She obviously wasn't into that life." Macey stirred her drink and stared into it like it held the answers to her pain. "Poor thing. The woman would have conversations with me. She'd tell me about how wonderful and innocent her daughter was, and that I reminded her of the little girl she had waiting for her." Macey smiled, remembering the woman and the young girl she had spoken of.

"The woman couldn't have stopped him, but she *did* feel bad for what Walsh was doing." Macey's eyes were moist. She really had cared about this mysterious woman. "Then, one night, I saw the woman's little girl. The one she had talked so often about. I was afraid for the little girl as she looked for her doll, but I'd been so cut up, so beaten and bruised, I couldn't move to let her know I was alive, or that she shouldn't be there." Her voice cracked.

"Then the cops came, and they found me, and all the bodies at the house and at the other place—the cabin…" She brought her hand to her neck, gently stroking her neck. I wanted to tell her it was okay to feel now, that Walsh couldn't hurt her anymore, but I wasn't so sure. So I just sat there listening intently to each word she said.

"This woman you talk about—why didn't she come forward?" I looked at her for some explanation, but all I saw in her eyes was loss and sadness.

"In the reports when you were questioned, you never mentioned a woman."

"She was innocent," Macey replied, tears rimming around her eyes.

"It's the court's job to determine innocence, Macey, not yours. It's hard to do that when we never knew anyone helped him."

"I was a child!" She angrily wiped away her tears. "She was all I had. I had to protect her."

I shook my head in disbelief. "Well, what use is it to protect her now? It's been twenty years. She could help end this."

"The FBI really has no clue, do they?" She shook her head.

"Clue about what?" I scrunched my eyebrows together. What was she talking about?

"That woman was Aimee's mother and Walsh's wife. Audrey Walsh helped her husband."

Chapter Twenty-One

MADISON

I didn't want a babysitter, but being left alone made me feel uneasy and tense. I got out of the shower and put on the pajamas I'd laid on the bed. After putting on my clothes, I turned on the news. I leaned back into the squishy hotel pillow, and only slightly paid attention to the news as I thought about Scott. Spending the day with him had been wonderful. It had been as though we were a regular couple. We hadn't made it official, whatever that meant. He just kept saying we should wait, and while I agreed, I couldn't help but feel the right time would never come. I ached for him, my body immediately roaring to life when he entered the room. Hell, all he had to do was speak and the deepness of his voice would rumble through my core, making me wet with desire. I smiled to myself, remembering the few stolen kisses we had shared. Neither of us wanted to wait— regardless of what we told ourselves. Scott had hardly left my mind at all these past few days, but I didn't mind. He was a nice distraction from my fa— from Walsh, and this screwed-up mess we were facing. I silently chastised myself for slipping again. Walsh was Walsh—he wasn't my father. Wasn't that what I had made clear to the guys earlier?

A woman's voice broke into my daydreams, uttering the words I'd never wanted to hear.

"Breaking news: Michael Walsh, the notorious serial killer, escaped prison last week," the newswoman said seriously into her microphone.

I froze. Why was this being released? I had thought Walsh's release was supposed to be kept under wraps. My heart thumped in my chest as I moved closer to the TV, leaning over on the bed. This couldn't be happening. I yanked my phone off the charger, almost knocking the lamp to the ground, and frantically dialed Uncle Tom.

"Assistant Director Harper," he answered.

"Uncle Tom? It's Maddie." My voice quivered.

"Hey, sweetie. How's it going? Reynolds told me everything has been going well. Did you take a look at the pool, yet?"

"Yeah. Liam's been having me do weight training and running. I was sore, so Scott and I hung out at the pool today. It was wonderful. Thank you." I paused, fear clawing at my chest.

"Maddie, is something wrong?" I hesitated and then dove in.

"So, I just turned on the news and it was released that Walsh escaped. I thought we were trying to keep this under wraps. I don't want the press digging into places they don't belong. Next thing you know, my face will be all over the news!" My voice had risen, and I'd said everything as one sentence without once stopping for air. I took a deep breath, filling my lungs. The air stung, and I shook with shock and fear.

"I was afraid of this," he said angrily. "The goddamn COs transferring him couldn't keep their mouths shut. Anything for a payday. Don't worry though, Maddie. This won't change much. They still don't know anything about you. You're safe."

"For now," I muttered under my breath.

"No. *Always*. I promised my brother I'd keep you safe, and I will. That's why you're with O'Leary and Reynolds. They will keep you safe. I know it's hard for you to put yourself out there like this, but we *will* catch him," he said confidently.

"I know. I'm afraid of what he'll do in the meantime. I don't want anyone else to get hurt," I explained. The fear had subsided a bit, but its embers were still there smoldering in my belly. Fear was annoying as hell.

"No one does."

"Okay." I breathed a sigh of relief. As long as everyone was on the same page, we were good. Lives needed to be preserved at all costs. "On that note, I think I could use a swim! I won't be a civilian much longer, and I have a feeling these luxuries will be few and far between." All of a sudden, the thought of spending the next month and a half isolated and disconnected from all that was going on seemed scary. I needed to know what was going on with this case at all times. Hell, I bet if I allowed myself to roam free, Walsh would find me. Then it'd just be me and him. The thought wasn't such a bad idea. I quickly shook it out of my head. No. I wasn't ready. Not yet.

"Oh Lord! Stop whining, child. This is what you wanted," he teased.

"Yes, it is." I smiled. "Hey, quick question before I go. What's O'Leary's deal? Has he always been so…"

"So unrestrained? Uncontrollable? Impulsive?" I laughed as he listed off the many adjectives that described O'Leary. They were right on the money. "The answer would be yes, I'm afraid. He had a rocky start in life. He may be rough around the edges, but he's good at what he does."

"Yeah," I replied.

"Why? He hasn't tried anything, has he? I swear he needs to learn some self-control." Uncle Tom sighed. I laughed.

"He tried, but didn't succeed. Scott will ensure that it stays that way."

"Reynolds is a great guy, Maddie. He'll protect you. Just remember, emotional attachments make things difficult in the field."

"I know," I said, leaving the conversation at that. I did *not* want to talk romance with my uncle. "Have a good night. Chat soon."

"Good night. Love you," he stated.

I hung up the phone. I never could utter those words. The only person I had ever said "I love you" to was my mom, and she had been taken from me. I wouldn't risk that again.

Chapter Twenty-Two

MADISON

Seeing Walsh on TV had made me want to get stronger, get better, so I was ready when it came time to catch the son of a bitch. Liam had told me he was just running downstairs. He'd said he would be back any minute. Once I told him about the news, I was certain I could convince him to do some training. I squeezed into my bathing suit, sighed, and threw my Beatles T-shirt on over it. I could, at least, cover myself up. Didn't want to scare the kids! I laughed out loud. I sure knew how to crack myself up.

I sat on the couch and waited… and waited—for what seemed like forever. Where the hell was he? I picked up my cell and shot him a text.

Where are you?

Why? Miss me already? The text came with a winky face emoticon.

No. I want to go swimming and do some training.

You just took a shower. Pretty sure that counts.

It doesn't. Hurry up!

I'm busy at the moment. You'll have to wait.

I don't want to wait. I'll just head down now. Meet me there.

The phone rang and I rolled my eyes at the sight of Liam's name across my screen.

"Yes?" I answered, my voice laced with annoyance.

"Madison, don't leave the room without me. I'll be a few more minutes. Just wait."

"Well, then send Scott up here," I replied.

"Reynolds? He's at Quantico."

"You said you were meeting him." The lack of an immediate reply pissed me off. He was lying and he was trying to figure out how to cover it up.

"Oh. Right. He went back already. STAY PUT."

I hung up the phone. I didn't even respond. I knew he hadn't met up with Scott. I grabbed my room key and slipped my feet into my flip-flops. I took the stairs two at a time, running up and down them a few times before going to find Liam and head to the pool. A few laps would keep my heart rate up and soothe some of my sore muscles. When I got to the first floor, where the pool and bar were, I saw what I should have expected—Liam and some hot chick getting cozy. Against my better judgment, I walked right up to them.

"Excuse me for interrupting. Just thought you'd like to know that he has herpes," I practically shouted, and walked away feeling somewhat triumphant. I looked back to see her laughing and Liam shaking his head. She leaned in closer to Liam and pecked him on the cheek before walking away. I stopped dead in my tracks. I had been watching the interaction, and as she faced me, I realized what I hadn't before. She was stunning.

"Don't worry, sweetie. He's all yours." Her voice was angelic, and I took a step backwards. As she slid gracefully away, I stood there like an idiot.

"Are you done embarrassing yourself?" Liam asked from behind.

"I can't believe you!" I whispered. I stormed off toward the pool with Liam following not too far behind.

"It was a business meeting, Madison. Not that it's any of your concern." He eyed me curiously.

"It is *my* business when *my* life's in danger. Not yours. You left me behind for a piece of ass."

"You're wrong, but believe what you want," he advised, a smile forming on his face. My body tensed. A smile? His reaction only further solidified what everyone had warned me about. He was unpredictable, unreliable, and obsessed with alcohol and sex. He only cared about himself.

"Believe what I want? You're totally fucked-up. Whatever happened to you must have truly screwed you up," I yelled. A couple in the corner of the pool area gathered their things and scurried out. I didn't care about making a scene. Liam needed to know that he had to get his head out of his own ass long enough to see that he was self-centered and needed help. Like, psychiatric help. I put my hands on my hips and looked him right in the eyes. I wasn't going to cower before him.

Liam clenched his jaw and tightened his fists. He

grabbed my arms tightly, looking as if he would hit me. I shut my eyes tight, preparing myself for what was to come. Instead, I felt myself being lifted off the ground and flying through the air.

The shock of the water made me gasp. I emerged and rubbed my eyes, searching for Liam. I couldn't find him. Panic began to set in. "O'Leary? O'Leary? Liam! Where are you?" I got closer to the edge of the pool, and I tried to see over the top. All of a sudden, I was pulled down under the water. I kicked hard and felt a connection with skin and bone! Score! I started to swim as fast as I could, gasping for air the entire time.

"Madison! Madison! Calm the hell down! Jesus Christ!"

"O'Leary?" I stopped swimming and turned around. In the pool, nursing his newly broken nose, was Liam. "Oh, my God! I'm so sorry. I thought someone was trying to kidnap me."

He laughed. "Yeah. Well, obviously not," he stated as he swam to the edge of the pool.

I paused. "You threw me in the pool."

"You made me angry," he stated, as if that justified his actions.

"So you threw me in the pool?" I asked.

"I was trying to be playful."

"Playful? Seriously? Next time, try to be playful with someone who isn't being stalked by their serial killer sperm donor."

"You're right. *Jesus.* You broke my nose. You have a hell of a kick." Snap. Crack. He put his nose back in place.

"You're insane, Liam."

He cocked his head, looking at me intently. "You called me Liam."

"I did, huh?" I shrugged, treading water.

"Maybe you do like me, after all." He smiled pleasantly.

"Don't kid yourself, bud," I said as I swam away.

We swam around, doing laps and bantering back and forth. It was lighthearted. When Liam wasn't being a complete ass, he was actually fun to be around.

I heard the door to the pool room open. The bartender came in carrying a tray with two drinks.

"Madison?" he asked.

"Yep. That's me." I waved my hand and got out of the pool.

"Here you go, ma'am. For you and the gentleman."

"But I didn't order any drinks."

"They were ordered already."

"Uh, okay. Thanks." I took the drinks and sat down. *Liam.* Trying to get me drunk. It was my favorite drink, though. Red's Hard Cider with extra ice. Delicious. And there was a Jack Daniels, too. Figures.

"O'Leary," I yelled. "The drinks are here."

"Nice." He jumped out of the pool, removing his soggy pants. I tried not to look but I couldn't help myself. His nice V-cut was accentuated by his low-hanging boxer shorts. He had such a beautiful, toned physique. His abs were well defined, and his chest was completely bare. As the water dripped down his chiseled body, I started to get hot. Very hot. *Snap out of it, Madison!* I took a swig of my drink. *He's an ass, Madison,* I told myself over and over again. *A womanizing ass. A hot one, but an ass nonetheless.* The feelings I felt toward Liam were now purely lustful; not like with Scott. My mind drifted, and it was then that I noticed there was a note on the tray. The name written on the slip of paper made my blood run cold. I opened it carefully, so as not to mess with any physical evidence that might be present. My mouth got dry and my palms started to sweat…

Aimee:

No matter where you go, what you do, or who you have protecting you, I will find you. There is no escaping me.

But Liam… so conflicted… so troubled… just like me. He'll make such a wonderful addition to my masterpieces. Don't worry; we will all be together soon.

Enjoy the drinks.

Dad

P.S. Enjoy the present I left for you in your room.

I jumped up from the chair.

"Liam! Liam!" I screamed.

"Easy there, sweet cheeks. I know I look good in my boxers, but there's no need to shout." He continued drying off.

"We need to go back upstairs. *Now,*" I shouted again, on the verge of hysteria. I took a breath.

Finally realizing I wasn't playing around anymore and noticing what was in my hand, he rushed over to me and grabbed the letter.

"Shit. Fuck. Hang on," he told me. Grabbing his cell from the chair, he told me to get my things. He dialed Scott and told him to get his ass over to the hotel ASAP and to bring backup. Liam took my hand and practically dragged me to the stairs.

"Madison, I don't know what we'll find upstairs—so be prepared, okay?" He held my hand tighter.

"Okay," I whispered, leaning in closer to him. I knew Walsh, and anything he had left for me wasn't going to be good.

We ran up the stairs, and my legs started to burn. I felt so tired and weak all of a sudden. My head started pounding, and I was pretty sure I was going to vomit. Something was wrong. I fought back the urge to throw up, swallowing chunks of my lunch, and trudged up the next few flights.

Liam put his key in, and we heard the click of the door. Liam had to drag me along.

"Madison, keep up," he scolded me. The room started to spin. Everything was a blur. Were there two couches? No. No. I remembered only one. Forcing myself to focus harder, I looked at the couch. A woman was on the couch, propped up like an exhibit; the woman Liam had just had a drink with not that long ago. She was naked. Rope secured her hands behind her back. My eyes immediately went to her throat. A perfect line marred her skin. The cut was so deep I could see her neck muscles. I fought back the bile that had crept up into my throat. The blood that flowed from her neck was fresh, staining the couch and the floor. Dripping slowly. God, there was so much blood. I looked down at her body, following the trail of blood. Her legs. Oh, her poor legs. The thin red lines looked like a little kid had scribbled all over her. Scars had been there before. There was no mistaking the scar tissue. Now, long gashes had replaced those old scars. Blood oozed from the newly opened wounds, thickening ever so slightly.

I heard the faint sound of music playing. What song was that? I couldn't process the words. It sounded so familiar. My head was spinning, and I was losing control. What had been in that drink? I frantically looked around, trying to get my bearings and to focus on anything *but* the sight in front of me. The room continued to spin and spin and spin, and my eyes finally settled on the glass coffee table. It was then I noticed the words written in blood on the table: "My Masterpiece is Complete." Written in the poor woman's blood. I couldn't stand up any longer. I lost my balance. It all seemed to happen in slow motion. As I was falling and drifting away, I swear I heard Walsh laughing.

Chapter Twenty-Three

LIAM

I lowered Madison to the floor.

"Goddammit," I said out loud, checking Macey's pulse. I knew she was dead just by looking at her, but I had to be sure. I checked her wounds and her body was still warm to the touch. I shouldn't have touched her but just an hour earlier, she had been full of life, full of hope. Now her face was ashen and lifeless. Walsh knew how to drain every ounce of life out of a person. That's what he did best.

"What happened?" Reynolds snarled as he entered the room. "Mother of God. Who is that? What happened to Maddie?" Before I could answer, he was by her side trying to wake her up. Good boy, Reynolds. Forever reliable.

"She was drugged, I think." I sighed. "Don't worry. She only had a sip of her drink. She'll be okay."

"Drugged?" He yelled. "You had one job. To make sure nothing bad happened to her, and now she's passed out, drugged, and this woman was murdered?" He stood up, getting dangerously close to me. Anger burned in his eyes.

I had let his precious Maddie get hurt, something he would never forgive.

"I get it. I screwed up. Let's just get this mess cleaned up." I walked away. I didn't want to argue with him. Not now.

"Right." He knelt down next to Madison and stroked her hair. "What happened? When I left everything was fine."

"That's Macey Winslow." My voice cracked ever so slightly. Remorse hit me as I looked at the woman who, not that long ago, had sat with me—alive. I cleared my throat, trying to shift my focus away from my emotions.

"Wait. Macey Winslow? You mean Walsh's last victim and only survivor? The girl I saw in the basement that night?" Reynolds asked, concern peppering his face. He'd gone pale.

"Yeah. The one and only. She texted me tonight and we met downstairs. She told me she had been following Walsh for some time. That some girl named Alice gave her information on where to find him. She was leery but couldn't pass up the chance for revenge." Macey had been struggling, hoping we'd catch Walsh so she could live her life. But that was gone now, all in the blink of an eye. I texted Assistant Director Harper on my phone, trying not to feel the swarm of emotions that threatened to batter me. I glanced over at Madison, and fear hit me suddenly. The dead woman could have been her. I frowned as a text message came through. Assistant Director Harper was not pleased.

"Clearly, he got the jump on her now," Reynolds said

with dismay. Reynolds stood and lifted Madison off the ground with ease.

"Macey said Walsh was planning something big. She didn't get a chance to say what, but she saw fit to warn me. She mentioned some stuff about Madison's mom, Reynolds." Pangs of sadness hit me. I knew how to handle a dead body, but the reality that Madison's mother had been involved was so unexpected. Madison wouldn't take the news well.

"What about Maddie's mom?" Reynolds asked.

"That she helped Walsh with the murders. It seems not by choice, but she was involved." I walked over to open the door, and the sound of my hard steps calmed my nerves. "She helped Macey cope with the situation by being an ear to listen and a shoulder to cry on. She'd tell Macey stories about her daughter, Aimee. She was way more involved than I think anyone ever knew."

Reynolds was silent for a few moments, and then he nodded, as if coming to a conclusion. "I can't hurt Maddie like that. She's not ready to hear this yet. I won't be the one to cause her more pain." Reynolds nodded again as he left the hotel room with Madison still in his arms. We both knew the news would crush her. She had loved her mother with every ounce of her being. Knowing, whether forced or not, that her mother had helped her father would change her. Reynolds couldn't tell her. Neither could I. I couldn't do that to her. I wouldn't do that to her.

Chapter Twenty-Four

Scott

I had almost lost Maddie—again. Getting the call from O'Leary, my heart had caught in my chest, and it had felt like it would explode. Then I had seen red. I knew I shouldn't have left her with O'Leary. His unreliability and quick temper had left her vulnerable and exposed. I should have been the one to comfort her, protect her, but this entire mess had left so much red tape that had to be handled, and it all fell on my shoulders, as things often did. I didn't care, though. For Maddie, I'd steal the sun from the sky just to see it shine on her face. She was my world. I just hoped she knew.

Director Harper let me know he was sending a doctor to look over Maddie. Liam told me she had only taken a sip of the drink, so she hadn't ingested enough to cause too much worry. When I got to our new room on the sixth floor, I laid her down on the bed and looked down at her. She looked so fragile. I cursed myself again for not being there to protect her. She was still wet from the pool, and her curls hung limply against her face. I gently crawled next to her and held her tighter, trying to will my warmth into her. I knew I had to change her before tucking her into bed but none of our things had been moved to the new room.

A knock at the door caused me to reluctantly leave her side.

I looked through the peephole. "Who is it?" I asked.

"Agent Torres, sir." He fumbled with his badge. I opened the door and took his badge in my hand.

"I was asked to bring your things." He was new to the job. I could tell by the way he stumbled with his words. I remembered what it was like, being new and uncertain.

"Thank you, Agent Torres." I took the bags from him and returned his badge.

"You're welcome, sir."

"It's Special Agent Reynolds." I shook his hand with my free hand. "Thanks again." I nodded to him as I shut the door.

Going into her bag, I took out a clean white T-shirt and cotton underwear. I smiled at the wet Beatles T-shirt she had on. She loved her music.

I pulled off the T-shirt that covered her bathing suit, and slowly exposed her mocha skin. The bathing suit was covered in little sunflowers, strategically placed on the bust. My body tensed, passion surged through me, and my cock grew with each touch of her body. I managed to get her undressed, all while trying not to look at her for fear I would come. She was that exquisite.

She looked so peaceful. I got into bed next to her,

pulling her in close to my body. I knew I should go to the chair to watch her, protect her, but I needed to be near her, just for a moment. I needed to feel her lungs fill with air, to feel the warmth of her body against mine. I needed to feel her life seeping into mine.

I wanted her, all of her, and I knew I couldn't wait anymore. I could no longer be the guy who waited on the sidelines until it was right. Time was never promised. If I was taken from this Earth tomorrow, I would feel complete and fulfilled if Maddie were mine—even if for just a day.

Thoughts encroached about Liam, and his lack of judgment in protecting Maddie tonight. My rationality seemed to cloud over, the need to show Liam how badly he screwed up filling me with rage. I always talked it out. That was what made me a good profiler. Liam was better at the physical aspect of our job. It was why we were partnered together. But ever since that incident with the little girl, Liam changed. His childhood issues became more apparent as well as his drinking. His past wasn't news to anyone, but his alcohol abuse, his sex-fiend ways, I helped him hide. I guessed I thought it was just a phase. That someday he'd overcome it all. But looking at Maddie, drugged because of him, I wasn't so sure he would be able to work through his problems.

I sat down in the chair next to Maddie, trying to stifle the urge to storm out of the room and punch Liam in the face. I considered showing Liam that I had it in me to kick his ass, to show him that I loved Maddie more than anything. Maybe then he would understand me. I gripped my gun in my holster and shut my eyes, taking deep breaths to try to calm myself. I had to stay away from Liam, because if I saw him anytime soon, I wouldn't be able to resist showing him with my fists how much Maddie meant to me.

Chapter Twenty-Five

LIAM

The Medical Examiner came and took the body. The forensic team collected all the evidence, including the couch, the table, the remote, and the note. Everything was bagged and tagged. No matter who came in, everyone commented on how fucked-up it was. How it was such a waste she had died. I agreed absentmindedly with everyone, my mind lost in playing the night over and over again.

My cell phone rang, and I glanced at the Caller ID: Assistant Director Harper.

It was inevitable. I was going to have to talk with him, but I knew he was going to chew me a new asshole. I answered the phone, not bothering with a greeting. I braced myself for what was coming.

"O'Leary, you better have a good goddamn explanation for why we have another body on our hands and for why my niece was drugged!" I held the phone away from my ear while he yelled.

"Sir, Macey came to me with information that was

pertinent to the case and the possible apprehension of Walsh. I thought that would take precedence over Madison. She was safe in the hotel room at the time. If she wasn't so goddamn stubborn and stayed put—"

"Are you trying to tell me that this was Madison's fault? It is your job to protect her, not to go off on some vigilante adventure collecting clues. You are not Sherlock Holmes." He sighed into the phone, his frustration seeping into his words. He was stressed, pissed off, and I was the target for his feelings. Screw it. I was used to being a launching pad for emotions. No sense in arguing.

"I'm not blaming her, sir. I'm willing to take full responsibility for my actions."

"Good. Now, I'm concerned there will be more to this. That Walsh is planning something else."

"It is likely. Macey mentioned that. All we can do now is wait," I replied.

"That we can agree on.

"An agent questioned the bartender. Apparently, some girl came in and paid him a couple grand to lace Madison's drink. He remembers nothing other than the fact that she was young, possibly college age. He was fucking high as a kite." He sighed. "Once you all get to Quantico, you'll be safer. Don't fuck up again, O'Leary, or it will be your last fuckup."

The call ended without so much as a "good-bye" or a "good luck." I clenched my fists and took deep breaths. I knew we were in danger, but I wasn't myself. Whispers filled my head. They pushed at my mind, reminding me of my constant incompetence. The voices—something I hid from the world—often raged within me, and tonight was no different. They were harsh and relentless, but I was worried about Madison. And just as with her singing, thoughts of Madison soothed my mind, giving me something to focus on, other than the goddamn drums and whispers that plagued me. Regret stabbed me in the heart like a knife. I heard the next whispered words loud and clear in my damaged mind: You shouldn't have left her alone, you worthless piece of shit.

I left that place of death and took the stairs to the sixth floor. I just wanted a shower, and to wash the night off. I entered our new hotel room, but before I had even finished setting all the locks, a faint knock caused me to jump.

I grabbed my weapon and checked to make sure there was plenty of ammo. I opened the door slowly after looking out the peephole, holding the gun close to my side.

"Special Agent O'Leary?" the woman asked. Her red-rimmed glasses slid down her nose, and she propped them back up with a press of her finger.

"Depends who's asking," I said through the small slit in the door.

"I'm Dr. Abigail Wilson. Assistant Director Harper sent me. I'm here to check on Madison." She tried opening the door again.

"Right. Badge?" She showed me her credentials. I opened the door and pulled her inside the hotel room, latching the door behind her.

"Where is she?" Dr. Wilson asked.

"In this room." I walked her over to Reynolds and Madison's new bedroom and quietly opened the door after a short knock. When I peered in, I saw Madison lying on the bed. She was no longer in her wet bathing suit, and she looked relaxed in the Coldplay T-shirt she now wore. A tightness formed in my chest, knowing Reynolds must have been the one to change her. Reynolds sat in a chair next to the bed, his hands gripping the arms tensely. His eyes were shut, but he appeared alert, even in sleep.

"Reynolds?" I whispered. He shot up from the chair, grabbing his weapon from his holster. I found myself face-to-face with a Glock 22.

"Settle down," I said with slight irritation, pushing the Glock out of my face. "The doctor's here to check on Madison."

"Okay." Reynolds holstered his gun slowly. After having Dr. Wilson pull her credentials out a second time, he exited the room looking worn out and exhausted. He rubbed his face.

"We'll wait out here, Dr. Wilson." I let the doctor in and backed away, catching one last look at Madison before shutting the door. I returned to the living room. Before I knew what was happening, I was swung around and my face met with Reynolds's fist.

"What the fuck man?" I touched my jaw, checking to see if it was broken. No, but it sure as fuck hurt. I wound up and punched Reynolds back, square in the face. He spit on the floor, and his fresh blood stained the carpet of our new room. The hotel was never going to let the FBI stay there again. Reynolds came at me, his head barreling into my chest. We found ourselves on the floor fighting and rolling around like the fucking idiots we were. We took turns pummeling each other, grunting like some goddamn Neanderthals. It was therapeutic.

"Ahem." Dr. Wilson cleared her throat, and both of us stopped midpunch. "Gentlemen, if you are done acting like children, I'd like to discuss Madison's condition with you." She looked us both up and down from behind her glasses, disgust evident on her face. She was a petite woman, her hair black with gray hairs woven through as if strategically placed there. A fierceness in her eyes commanded attention. Her severe demeanor was enough to make a grown man obey without a second thought. And that was exactly what we did.

Reynolds and I both sprang up, wiping the blood from our faces. I glanced over at him. Other than a ripped shirt and some blood staining his mouth, he looked fine. I wiped my mouth with the back of my hand, staining it red. I straightened out my clothes as best I could, and took a breath to regain my composure.

She nodded as if pleased she had our attention.

"She's fine. She was definitely drugged; but based on the samples from forensics, the drug will have no lasting effects. She should be awake in a few hours." Dr. Wilson paused, looking quizzically at my bruised face. "Is there anything else you need from me before I go? Assistant Director Harper said I was to be at your disposal." She came up to me, placed her hand on my chin, and tilted my head.

"Perhaps to look at your nose, Special Agent O'Leary?"

Reynolds chuckled, dabbing at his mouth with his sleeve.

"No, I'm fine. Thanks," I muttered under my breath.

"Suit yourself. My advice, though—whether you want it or not—is to get your shit together. Don't let Madison see you two fighting. Director Harper told me she has enough on her plate. Don't make it any harder on her than it already is." She walked out of the room and left with a slam of the door.

"As fun as this was, I'm going to go sit with Maddie again," Reynolds announced. I thought about arguing with him and saying I should go sit with her, but really, there was no point.

"Cool. I'm going to change and head out. Don't wait up." I went into the second bedroom and grabbed a blue button-down shirt, leaving it loose around my waist.

It seemed like so long ago Madison had broken my nose with her foot in the pool, but it was throbbing again. Shit. I should have had the doctor look at it. My hands were still stained with splotches of Scott's and Macey's blood. No one else would be able to see the splatters of red, so I left them; they brought me a sense of peace. The blood made me feel something other than the constant reminder of my feelings for Madison. Screw it. Yeah, I was about a thousand shades of fucked up.

I sighed, grabbed my car keys and wallet, and rushed out, leaving the small bloodstains on my hands. The hotel bar was out of the question after tonight's events, but I needed a drink. Bad. I also needed sex. Bad. I left the room knowing I could easily find both.

I hopped in the car and drove a ways, finally finding a local bar, the Chewy Bone. The green neon sign flashed before me. It would do just fine. I parked the car around the corner, locking it with the fob.

I walked into the dark atmosphere, and the smell of smoke and piss were only slightly masked by my swollen nose. Damn. A broken nose and the place still smelled like a fucking latrine? I thought of walking out. Ah hell, who was I kidding? I sat down on the stool and ordered up some Jack Daniels. I took a swig of the dark caramel liquid. The cold, stinging sensation filled my throat, warming me instantly. I leaned back into the bar stool, making myself more comfortable. It took a few more swigs before the headache dissipated and my nose felt normal. I smiled, ordering another.

"Looking for a good time?"

I turned and saw a woman standing over me, snapping her gum. Jackpot. I grinned.

"I'll take that as a yes. Name's Candy." She sat down next to me, crossing her smooth, olive-toned legs. Her leg rubbed against my jean-clad thigh, causing me to throb in anticipation.

"Candy, huh?" I said with a raise of my eyebrows. "You sure that's your real name?" I took another sip of my drink. I didn't look at her. I looked straight ahead. I'd see what this bitch could do.

"Does it matter? I got what you need." Her delicate hand

touched my leg. I glanced down, noticing her perfectly manicured nails. Jet-black polish covered the tips. Dark. I loved dark. She stroked my leg and came dangerously close to my throbbing cock, but held back. She smelled like cigarettes and sex, but it didn't matter. I needed a release, and she'd come to answer my call.

"How much?" I asked, removing her hand from my leg. A move that said, don't touch me unless I say so.

"For you, baby, fifty. That includes the works." She started touching my leg again. The faintest whispers began in my head, drawing me in. Give this bitch a fucking she'll never forget, the voices said. I downed my drink.

"Sounds good, Candy. Do you have a place, or should I get us a room?" I asked.

"Room?" she asked, laughing loudly. People turned to look at us. "What do you think this is? There's a bathroom over there, and I saw you park that fancy-looking car. Either works for me."

"Car it is, then," I decided. She'd learn quickly that I called the shots. I placed a twenty on the counter and took her hand, dragging her out to the car. Her hand felt cold in mine, distant. It wasn't like Madison's. I squeezed it tighter, willing it to send my body into a frenzy. It didn't. Fucking A, man. What the hell was Madison doing to me?

Candy grabbed my ass with her free hand then reached around, grabbing my cock. She couldn't keep her hands off me. "Easy there, Candy. I'm not going anywhere." I pulled her hand away from me. We rounded the corner and, with a click, I unlocked the car.

"Oh, I know you won't." She pressed me up against the car and grabbed my hard cock. She leaned in and went straight for my mouth. Her tongue swirled in and out, and I moaned against her kiss. If she wanted it that bad, who was I to deny her? I needed this, too. I needed this bad. Pushing Madison out of my mind, I responded.

"You like that, huh, baby?" I opened the car door, and pushed her onto the backseat. She squealed, and I unbuttoned my fly. Her eyes got big, and a huge smile formed on her face. She grabbed my face, pulling me down on the seat. Then, she sat up and took my shaft in her mouth. The depth of her mouth astonished me. It wasn't often I reached the back of a woman's throat, but my entire cock fit in her mouth. When I heard no sound coming from her, I realized Candy had no gag reflex. God, her mouth felt so good. I grabbed her hair in my hands, pulling it, feeling it rip in my grasp. She whimpered. "Harder," I yelled. Her eyes glanced up at me, looking for clarification. "Use teeth, lots of teeth." She obliged. Oh, did she oblige. Her teeth raked my skin, and I seethed as the pain finally set in. When I'd had enough, I pulled her up. She wiped her mouth, and looked at me, her eyes wide with worry.

"I'm sorry, baby. I didn't mean to hurt you," she said, rubbing me with her spit-slicked hand.

I snapped. I didn't mean to hurt you? That dumb bitch. I flipped her, pushing her down onto her stomach and lifting her now exposed ass in the air. After ripping a condom from my pocket and putting it on, I rammed myself inside of her. She squealed, taking what I gave her. It was hard. It was fast. I smacked her ass, the stinging sensation covering my hand. It wasn't for pleasure. It was for pain. I glanced down, and I noticed a red handprint covering her round ass. This wasn't passion-filled or erotic. This was pure fucking. Finally, my release came, and I pulled out. I gathered myself, took off the used condom, and buttoned my pants.

Candy lay there panting heavily, trying to pull herself back together. "Good God, baby. Anyone ever tell ya you sure do like it rough?" she asked, quickly pulling down her skirt and covering her naked ass.

"That's not even half of it," I mumbled, as I pulled out my wallet and handed her sixty dollars. "Keep the change."

"Thanks, doll. You sure you don't want more?" she asked hesitantly. She started to caress my shoulders, but I smacked her hands away hard and grabbed her by the neck. She gasped for breath, and I quickly let her go.

"What the fuck?" Candy yelled, staring at me.

"Get out." The words came out quiet, but violent. My jaw clenched in anger. She stared at me, her eyes wide and confused. "Get out!" I screamed.

I opened the car door and threw her purse and shoes out on the sidewalk. She scrambled out of the car, cursing me as she quickly walked away. I sat there, alone, in the dark. I felt better. Like I had released evil from inside me. I continued to sit in silence and stare off into the distance.

The longer I sat there, the longer the void had to return, though, and after some time, I felt the voices start creeping in again…

I heard little whispers now in my head. They'd always

been a part of me, but now the emptiness seemed separate. The whispers were now dragging me down. I tried to focus on what they were saying, but then I stopped. Did I really want to know? I slammed my hands on the sides of my head, trying to relieve the pressure. I got out of the car and headed back into the bar. More alcohol. That was exactly what I needed.

Chapter Twenty-Six

I was falling. Falling with no end in sight. I tried screaming and reaching out for help, but no one was there. The dream was horrible. It wasn't like others I'd had. Instead of Walsh, my mom was the one inflicting the pain. She held the knife and carved into a girl's flesh. Walsh stood over her, watching her, giving her instructions on what to do next. The girl cried out in pain. I stood at the top of the stairs, calling for my mom, telling her to stop. She greeted me with a smile and gave me a present. It was my doll, and she was so beautiful.

"Aimee, whenever you get scared or lonely, just hold her close, okay? As long as you have her, you'll be safe." I took the doll, and I hugged her small porcelain body tightly.

"She looks like you, Mommy," I commented. My mom smiled at me and patted my head.

I kissed my mom and ran off to play. I heard screams coming from the basement, but I didn't care anymore because Dolly was with me.

Thump thump thump up the basement stairs. Daddy stormed into the living room and smacked me across the face. He told me I shouldn't snoop around and never to go in the basement. He reached for my doll. I couldn't let him take Dolly from me. I had to do what Mommy said. I had to protect her. I started kicking and screaming.

"Please don't take Dolly away!"

"Madison, wake up. Come on, sweetheart. Wake up," whispered Scott. He gently shook my shoulders. My eyes flickered open, and I realized Scott was sitting next to me looking as panicked as I felt. His eyes darted across my body, as if looking for any wounds. There were no physical wounds; just the mental scars that seemed as though they would never heal.

"What's going on?" I asked weakly.

"You must have had a nightmare. You were screaming and flailing around."

"Yeah. I do that sometimes." I tried to sit up in bed, but my head started spinning. I fell back onto the bed with a loud thud.

"Where do you think you're going?" Scott asked, fixing my pillow and tucking me in. "Doctor's orders. Stay in bed for the rest of the night."

"Gee, that sounds like fun," I groaned.

"Maddie, it's like 1:00 a.m. Sleep it off. Tomorrow's a new day."

"One, huh? I've been sleeping a while. I should really get up and clean…" I trailed off, clasping my hands over my mouth and remembering the events from earlier. "Oh

God, Scott! The mess. That poor, poor girl. Those things he d-did t-to h-her," I stuttered, trying to find the words. "J-j-just—it's a-a-a-all my f-f-f-f-fault," I cried, stuttering as I remembered every last detail of what I had seen.

Scott grabbed my hands, stroking them. "Maddie," he said soothingly. "It wasn't your fault. None of this is." He looked at me fixedly. "Now, lie down, and don't worry about anything. O'Leary called it in, and he even called your uncle. It's all taken care of," Scott whispered as he gave me a hug and spoke into my hair.

"Thank you." I was grateful for Scott's comfort. "Where's O'Leary, anyway? I thought he'd be guarding the other side of my bed," I joked.

As I looked at Scott for an answer, I noticed the subtle hint of a bruise forming on his cheek. "And what happened to your face?"

"Liam," he said without explaining. The distant look in his eyes let me know not to press the issue any further. "He went out. Had to let off some steam." Scott looked away. He was embarrassed. I couldn't help but smile. Always the protector.

"Gotcha. Meaning he went out drinking and looking for a lay. You don't have to sugarcoat it with me, Scott. I'm not a child. I do know what sex is. It's this thing where you have a man and woman…"

"Enough!" Scott raised his voice. "I know you aren't a child. It won't happen again." Scott stood and began to leave the room. Was he mad at me? I hadn't meant to make him mad. I was just tired of everyone tiptoeing around me.

"Where are you going?" I asked, unsure of myself and where we stood.

"I'm going to get some water."

"Oh."

"Why? Do you need something?" Scott asked, stopping in the doorway. The low light cast his silhouette onto the walls. The masculinity of his body was apparent even in the dimness. My body reacted, need and desire radiating from my core.

"I just don't want you to leave me," I said shyly. "Can you come lie down next to me? I don't want to be alone right now."

"Uh… sure." Scott's demeanor changed. "Just let me grab some water really quick. Would you like something to drink?" I shook my head and waited for him to return. Scott ducked his head as he came back in the room. He wouldn't look me in the eyes, and he adjusted his layers of clothing as he started toward the bed.

"You going to wear your jeans, gun, and vest to bed?" I joked, laughing lightly.

"Oh. Right." He stopped and thought for a moment. He stood on the side of the bed and I watched him take off his boots and his vest. He removed his weapon and placed it on the nightstand. I blushed when I realized he was going to take off his jeans, and quickly turned away.

"If you're too uncomfortable, I can leave them on. Trust me; I'm used to sleeping in far worse conditions."

"No!" I said a little too loudly. "No. I want you to be comfortable. Go ahead. Take them off. Please take them off— I mean… Oh God! I didn't mean it like that…" I placed my hand over my mouth, shocked at what I had just said. Heat touched my cheeks, but Scott laughed, breaking up the tension that had filled the room.

I looked over at him right as he removed his shirt. His arms were well toned, and as he raised them, the stretch showcased how incredible his entire body was. Holy hell. I gulped loudly, feeling my throat tighten. I looked at him, not caring that I was staring. He had broad, muscular shoulders and a chiseled body. He was lean and strong. He was like the Greek god Apollo, in more ways than one. Apollo was handsome, athletic, but he was also the god of light, driving his chariot across the sky into the sun every day. Scott was my god, my light, and he was beyond captivating. His eyes. Good lord. I gulped so loudly I was sure he heard it. Even in the darkness, his eyes were shining, the subtle hint of moonlight reflecting off his face and stopping within his eyes. They flashed with passion and sexual hunger. I rubbed my shoulders, trying to loosen the tension building there. I was frozen, my eyes never once leaving his exquisite form. My sexual hunger became more and more apparent. I was so focused on my own thoughts, I didn't even notice when he took off his pants. I probably couldn't have handled watching that. I would have come undone.

He cleared his throat, and I snapped out of my trance. He slowly got onto the bed, placing himself on top of the covers.

"No covers?" I croaked. I cleared my own throat, knowing my desire was showing.

"Usually not. I get hot at night." He placed his hands underneath his head, his bulging muscles flexing and reacting. My throat became dry, and I had to stop myself from reaching out and touching him.

"Gotcha," I said casually. I adjusted, trying to turn my back to him. Before I could fully turn away, he gently touched my shoulder.

"Maddie, if this is all too weird, I can sleep on the floor. It's not a problem."

"Honestly, it isn't. I'm just all sorts of mixed-up right now, and looking at you like that, it's just hard. That's all." I turned to face him, sure I had just given away that I wanted to jump his bones. Screw waiting.

"Well, it wasn't easy changing your clothes either." He was closer now, and as he faced me in all his glory, his eyes narrowed. The intensity of his gaze pressed in on me.

"Wait, you undressed me?" I exclaimed.

"Someone had to. You were cold and wet. Like hell I'd let O'Leary do it."

"Thanks, I guess." Great. He had seen me naked. Wow. Lord knows, no man had ever really seen me naked. And talk about awkward. I got goose bumps thinking about his hands roaming all over my body as he removed my clothes. Why couldn't I have been semiconscious at the time? Just my luck.

He wrapped his arm around me, bringing me as close to him as possible. My muscles tensed. I hadn't expected the intimacy of his touch. Then I melted like ice. Cold and lonely, I had just been waiting for the sun to set me free.

My body instinctively molded to his. It was so perfect. It was so right.

"Maddie, I know there is so much going on right now, but I mean this sincerely. I missed you, and I care about you. I know now isn't a good time, but maybe when things settle down—I want to be the one to take you out for coffee." He shook his head. "No, that's not what I want. I want to be the one to make you happy." He took my face in his hands. I fell into his touch, giving myself to him completely.

"Scott. I'm messed up. My past…" I sighed as I struggled to find the words. I wanted him. I did. But I wanted him to know what he was up against. Protecting me was his job, but being with me was a choice I couldn't let him make lightly. "It's all around me now. I'm just afraid by getting close to me, you will be impacted badly. I'll be ruining what happiness you have by dragging you into this crap. Here you are protecting me when I'm sure you have other cases—better cases—to work on."

"Maddie," Scott growled. "There's nowhere else I'd rather be. Stop selling yourself short. Allow people who care about you to help you. Stop holding back. If anyone is preventing you from being happy, it's you." Scott's words hurt because he was right. I had only given myself small bits of happiness. I'd drowned myself in school, and I'd measured my success based on academics, but I wanted more.

"I won't sit here and lie, say I don't feel it, too. The pull toward you. The desire to be with you. Even the other day when we were in the elevator at the FBI office," I paused for a moment and smiled. "Do you remember?"

"Yeah," he replied, a small smile tugging at his lips.

"I wanted you then. Really wanted you." We both laughed at my honesty. "But that doesn't matter. My past matters. You know? The one currently screwing with my life."

"I don't care about your past. All I care about is your future." He paused, staring at me with such intensity I thought I'd burst. "Your future with me in it." He kissed me ever so gently on the lips. It was quick and light, but it sent fireworks through my veins. He was right there, and his feelings, his desire to make me happy, surrounded me. I opened my eyes and looked deep into his. I knew he meant what he said. Despite the hesitation, and the chaos surrounding me, I wanted happiness. I wanted him. My past would always be there, haunting me, and Scott knew what that was like. He'd lived it with me. For the first time in my dark life, I felt like I could have a future with someone. My past was a part of me, but I hoped it didn't have to define my future. I hoped I'd find a way to gain control.

"I'd like that a lot, Scott. I'd like to have a future with you, too." He grinned as he gently kissed my forehead. His intimate kiss sent me into a full state of arousal. The lower parts of me ached for attention and I arched my back slightly, willing our bodies to collide even more. He couldn't chase my darkness away—that was my responsibility—but right now, with Scott holding me and caring for me I realized that Walsh had taken so much from me, but he couldn't take my feelings away. Walsh could torment me. He could stalk me.

In the end, he could even kill me. But the feelings I had for Scott were mine, and regardless of what happened—what the outcome of my fucked-up life was—I would always own my feelings for Scott.

"Who says we have to wait? Like you said, I'm the only one in my own way right now, and I'm tired of my past dictating what I can and can't do. I want to be with you. Only you. I want that now. Not God knows how long from now."

Scott looked at me curiously, as if dissecting my words.

"You're sure?" He stroked my hair, and with each touch, my curls bounced.

"I am. I want to be with you," I reassured him. I took his face in my hands, and our noses almost touched. I closed my eyes, parting his mouth with my tongue. His tongue collided with mine, like heat to flame. Our tongues thrust into each other and I felt him harden against my stomach. A low growl came from his throat and I grinned. I pulled away, opening my eyes to make sure I wasn't dreaming. His eyes were wide and he licked his lips, relishing the hunger the kiss had left.

"God, Maddie. You don't know how long I've wanted to do this."

"To kiss me?" I asked, pushing myself closer to him.

"Yes, but I also just wanted to be with you. I get the circumstances suck, but from the moment you left me all those years ago, I hoped someday we would be together."

I cuddled closer to him.

"Well, we're here now. What are you gonna do with

me?" I looked at him with trust and vulnerability, but also a little bit of teasing.

He kissed my forehead and looked a little pained. That should have been my first clue that tonight wasn't going to go my way.

"Now, we sleep. We will have all the time in the world for the rest."

Chapter Twenty-Seven

LIAM

After I downed my sixth Jack Daniels, the bartender finally cut me off. The fucking son of a bitch. He didn't know who he was dealing with. I could easily drink six more.

"Better sober up, buddy. Otherwise, I'm taking your keys," the bartender said.

"Fuck off," I slurred, gulping the water he'd dropped in front of me. He was right. I was wasted. I stumbled off the bar stool and felt my way to the bathroom. Whoa, my eyes felt heavy. I made it to the bathroom and pissed for what seemed like an hour. Slowly, the room stopped spinning, and I started to feel slightly less nauseous. All I wanted was to sleep. I headed back to the bar, had another glass of water, and decided it was time to go.

I got into the car and drove back to the hotel. I pressed the elevator button and I waited… and waited for the next ride. As soon as I got in, I vomited all over the elevator floor. Fantastic. The elevator dinged for the sixth floor, and I staggered off, looking at the mess I had left.

"Sorry, maids," I said out loud as I waved at the security cameras.

I put the key card in the slot, heard the familiar click, and fell into the room.

"Shit," I whispered. All the lights were out, and I stumbled, falling again. Madison and Reynolds were asleep. I picked myself up off the ground and tiptoed to the bedroom. Their door was wide open. I peered in and saw them in bed together. Her head was resting on his chest and she looked so peaceful. She snored softly. I entered their room quietly and leaned over, gently brushing a kiss on her forehead. She moaned and snuggled up closer to Reynolds. I retreated slowly, defeated, and shut the door behind me.

I went to the other bedroom, lay down, and stared up at the ceiling. The whispers were back again. They rose like a pot of boiling water, and their presence stirred dangerous emotions in me. Anger. Frustration. Rage. They all boiled over, and I felt panicked and completely lost. I tried to regain some sort of composure by counting the ceiling tiles. My sour stomach turned, and vomit again made its way to my mouth. I swallowed. Fucking gross. Jack Daniels did not taste as good coming back up. My phone buzzed in my pocket. I looked at the caller ID. You've got to be kidding me, I thought. I reluctantly answered the call.

"Hello, Mother," I answered.

"Liam. I hope I'm not waking you." I chuckled. It was 3:00 a.m. She knew me too well.

"No, Mom. I wouldn't have answered if I were asleep." Sarcasm dripped from my words.

"Right. I just was calling to see why you keep missing Dr. Brown's appointments. He's worried about you," she said.

"I'm on a case. He knows that when I'm on cases, I can't see him. I told him, and you, this many times."

"Your health is more important than those murderers and thugs you chase around. I don't see why you want to be in that profession, anyway. It's all blood and gore. It's not good for you, Liam," she pleaded, a slight quiver in her voice.

"We've had this conversation countless times, Mother. I feel useful here, and it helps. It helps with the urges," I argued.

"It perpetuates the urges. That's what the doctor always says. It keeps you in a constant state of anger. You need to work on not getting angry. Not chasing things that make you angry."

"I know this." The phone call was irritating me. I hadn't seen my mother in months. Mostly, that was because every time we talked, or even got into the same room with one another, we fought about the same thing: my job and my mental health. "It's under control. I have outlets that allow me to work and stay focused."

"You mean sex and alcohol? It was the same thing with your father. You saw what he did to me. I just worry—"

"Worry that I'll turn out like him? A violent, alcoholic woman beater? Too late, Mom. This is who I am. There's no curing who I'm wired to be."

"Oh, Liam." She started crying.

"Mom, I've got to go. It's late, and I've got work tomorrow."

"Please promise me you'll call Dr. Brown. He can help. He's the best."

"Sure, Mom." I rolled my eyes.

"I'm sorry. I'm so, so sorry," she pleaded and wept on the other end of the phone. I knew what she was sorry for. She wasn't sorry I'd grown up watching her and my dad have sex with everyone who walked through the door. He'd forced her, pimped her out to the highest bidder, and often joined in on the fun. She wasn't sorry I'd been forced to sit in my room quietly and pretend I didn't know what was going on. She wasn't sorry I'd watched him beat her and maim her for his own sexual pleasure. No. She was just sorry it had shaped me into the man I was today. The same man my father had been. Sadistic, sex crazed, and angry. But I was different from him. I was much, much worse. My anger fueled my body daily. It was my drug. It allowed me to do my job with such conviction and drive. It was who I was. The sad thing was I loved my job. I loved the murders and the adrenaline rush of a gunfight because it made me feel normal for even just the briefest of moments. I was free and felt at home amongst the bloody chaotic mess.

"Good night, Mother." I hung up. After my father had passed, my mother had been so lost. Lost in a world without a domineering, controlling man. She'd found God, and she'd also begun to see what all the years of abuse had done to her and to me. The guilt was eating away at her, and so she was trying to shove her god down my throat.

174

"God will get the devil off your back," she'd say, but I didn't care. I kind of liked the devil on my back. She should have realized her part in the abuse years ago and protected me from that world. I was who I was, and nothing could change that. The devil was knocking—that was for sure—and he had one foot in the door. I rolled on my side, and drifted off to sleep. For a brief moment, I was at peace with who I was.

Chapter Twenty-Eight

MADISON

I was on cloud nine. I opened my eyes, and the sun was shining through the window. It was warm against my skin, and its presence sent the promise of a beautiful day radiating down my body.

I turned around to face Scott, only to realize he wasn't there. I put my hand against the sheet, and his spot was cool to the touch. He must have already headed off to Quantico. I'd have to get used to that type of life myself. Who knew where I would be placed when I was done with the Academy? The thought of being separated from Scott tugged at my heart, but I pushed that thought aside. I'd just have to cross that bridge when I came to it.

I groaned at the thought of the agenda for the day. More training. Liam had mentioned we were going to focus more on shooting and stamina, so we were headed to a local range and then back for some laps in the pool. I was thankful we would be swimming. My legs burned from the three-mile run we had done the day before, but after all

I had put my body through in the past few months, I felt stronger and more in control of myself. I got out of bed and looked at myself in the mirror. My stomach was much flatter now, and my arms were toned. My legs, while thick, were muscular and strong. For the first time in... well, forever, I wasn't completely disgusted with what I saw in front of me. Probably not the healthiest mental attitude to ever have about your body, but there you have it.

Despite my worries over the training schedule, the day went by fast, and the gun training turned out to be my favorite. Something about holding a gun in your hands made a person feel powerful. Liam spent most of his time yelling at me to stop fidgeting, to stay still, and to focus. He wouldn't touch me, though. He kept his distance, never once letting our bodies touch.

At the end of the day, I collapsed into bed, alone. Scott still wasn't back from Quantico, and I drifted off to sleep. The familiar tug of nightmares pulled at me, and I was tossing and turning when I felt the warmth of strong, protecting arms come around me. I opened my eyes to the sound of Scott's gentle breathing. I snuggled closer, finally drifting off to a peaceful sleep.

I woke up to a kiss on my cheek. I rolled over and smiled widely at Scott.

"Good morning. It's time to get up."

"Ugh. I don't wanna!"

"We've got to get going. Today is the day we move into the Academy." I buried myself further into the bed, pulling the blankets over my head. He snuggled down and started to tickle me.

"Stop! Please! I'm going to pee my pants." I laughed, trying to hide myself in the blankets.

"Never." I gasped as he grabbed my shoulders and dragged me on top of him. Scott lay there, looking up at me, and I smiled shyly and blushed.

"What?" I asked. He was so intent.

"You're beautiful. That's all," he commented, as if it were the most obvious truth in the world.

"I'm sure," I said sarcastically. I patted down my crazy bed head. Like that would do any good.

"You're perfect." He grabbed my face and kissed me passionately on the lips. I felt liberated and confident as I slowly moved my hips and gyrated against him. He stopped kissing me, and I looked into his beautiful, sparkling blue eyes. He slowly brought his hands down to my hips. They glided over the sides of my body, leaving a trail of heat all the way to my breasts. As he moved further north, I sensed his question. My eyes said yes. Yes, I want you to touch me everywhere. When he finally cupped my breasts for the first time, I moaned. He lingered there for a moment before gently caressing their soft fullness. His touch was calm at first, slow and methodical, as if he were getting to know me. Then he started getting more needy and deliberate. My body answered, and I pressed myself into him. I couldn't take the building tension, so I took off my shirt and bared myself to him completely.

"God, Maddie. You're so sexy." I smiled. I wasn't shy. I didn't blush. I was on fire. I took his hands and placed them on my now exposed breasts. My nipples instantly hardened, and my pussy clenched tightly in anticipation. Scott grabbed my hands and pierced me with his gaze.

"Are you sure?" he asked.

"I'm very sure," I replied. I stood slowly and pulled down my cotton underwear, showing him just how ready I really was. He breathed in sharply, standing and staring at me for what seemed like forever. I went to move toward him.

"Stop," he ordered. He grabbed my hands and placed them at my sides, and knelt in front of me. His eyes roamed over my body, stopping right at my center, and he licked his lips. He grabbed my ass and laid me on the bed, my swollen pussy now entirely at his mercy. I was completely his, and him taking control was hot as hell. As if sensing my tension, he gently kissed me once between my legs, which only served to ignite further the passion within me. I arched my back, trying to encourage the attention, but he moved past the area I needed him to go. The slow-burning fire was now fully blazing as he slowly kissed my outer thighs and moved closer and closer to my center. He opened me wide and licked. Oh, did he know how to lick. He lapped up every ounce of me, making me squirm with need. I grasped the sheets, moaning with every move his tongue made. I couldn't take it anymore. I was going to explode. I sprang up and pushed him down on the bed as he laughed.

I took my place on top of him, my legs once again straddling him. He smiled and kissed me eagerly on the lips. His penis had broken free from his boxers, and it hid naturally within my folds as if seeking entrance. I grabbed him—all of him—in my hands. God, he was huge. I methodically moved my hand up and down, wanting and needing to feel every inch of what would soon be inside me. My curiosity was getting the better of me. He shuddered under my touch, and released a low growl from deep within his chest. As I continued stroking him, his tension grew, and he grabbed my hair. His body quaked, letting me know he was close.

"Scott, do you have a condom?" I asked, praying that he had one. He gently moved me off as he reached down quickly into his pants pocket, pulling out his wallet and removing a condom. I smiled, ripping it open. As I rolled it on, I didn't once take my eyes off his. The heat between my legs only intensified.

I was ready for him. I adjusted myself as I straddled him and smoothly placed him inside me, my wetness guiding the way. There was no resistance as he entered me for the first time, and he moaned and grabbed hard at my sides. He filled me completely, perfectly. I felt every inch of me stretch and warmly wrap around him. I wanted him—all of him—and my hips started moving in an instinctive, fluid, sensual motion. I rode him slow and steady, and with each pulsing of my hips, I sent us further into a frenzy. We grasped at each other, trying to hold on. He'd grab my hips. I'd grab his strong upper arms. He'd reach for my breasts. I'd dig my fingers into his back. I watched him intently, and my eyes never left his. I felt confident, in charge, and seductive. My long hair flowed around me and gently caressed Scott's body with each move I made. I felt so alive.

I continued straddling and dominating every part of him. His eyes closed and he grabbed my ass. Moving his hands to my waist, he rammed into me, pushing himself deeper inside. I screamed my pleasure. Fuck! That had hurt so good.

"Maddie…." He grasped at my sides, keeping me still as I felt all of him inside of me. I looked into his eyes, the once light blue turning a darker shade. I overflowed with sensation and heat. Every ounce of my body sensitive, like just a simple touch would send me over the edge. Just then, Scott reached out and grasped my nipple with his teeth and my pussy clenched around his penis, gushing warm liquid.

"Jesus, that's so goddamn hot," Scott said. As I rode him again through my climax, his body stiffened. I felt closer to him, a part of him. We were as close as two people could ever be. I had never done anything like that before, and had never been so satisfied. My lips curled up into a smile. I slid off him and lay on my back, pulling the sheets up to cover my body.

"That was amazing!" he exclaimed, kissing me.

"I've never done anything like that before," I breathlessly answered. He looked at me, shocked, and then he smiled.

"I'll gladly allow you access to my body anytime," Scott teased. I smacked him playfully on the arm.

There was a knock at the door.

"Madison? Reynolds? You up?" Liam yelled.

"Yep," we answered in unison. Heat filled my face quickly. Crap. Had Liam just heard all of that?

"We have to leave in about an hour to get to Quantico. They're expecting us. So—" There was a pause and a jiggle of the doorknob. "Can't I just open this? It's fucking annoying talking at the door." The knob jiggled again. Thank God, it had been locked—presumably by Scott before I'd woken up.

"Ummm," I stuttered. "I'm not decent…"

"Oh." Liam replied. Irritation echoed in his voice. "One hour, or I'm leaving without you guys." He stalked away, his steps heavy and deliberate. I buried my head under the pillow.

"Maddie, why are you hiding?" Scott asked, trying to remove the pillow from my face. I held it tighter.

"Because! He probably knows we just had sex," I groused, rolling onto my side.

"People have sex all the time. If anyone knows that, it's him." A creak of the bed let me know Scott was getting up.

"I guess. It's just so embarrassing."

Scott laughed. He was always laughing, which was one of the many things I enjoyed about him.

"I'm hopping in the shower," he announced. I turned to face him just as he started walking away. I admired his ass in his boxers. My mouth watered at the thought of fondling his luscious ass while he fucked me again. Just that thought had my nipples hardening. I was swollen and wet, and I pressed my legs together tightly as my body responded to his stare.

"Join me?" His eyes sparkled with lust as he held his hand out to me, and I trembled and ached for his touch.

I took all of him in. He stood in front of me, sweaty and flawless. I glanced down at his penis. I released my tightly closed legs. He was fully erect. Who was I to say no to a Greek god's request? I jumped up and ran toward the bathroom, excited. Despite all the bullshit going on in my life, something at least seemed to be going right.

Chapter Twenty-Nine

LIAM

I don't know what I had expected. I knew Reynolds wanted her. They had history, after all, but it fucking pissed me off. I listened as she squealed, and I knew what they were doing. I punched the wall, leaving a huge gaping hole. I didn't care that the damage would likely come out of my paycheck. The anger left me after releasing some of that violence, and I felt a little better. I packed up my few belongings and waited in the common room until I heard the bedroom door open. Out they came, hand in hand, looking… happy.

"About goddamn time," I said, immediately standing.

"Good morning to you, too," Madison said with a roll of her eyes.

"Nothing good about this morning, Harper," I replied.

"Harper? Since when do you call me Harper?" she questioned, cocking her head and studying me intently. "And what happened to the wall?" She walked over and touched the hole I had just made.

I shook my head, not wanting to answer her question. She blushed, pulling her hand away from the evidence of my rage.

"From now on, I'll be calling you Harper. I'm supposed to be your instructor—not your fucking friend." I started gathering my bags. I had to get myself the fuck out of there.

"Ouch. Okay. Guess you woke up on the wrong side of the bed." She chuckled.

"Nope. Just woke up to you two fucking so loudly, I wish I'd had earplugs. Not how I planned on starting my day." Reynolds shook his head, but I ignored him.

"Sorry," Maddie said, biting her nails and looking up at Reynolds. Reynolds smiled and gently took her hand.

"It happens. People *do* enjoy sex. It isn't just for fucking." Reynolds let go of Madison, crossed his arms, and propped himself up against the wall.

"Forget it," I murmured. I wasn't in the mood to fight.

"We just got a little carried away. It's been so long since I've had a boyfriend that I forgot what it was like." She looked over at Reynolds and winked. *Wait. Boyfriend?*

"Boyfriend?" I opened the door to the hallway. Fucking boyfriend? What happened to staying away from her? I glared at him, willing him to look at me. *Look at me, you sly bitch.*

Reynolds answered, "Yeah, we just decided to make it official. It's what we both want." He looked at me, and our eyes locked. He didn't back down, eyeing me with conviction and force. I glared at him. It wasn't like him to lean into confrontation, but Madison had this way of making a man want to change. I'd give it to Reynolds. Maybe he did have some balls.

"Right. Okay, let's go before we're late." I grabbed my bags and slung them over my shoulders. I had a strong desire to break something. Possibly Reynolds's face.

I headed down the stairs. As I brought the car around, Madison came out alone. She looked so different, dressed for the field. Her hair was tied back neatly in a bun at the top of her head, her unruly curls smoothed back. I frowned. I loved her curls.

Her pressed khaki pants hugged her hips tightly, accentuating her curves. Her FBI-issued navy top was tucked in, making her look professional. The top was tight, though, in all the right places. Her breasts bounced as she ran to the car. She opened the door, threw her bags in, and sat in the backseat.

"I'm sorry," Madison said as she buckled her seat belt and looked up at me.

"For what?" I clenched the wheel harder. How could she make such a god-awful outfit look so damn sexy? I gritted my teeth and she sighed.

"Listen, I know it's weird with me and Scott and all. I just want to say thank you for taking care of what happened last night." She paused, adjusting the seat belt around herself. "Yeah. Ummmm… that's all."

"That's my job. I protect the weak." I looked at her when I said those words. Pain filled her eyes. I didn't care. I wanted her to feel how I was feeling.

"Plus, it's none of my business what you and Reynolds

do, Harper. We weren't going out or anything. I asked you out for coffee, and it didn't work out. He's a better guy than me, anyway." I hesitated. "I'm no good for you."

She sat up straighter and leaned into the front seat. "See? That's your problem, Liam. You always think you know what people should and shouldn't do. You're too busy judging others you don't see how much help you need. All the sex? The alcohol? The violence? It's not healthy." The tip of her thumb was in her mouth, and I heard the crunch of her nails. She slouched back, a look of concern plastered on her face.

"I know I'm fucked-up, Madison. This is who I am. The fucking alcoholic who feeds off violence. But don't sit there and make it seem like you and I go *way* back like you and Reynolds. We don't." I glared back at her.

"I thought we could be friends?" she asked, her mouth forming a thin line. I didn't want to be her friend. I wanted to be more than friends. I wanted to be so deep inside her Reynolds would seem like a distant memory. But *friends*? No. I couldn't be her friend.

"Sorry. You were mistaken," I replied, regaining my composure and focusing on the front seat.

"Clearly," she said despondently.

Reynolds got in the passenger seat, fastened his seat belt, and looked curiously between me and Madison. Madison sat in the backseat, looking wistfully out the window, avoiding eye contact with Reynolds and me. Good. I hoped she felt like a total goddamn idiot. I'd wanted her. I'd needed her, yet she'd chosen the golden boy. He didn't need her like I did. She made me better. She made all the fucked-up shit in my head fade. I clenched the steering wheel tighter, and my hands went numb.

As we headed off to Quantico, I couldn't help but feel a sense of satisfaction about what Madison would be walking into. She'd need me. She'd come back to me. The faint whispers filled my head, reassuring me, calming me down. I smiled. Yes, she'd need me again. I could be her savior. No doubt, the next month would be challenging for her. She would have to prove herself to become an agent and work to apprehend one of the worst serial killers we had seen in a long time. I just hoped she was up for the challenge.

Chapter Thirty

I watched Aimee leave, and fury surged through me. She was happy. The misery I had tried to cause her over the past few days—it didn't matter. I had my newest girl, Alice, follow and torment them. But she had failed. She was too young, too weak. I needed someone else, someone stronger.

Aimee had fallen hard for Scott. I wanted to make her miserable. I wanted her to feel what it was like to lose the only person you cared about. But Scott wouldn't be enough.

A cunning smile formed at my lips as I watched Liam pull the car around. The look in his eyes as he had watched her descend the stairs—that look let me know all I needed to. Liam wanted her. No, it was more than that. He was tormented by his desires, yet he struggled to keep those obsessive feelings at bay.

I watched her try to comfort him but his body had betrayed his true feelings. I wanted Liam. I wanted Aimee. I wanted her to know what it felt like to watch someone you cared about slip away. I saw it in her eyes that she cared. Those same eyes looked into her mother's when I killed her. I was going to be the one to break him and make her watch as I did. I pulled up my jacket to cover my face, and walked by them. Neither of them noticed me. They were too transfixed in that moment, too focused on each other, to notice me right next to them.

I turned the corner and walked down the alley. The sounds of dripping water and the stench of alcohol, drugs, and urine surrounded me. Then I saw who I needed.

Hunched in the corner of the building sat a young woman with ragged red-and-black hair. The hair was matted to her face, and she looked right at me, need evident in her wild eyes.

I crouched in front of her, and my hands twitched just looking at her beauty. She was dirty, but I could see her potential, the beautiful masterpiece underneath. She was much older than my usual, but I wasn't shopping for me anymore. I pictured myself carving into her flesh, her warmth surrounding me as I finally released her soul. It would be my hands that took her life. The warmth and smell of her blood hit my nostrils, and my groin tightened in ecstasy. I shook my head. She wasn't for me. She was for him.

"What's your name, sweetheart?" I asked.

"Samantha," she said. Her wild eyes focused on mine.

"Do you want to come with me, Samantha? I can keep you safe. I can help you." I smiled, reassuring her.

"What do I have to do?" She asked the question so calmly, so knowingly. She had reached into my mind and pulled out the ideas floating there. She knew I needed her. She knew the type of man I was.

"I need to help a friend meet his destiny." My face was serious. The smile had dripped away like melting flesh. She didn't once take her eyes off mine, and in that moment, I knew she was perfect.

"Will it hurt?" she asked anxiously as she glanced away.

"Yes." I lifted up her face. I wanted her eyes on mine again. We stared at each other for a moment—wordlessly, but so much was conveyed in those silent moments.

"Okay." She nodded, her mouth forming into the most devious smile. She got up from her corner and took up the ragged bag that had lain beside her.

We walked away, and she smiled at me again —that all-knowing smile.

I knew she would be perfect. She would be such a wonderful masterpiece. So magnificent. I couldn't resist. I'd leave Aimee, Liam, and Scott alone for a while, allowing them the comfort and normalcy that came with life. They wouldn't be looking over their shoulders anymore. I would give them the calm before the storm.

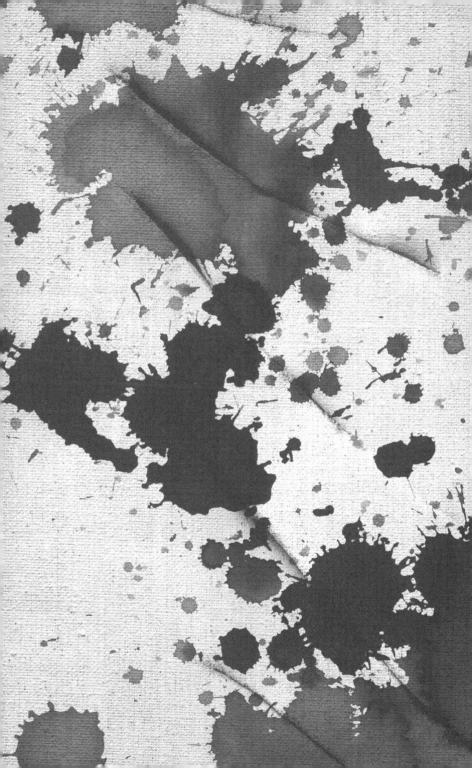

Part II: The Tragedy

"Don't be ashamed to weep, 'tis right to grieve. Tears are only water, and flowers, trees, and fruit cannot grow without water. But there must be sunlight also. A wounded heart will heal in time, and when it does, the memory and love of our lost ones is sealed inside to comfort us."

-Brian Jacques, Taggerung

Chapter One

MADISON

When we got to Quantico, I was immediately separated from Scott and Liam. I tried to be brave, but I was petrified. I had worked for my entire life to get to where I was at that moment. I, Madison Harper, was training at one of the most prestigious and coveted academies in the United States. I walked into the dimly lit room, which was nothing like the Hilton. There was no privacy. There were no personal bathrooms, and each of the four beds had an ugly brown blanket covering it. I itched just looking at it. Each bed had its own three-drawer dresser. Good thing I had packed light.

"You must be the new girl," said a voice from behind me. I turned around and came face-to-face with tamed, yet fiery red hair and a face full of freckles. She stared at me with pale green eyes. She was a little taller, and more slender than I was. She looked strong, and her toned arms showed from under a dark blue T-shirt. The woman's wild green eyes told me she could and would kick ass at the drop of a hat. Everything about her screamed perfection. Her pants were pressed perfectly and not a hair was out of place in her neatly tied bun. I needed her secret to that one. I smoothed my hair back, realizing I had about ten stray hairs that had come free.

"Yes, I'm Madison Harper. And you are?" I extended my hand in greeting. She looked at it as if I had some incurable disease.

"Avery Grant." She eyed me up and down. "I know who you are, Harper. Not sure why they'd let someone come in so late. You've missed a lot." She placed her hand on her hip. "Don't bother asking for help. I'm the top recruit."

I so didn't need girl drama. I wasn't here to step on anyone's toes; I just wanted to graduate. I met her hands on her hips with a dramatic cross of mine against my chest, cocking my hip. Two could play at that game.

"Let's make a few things clear, Grant. Number one, I won't be asking for help. I know what the hell I'm doing. Number two," I said putting two fingers in front of her face. "I transferred. I also have no intention of taking over your top recruit spot, so relax." Who did this woman think she was? We stood staring at each other for a moment, looking like we were having a good old-fashioned standoff. Who was going to draw first?

"Great. Glad we got that cleared up," Grant replied, relaxing slightly.

"Oh. My. God!" Two women came running in. "Did you see the two new guys? They are both instructors and fantastically delicious," said the tall one.

"Yeah, they're O'Leary and Reynolds. They came with me," I added with a wave.

"Wait, you know them? Dish! I'm Eden Marshall by the way," said the tall one. "And this is Desiree Garcia." She pointed to the petite woman standing next to her. Garcia looked a good two inches shorter than me. Elation filled me at the thought of someone being shorter than I was. Garcia's brown hair was tied back at the base of her head, and she wore khaki pants as per dress code, but her shirt wasn't quite as filled out as mine. Garcia's skin was olive toned, perfect and smooth. Marshall, however, towered over Garcia, and Marshall's hair was jet black and straight as an arrow. She had bangs that covered her forehead and swept over her eyes. Brushing the hair from her face, Marshall sat down on a bottom bunk, while Garcia remained standing. Both Marshall and Garcia anxiously waited for me to give the details on Liam and Scott.

"Hey, I'm Madison Harper. And yeah, I know them. Too well, actually." I rolled my eyes, shaking their hands.

"Sweet. I can't wait to see what they can do. I'm sure they are awesome at PT," Garcia said. We all laughed. They seemed like nice enough women, despite Grant's attitude problem. I hoped I had made it clear I did not intend to step on her toes. I was there to get through training and catch Walsh. That's all. I didn't care about status and rankings. As long as I made it through—that was all I wanted.

"Ladies, Gun Qualification time." Liam peered in the doorway. "Harper, you can sit this one out since you just got here." He started to walk away.

"No, thanks. I'd rather just get right to it," I added, grabbing my stuff.

"Suit yourself," he yelled over his shoulder as he continued to walk off.

"Yikes! Talk about tension," Grant said. Garcia and Marshall glanced my way as if looking for an explanation.

"Nope, no tension. He's just an asshole." I laced up my boots. "The other one, though. He's a keeper." I winked at them. "He's mine, girls."

"Gotcha, one's taken, but that other one—I don't care if he's an asshole. He's hot," Marshall said.

"If you guys are done gossiping about boys, let's go. We aren't in a sorority. We are in the FBI," Grant scolded. We all filed out of the room and headed toward the range.

Once we got there, I was issued a Glock 22, some earbuds, and goggles. "Head down that hallway and take a right," said an instructor. He was older than most of the instructors I had seen so far, gray hair beginning to peek through the dark brown. Wrinkles lined his eyes when he smiled and handed me the Glock. His grip was strong, and his hands were calloused, but I saw something youthful in his eyes, something that let me know he still had a lot of fight left in him. "Someone will be there to help you." He gave me a quick nod.

"Thanks," I replied. I grabbed the tools I had been given and made my way down the hall. Liam waited for me at the end of one of the lanes. Fan-freaking-tastic.

"Harper, get the gun ready. Remember our training." The weapon felt heavier, but that wasn't a bad feeling. The gun tethered me. I held it out in front of me. Because weaponry was still something I was getting used to, the process of getting ready took some time. Liam came up behind me, reaching around me. He pressed his groin against my back, and I sucked in a breath. I glanced at him, but he continued to look forward, not giving any indication that he was remotely aroused. The hardness against my back told me otherwise.

"Here. Like this." He placed his hands around mine. Magnetic shock waves vibrated through our bodies, and we locked eyes. His glinted with anticipation. I cleared my throat. *Okay, Maddie, back on track.*

"Right. Yeah," he said, shaking his head as if clearing his mind. He stepped away from me, and the space seemed so permanent.

"Obviously, don't miss. We'll start at the three-yard line, working our way out to the twenty-five-yard line," he said.

He dictated the instructions; I inserted my earplugs and put on my goggles. I took the Glock in my right hand. I focused, trying not to miss anything. I stood, steady, taking deep, calm, consistent breaths. My motions were smooth—like making love, rather than too hard or jerky. *Gentle. Gentle,* I reminded myself. As I breathed out—One. Two. Three—I shot.

I breathed in again, gaining my composure. I repeated the previous rhythm over and over again. I was consistent. I was methodical. When the buzzer rang, I took off the goggles and pulled out the earplugs. The targets came forward.

Liam looked at his clipboard. "The goal for this was 48/60. You scored 53/60. Not bad." He marked it down and walked away. The abrupt nature and distance tugged at my heart. Poor Liam. I sighed.

I felt a tap on my shoulder. Turning around, I saw it was Grant. Her red hair was loose and resembled a fiery blaze. I laughed inwardly. It fit her personality perfectly. Her fair skin complemented her hair well, and her cheeks were flushed and pink with anger.

"Harper. Thought you said you weren't going to show me up?" she asked. She paused, and then flashed me her scorecard. "I got a perfect score." Her cheeks returned to their regular color. I couldn't have cared less. I was proud of my score.

"Maybe you could help me get a perfect score?" I asked, gathering up my things. It would be easier to be on Grant's good side. I understood where she was coming from. I was new. I'd come in late. She wanted to be the best, but I didn't need any added stress.

"Ha! Right. So you can be better than me?" She eyeballed me and then started walking away. Without even turning around, she yelled, "That last one… you pulled the trigger too tight. Be gentle." I smiled as she left. See? She wasn't so bad. At least that's what I told myself.

I grabbed my weapon and headed over to turn it in. I hoped Grant lightened up a bit, or it was going to be a long month and a half. Marshall and Garcia came up behind me.

Marshall placed her arm around my shoulder and gave

me a kind, soft smile. "I know Grant seems like a total bitch, but she isn't that bad. Her daddy is Deputy Director of the FBI, a real hard-ass. So she's no stranger to hard work and discipline. She'll grow on you, though," Marshall said, pulling me in closer.

I slowly shifted away from her. The show of affection had made me nervous. "I'm not worried. Just thinking how it will be a difficult month and a half living with her." I shrugged and laughed. Garcia laughed as well. She was different from Grant and Marshall. She seemed so out of place, almost fragile.

"We went out before we started the Academy and, well, the key to Grant's heart is cheap beer and dancing," Garcia said, handing in her weapon.

Marshall squealed and started jumping up and down.

"That's it! We should all go out one weekend. That will get Grant out of her shell and you too." She nudged me with her elbow.

"We can go out?" I eyed her curiously. How was that possible?

"In a month, when we get more privileges, we can. There's a bar in town. We can take a cab, get dressed up... it'll be fun!"

Marshall did have a point. It'd be good to let off some steam. And with PT and classes every day of the week...

"You know what, ladies? That sounds like just what we need."

Marshall handed in her weapon and smiled.

Chapter Two

LIAM

"Wait up, Special Agent O'Leary," Director Stone called. He was the Director of the Academy and a real asshole. I rolled my eyes. What the fuck did he want?

"Yes, sir. What can I do for you?" I stopped and faced him, my arms pressed closely to my sides.

"I am here about Cadet Harper. We are switching up her training a bit and expediting her to hand-to-hand combat starting tomorrow," Director Stone said. His hair was gray, and his face looked worn and tattered. I'd seen him about a year ago, but he was getting up there in age, and the years in the FBI had certainly taken their toll. His body wasn't muscular anymore, and his belly was rounded and protruded slightly from his suit jacket. He sounded out of breath after trying to catch up to me. I scowled. This was the other man who was supposed to help keep Madison safe?

"With all due respect, sir, she just got here today and she is already a few weeks behind the other recruits. Shouldn't she be focusing on the things she's missed?"

"It's not needed. She has her PhD, she's intelligent, and she's obviously a hell of a shooter from what I can see." He flipped through a packet of papers he had on hand. "First time score, 53/60 on Gun Qualification? That's good. Hell, and let's face it, she could probably teach most of our classes here. I want her focus to be on the physical stuff. Shooting, weapons, and combat. She needs hands-on skills training now—not book training."

"But, sir…" I held up my finger to interject. He was *so* wrong. She didn't need that shit.

He stiffened. "Last time I checked, O'Leary, I run this training facility—not you. Therefore, I make the calls. I just thought it'd be nice of me to give you a heads-up that you will be providing her with the one-on-one training. Perhaps I should not have done that, as you think you are entitled to an opinion on the matter. So, do as I say. Train her. Make her the best. Make her like you." He put the papers under his arm and stood there, waiting for a response.

I looked down at the floor. I couldn't look him in the eye; I'd probably grab his throat and throw him up against the wall. He was asking me to take away what I loved about Madison. Her personality, her emotions, her purity. I had to remind myself this was what she wanted. She wanted this life. I looked up at Director Stone and nodded my assent before storming off. Fuck Director Stone for making me ruin her.

Chapter Three

MADISON

Showering in a bathroom with twenty other females was mighty interesting. Being überuncomfortable with my body didn't help. Although I was confident in my abilities as an agent, I didn't quite fit the mold of what the other female agents looked like. As I showered quickly and tried to rush out of the shared facility, one of the female instructors greeted me and handed over a revised class schedule.

"Good luck." She snickered as she walked away.

I read through the new month's schedule and the accompanying letter, and I couldn't help but let out a loud groan. My days were going to be split between hand-to-hand combat, kickboxing, PT, weapons, and defensive training. My body already ached.

I made it back to the room and shared my new schedule with the girls as I got dressed. Garcia and Grant laughed at my expression while Marshall slapped me on the shoulders for good luck. She knew I was screwed.

"Ugh, I'm so jealous. Spending the next month with

Reynolds *and* O'Leary," Garcia grumbled as she tied her hair up in a bun.

"Don't be. I get PT basically for the next month." My ass barely fit in my PT shorts. Catching a glimpse of myself in the mirror, I saw that my curvy frame filled out the shorts much more than the other recruits' did. Bending over would definitely result in part of my ass hanging out. I gave in and put on some compression shorts underneath. No sense in worrying about my ass hanging out all day, especially with Liam as my trainer. I piled my curls on top of my head with a hair tie and grabbed my water bottle. I would definitely need that.

"Have a good day." Marshall and Garcia sounded off as they exited our room. Grant looked pointedly at me and raised her eyebrows at my ensemble. I couldn't help but chuckle. She sure was something else.

Chapter Four

MADISON

"I'm so tired!" I moaned as I threw myself on my small bed. I managed to take off my workout shorts and top, and I lay down in just my underwear and sports bra. This had become my routine over the past two weeks. All day, every day, my body was tested beyond its limits. When I was done, I'd study until I crashed. There wasn't going to be any studying tonight. Just crashing. Other than the firearms and some combat lessons I had every other day with Scott, I barely saw him. I missed the intimate moments we'd had at the hotel.

"That's what happens when you work hard," Grant said as she studied the FBI handbook. She didn't once look up from the large manual. A loud knock at the door vibrated through our small room.

"Who the hell is that?" Grant asked as she got up and opened the door.

"Is Maddie in there?" Scott's voice reverberated through the door. I stood at attention. His voice was different, less shy and reserved than normal. Grant opened the door and motioned for him to come in.

"Can you go somewhere, Grant? I need to be alone with Maddie." I'd stood up when he'd called through the door, but now I was eyeing him curiously.

"I'm studying," Grant said as she crossed her arms defiantly.

"Leave, Grant." Scott motioned toward the door. "I'm pulling rank. Leave. Go work out. Go study in the library. I don't care what you do, but just go."

I looked between Grant and Scott as she stared at him.

"Please." His voice got louder. I couldn't help but get turned on as my boyfriend commandeered the room. I heated with the thought of Scott between my legs, and my tiredness was replaced with pure adrenaline and need.

After a few quiet seconds, a small smile curved Grant's lips. She silently gathered her books and left, making sure to close the door securely behind her.

Scott's eyes turned a dark, midnight blue. As he moved closer, the first thought I had was of a lion stalking its prey.

"I can't stand it anymore. Being near you all the time. Your body brushing up against mine and not being able to touch you. I'm always following the rules. Not wanting to upset anyone, cross any boundaries. I don't want to play by the rules right now. I can't. I want you. Now."

I wasn't used to this side of Scott—the out-of-control, impulsive, taking-what-he-wanted Scott. I caught glimpses of it every now and then, but right now, as he looked me up and down, and drank me in, I knew I was about to get the ride of my life. Fuck, I was already hot.

"Then don't play by the rules, Scott. No one's here. Just you and me."

He stood for a moment thinking, a small smile forming on his lips.

"Why are you still wearing your panties and bra, Maddie?" he said, his voice low, as he finally closed the distance between us.

"I, um…" I was speechless. Utterly and completely speechless.

"Cat got your tongue?" Scott smiled as he knelt in front of me. I glanced down just as his teeth found their way to the edge of my panties, nibbling on my hip as they encouraged my panties down. He sure liked making sure I was completely exposed to him before he dived in.

"Now, that's much better," Scott said as he stood up. "The bra. It's gotta come off." He reached for the seam of my sports bra and helped me pull it quickly over my head. The urgency of the moment took me over. I needed him, and by his dark look, I knew he not only needed me, but he knew I was completely ready for him as well.

"Oh, yes," he said as my nipples stood at attention before him. Before I could say or do anything, Scott took off his shirt and pants and threw me on the bed. He smiled at me, a reassuring smile that said this—*this was going to be amazing.*

As he came over me, his thigh moved between my legs, pushing them apart. He grabbed his cock and looked at me as he pumped it once. I moved his hand out of the way and frantically stroked the length of him. He moaned against my touch as I picked up speed, his hips meeting each stroke of my hand. Our eyes held each other captive as I fucked him with my hand.

He quickly pulled away, taking back control. Before I could protest, he placed a condom on himself and found his way to my opening, the tip of him teasing the outside of me. I arched my back to meet him more closely, letting him know I was ready, that I wanted him inside of me. He rammed into me, harder with each thrust. I felt myself stretch and close around him with each movement of his hips, but I wanted more. I *needed* more. I wrapped my toned and newly bruised legs around him.

"Do you feel that, Maddie?" Scott asked breathlessly.

"Yes." I moaned loudly as I felt myself getting closer and closer to my climax. He grabbed one of my legs and held it to the side, opening me up further. I felt him go deeper.

"Oh. My. God." I tried my best to stifle my screams, but the way my body felt right then, it only seemed right to share it with the world.

His thumb found my clit and he rubbed, stroking it, teasing it. My eyes closed, and the tension built within as every nerve ending begged for release.

"Let it go, baby. Let it go," Scott whispered into my ear as he continued reaching parts of me I hadn't even known existed.

"Jesus!" I screamed as I felt myself coming undone in Scott's arms. Every ball of tension I'd built up over the last two weeks of training relaxed, and my scream turned into a sigh. Scott joined me in his own ecstasy.

We lay there for a moment, content and sated as Scott stroked my hair and brushed kisses against my forehead.

"Not that I'm complaining, but what was that for?" I asked as I rolled to face him.

"Do I need an excuse to want to make love to my girlfriend?"

"That was not making love, Scott. That was fucking." I laughed. Scott sat up on his elbows, the light blue of his eyes returning.

"No, Maddie. That's where you're wrong. It doesn't matter if it's quick and hard or soft and slow; every time I'm in you, every time my dick presses against my pants just from your smile alone, it isn't just fucking. It's love, Maddie. Genuine and pure."

Scott had a way with words. He always knew just what to say to make me understand what he felt. He had shown me in many ways what I meant to him, but I still struggled with expressing how I felt. I stared at the man in front of me, the man who had just kicked my roommate out to show me just how much he cared, and I knew. I knew without a doubt that it didn't matter what came along in my life or what had hurt me. It didn't matter what I thought had broken me. I would take the pieces that were left, and I would smile again. In fact, five minutes later, I actually *was* smiling as Scott hardened against my back. Yeah, there definitely wouldn't be any studying and crashing tonight.

Chapter Five

LIAM

"Come on, Harper! Flip me!" The sweat poured down my face as I egged her on.

"I'm trying, O'Leary. I just can't get—"

I lifted her over my shoulder and slammed her on the mat. Holding her side, she panted and winced, but she wasn't down. She got right back up and repositioned herself.

I smiled. I'd give her one thing: Madison didn't give up. The closeness of our bodies over the past month wasn't the same as it once was. The sparks, the sexual tension, they were gone for her now. I still felt the same pull, the same cravings for her, but she didn't look at me like she had during that first week. Her eyes were void of all attraction. She had given herself to Reynolds, fully. I still had hope, though. If I could just prove to her I could be the man she needed, the man she wanted, she'd choose me.

I barreled toward her, trying to use my speed and size to gain the upper hand. Bending over slightly, she used her back to stop me, knocking both of us to the ground. She quickly rolled over on top of me, pinning me down between her strong thighs. She was panting heavily, and I was stunned. The wind had been knocked right out of me. I hated feeling out of control; but for her, it was worth it. It had been a while since someone had gotten me on my back. I looked at her face shining with delight. Her legs gripped me tighter. My groin tensed, blood flowing to fill it. Jesus. Oblivious to my inner—and outer—torment, she released me and stood up.

"Yes!" she screamed triumphantly as she danced around, her hair breaking free from her bun. As much as I wanted her to have this moment, I couldn't. If she let her guard down like that in the field, she'd be dead. I swept her feet out from under her, and she hit the ground hard.

"What the hell?" She rubbed her neck and moaned.

"*Never* let your guard down. Even when you think your opponent is down, triple-check and cuff them immediately, or else something far worse could happen."

"You could have told me that, instead of kicking my ass." She groaned again.

"What have we been doing the past four hours? Hell! For the past month? You learn better by doing, feeling, experiencing. You've got all the fucking degrees in the world, but you need to experience it all physically now. Stop hiding behind all that education, and fucking work for what you want," I yelled, my dick pressing against my Under Armour shorts. I adjusted myself. I hated that my dick thought my anger was an open invitation to join the party. The anger floated around me as I flashed back to my past. *My mother, lying on the ground, bruised and beaten.* That could be Madison. That would be Madison if I didn't teach her.

"Seriously, O'Leary?" She'd sat up, and I could have sworn I saw steam coming out of her ears. "I worked hard for those 'fucking degrees.' I might not be as fast as you are, or have all the hands-on training—yet," she said with a pointed look. "But the educational experience that I have will help make me a better agent in the long run." She didn't yell. She was calm but assertive and absolutely terrifying in that moment. I looked down at her, giving her my hand to get up.

"Beauty, brains, *and* she can kick your ass," Reynolds said as he leaned against the doorway. "Sounds like she *is* already a better agent." He turned to Madison, missing the middle finger I sent his way with my other hand. Madison didn't. She smiled indulgently, like I was an entertaining child.

"Time to go. Weapons training time," Scott said.

She took my hand, jumping up from the floor.

"Ugh. I was hoping I was done for the day," Madison replied, brushing off her pants.

"No resting yet. You should be used to this by now, babe. You've been training for almost four weeks." He put his arm around her shoulders. "You only have one week left of training before the testing phase."

"Yes, sir," she said, teasing him.

"Don't call me sir." He playfully swatted her ass. She

giggled, leaning into his hold. God, those two made me sick.

"If you two are done, take her to the range. After all, the sooner she gets done, the sooner she can have some fun. It is Friday after all. She could use a break." I winked at her.

"Yes! What he said!" Maddie exclaimed, animatedly clapping her hands together. Reynolds grabbed her hand and dragged her out of the room, staring daggers at me as he walked away.

I sat on the gym floor for a while. I thought of Madison and Reynolds together—how I had blown my chance with her—and suddenly the whispers intruded. This time was different, though. Before the whispers began, a tingling sensation began in my groin and traveled up my arms and legs. Although pleasant at first, the initial sensation faded and the underlying pain took over. A prickling feeling— almost like tiny bee stings—covered my body. My mind raced, my heart pulsing. The whispers only stopped for one thing, though. Memories. Bad memories. I felt a mental tug, and I was thrown into a memory of my eighth birthday.

"Shut the fuck up, you dumb ass. I don't care that it's your birthday."

"Johnny, please just be nice to him today. He's turning eight! He's getting so big!" My mom smiled down at me and tousled my hair as she always did. I smiled.

"A wasted eight years of my life. Working and supporting this worthless piece of shit. I should have made your mom abort your ass. You're nothing but a goddamn leech." My

dad sat in his chair as he did every night, sucking down a beer from his third twelve-pack. My mom was trying to convince him to give her ten dollars so she could take me to McDonald's for a birthday meal. He liked my mom to stay home and "take care of him," so he was the only one with a steady paycheck.

"Baby..." Hugging him from behind, she placed her fragile, bruised arms around his neck. "Please? For me?" Turning, he kissed her abrasively on the lips. He then stood and started groping her, moaning and pressing himself against her. I went to leave, to go back inside, but he grabbed my arm.

"No. Stay. Watch."

The look on my mother's face was a mixture of fear and sadness. "Johnny, let him go inside. It'll be—"

His hand met my mother's face. I could have sworn I heard the breaking of a bone. "Don't ever tell me what to do, bitch. He stays."

I sat in the chair in the corner of the porch as he bent my mother over the chair. I watched him fuck her. His nasty, fat belly protruded from his stained white shirt, and sweat beaded down his face. He was groaning, licking his lips as he continued. I looked only at my mother's face, and as he finished, a single tear streamed down her cheek. I didn't shed a tear, though. I thought of all the ways I could kill the son of a bitch.

When he was done, my dad pulled out his wallet and threw a ten-dollar bill on her as she lifted her panties back up. A prize. A gift. For fucking him. My mom took my hand,

and we walked toward McDonald's.

"Liam, promise me something?" My mom asked.

"Yeah, Mom." I couldn't look her in the eyes. Not yet.

"Promise me you will get away from here. Please?" She had stopped walking. She looked me right in the eyes with tears streaming down her face.

"We will get free, Mom. I promise." I grabbed her hand and we continued walking. When we returned home from our dinner, Dad had a friend over. I was locked in my room for the night. I heard my mom screaming and crying. When I woke up the next morning, my bedroom door was open. My dad and his friend were passed out on the living room floor, completely naked. Used condoms were strewn all over the floor, cum spilling from the tops. My mom was draped on the couch, her left eye swollen shut, and her hands cuffed above her head. I took the blanket and covered her frail frame. I noticed bite marks and cigarette burns, and I fought back the tears. She moaned slightly and cuddled in, seeming to rest peacefully.

The bus would be there in fifteen minutes, so I headed to the kitchen to make myself some cereal. If I missed the bus, my dad would blame me, and I'd have more cigarette burns to add to those already covering my body. I couldn't miss school. I couldn't be late. That was my only escape from this world of pain.

I hated the flashbacks. I had tried to forget so much of my past. It infuriated me that my mom hadn't protected herself. She'd told me stories of how nice my dad had been at the beginning, lavishing things on her, buying toys and clothes for me when I was born. But that had soon ended, and the abuse had begun. My mom had done what she'd had to in order to protect me, but I was furious she hadn't protected herself. She hadn't known how, though. She'd been so dependent on my dad.

It felt like thorns were raking against my skin. I looked down, expecting to see blood. My heart beat faster, harder. The sweat beaded down my face, and the whispers grew louder and louder. The voices pounded at me, struggling to be heard. I needed something to make those go away. I needed a drink. I needed a release. I headed out to shower and to change. Another night of drinking away the pain and the memories, and cooling the rage that scratched at my soul.

Chapter Six

MADISON

The range hadn't been so bad. Shooting was something that—oddly— came naturally to me. I had an eye for it, Scott had said. As soon as I was done, I told Scott I was going to relax and go to bed early. In all truthfulness, Garcia, Marshall, Grant, and I were heading out to some local bar. We needed a night out; but with all that had been going on, Scott and Uncle Tom were still overprotective, and insistent that someone be with me at all times. Walsh hadn't tried to call. In fact, he hadn't done anything in a month. It was starting to look like we'd lost him again. I wanted to catch him, but I was grateful for the semblance of normalcy in my life.

I showered and put on my favorite ripped jeans and black tank top. It was low cut, and it looked amazing, hugging all the right places. I slipped on my black heels, adding a good three inches to my height. I had to live a little, right? My bare arms showed every bruise and welt inflicted on me the past month. I thought of covering myself up, but I was proud of those bruises and scars. They reminded me I was tough, a quality I often forgot I had.

Garcia and Marshall both looked like they were going to a club. Their skintight dresses left absolutely nothing to the imagination. I could see Marshall's thong line, and her red bra peered from underneath the black spandex material. Grant, of course, was wearing khaki pants, ballet flats, and a short-sleeved polo shirt. I laughed to myself. She was consistent; I'd give her that.

As we entered the bar, I immediately started choking on the cigarette smoke. Disgusting. It smelled like Walsh. The bar was loud, and the noise drowned out the voices of Garcia and Marshall as they screeched in delight. No sooner had we entered than guys were flocking toward us. Marshall and Garcia were getting the majority of the attention, and they were milking it for all it was worth. The few times I was actually approached, the men—and a few women—told me to leave the man who'd injured me. I smiled. Who knew the bumps and bruises would protect me from unwanted solicitors?

My heels were killing my calves, and I had a nagging blister, so I sat down at the bar and asked for a menu. The bartender laughed at me.

"Sugar, we ain't got no menus here." She smiled. Her boobs were pressed so close together and so far up her chest, I was afraid they'd choke her. She looked like she was easily over sixty, and the blue eye shadow she wore was not at all flattering on her old, wrinkled face. An image of Mimi from the Drew Carey Show popped into my head, and I smiled.

"She'll take a vodka seltzer." A guy with an unusually strong-looking jaw sat down on the stool next to me. His green eyes were intense, and only complemented his dark skin. He placed a fifty-dollar bill on the bar, which the bartender quickly grabbed and shoved into her bra.

"Thanks." I reluctantly took the drink from the bartender. The guy who had sat down next to me was handsome. He wore a light gray suit, paired with a baby-blue shirt. The shirt was unbuttoned, exposing his chest, and the tie he wore was covered in polka dots and was loosely hanging around his neck. He smiled at me and although he was beautiful, something about him put me on edge. His smile didn't produce the same warm feeling I had when Scott smiled at me. This guy's smile held the illusion of warmth, and I wondered briefly, what he wanted or needed from me. I brushed off my suspicions. I didn't know him. What could he possibly want from me?

"You're very welcome," he replied. "I'm Chris."

"I'm Maddie. Nice to meet you." I shook the hand he offered. It was strong, but clammy, and I had to hold back a shudder. I subtly wiped my hand on my outfit.

"What brings you in tonight, Maddie?" he asked, sipping his beer.

"Just taking a break with some friends." I pointed over to them. They had taken over a table and were downing shots. Marshall and Garcia gestured for me to come over while Grant sat back eyeballing the guy I was sitting next to. She was always on guard, always alert.

"Looks like they want you to join them." He waved at them. I heard Marshall giggling over all the loud music, and I rolled my eyes.

"Um, yeah. Would you like to meet them? They're all single." I laughed.

"Are you single, Maddie?" The aggressive way he said my name caused a slight tightness in my chest. My earlier worries resurfaced. What was this guy's deal?

I stuttered, "Well, uh, n-no I-I-I'm not." I shifted my drink in my hands.

"Shame." He shook his head "Well, let's go meet these friends of yours, shall we?" He held out his hand for me to grab so I could get off the abnormally tall bar stool. I looked around to make sure no one was watching me. Taking his hand, I dismounted from the stool and headed over to my friends' table. I felt guilty taking his hand. It felt wrong.

"We've been here five minutes, Harper, and you've already hooked up with some dude?" Garcia asked, looking him up and down. She was practically undressing him with her eyes.

"Harper? I thought your name was Maddie?" Chris eyed me skeptically.

"It is. Harper is my last name." I sat down at the table and kicked Garcia underneath. "Ouch," she said, rubbing her leg. I didn't need this guy knowing my life story.

"Interesting. So are you ladies in the military?" he asked, taking a swig of his drink.

Laughter came from the other end of the table. "Military? No way. FBI," Grant scolded him, and I briefly imagined her hair bursting into flames. I bit the side of my cheek to hold back a laugh. Grant was a firecracker, and I loved that about her. As passive as I could be, she had a voice that was enough for the both of us. During the last month, we had gotten close. We complemented each other well. She still teased me relentlessly about trying to be better than her, but she knew she was the best. It's hard not to be the best when you were raised by the Deputy Director of the FBI. Fighting crime was in her blood, and she may have been mouthy, but she was a good friend, and I knew she would always be there for me. For that, I was grateful.

Chris raised his eyebrows and waved the bartender over. "I need a round of Fireball shots for these FBI ladies here, if you don't mind." He presented her with a hundred-dollar bill this time. "Keep them coming," he whispered to her. The ladies and I shrugged at each other. Well, at least we didn't have to buy drinks.

The rounds did keep coming, and everyone kept drinking. Grant finally started loosening up. She'd even unbuttoned three buttons on her polo shirt and started dancing. I smiled. But she never wavered in her scrutiny of Chris, and her glance kept wandering back to him. Chris and I sat at the table chatting, talking about what we did for work. Actually, mostly I talked. I opened up, my hesitation to talk with him that I'd had moments ago fading. There was something about him, the way he asked questions, the way he leaned in, and listened intently. It was odd to have a guy listen so much, but I enjoyed the attention. I told him about how I had just received my PhD, and how I was only a week away from being done at the Academy. I told him about how I had sucked at hand-to-hand combat, but I also mentioned I was getting better. I showed him every scar and bruise. I even talked about Scott and Liam.

"Scott and Liam both seem to care a lot about you," Chris commented.

"I guess they both just want what's best for me," I replied.

"You said you've known Scott your whole life. Isn't it weird to date a lifelong friend?"

I shrugged. "We kind of went our own separate ways and just rekindled our friendship. It isn't that weird. It just feels right." Another round of drinks came. We had switched to drinking beer. It tasted like piss to me, but I nursed the one I had to be polite.

"What about your parents?" he asked.

I didn't know quite how to answer that question, so I lied. "They're dead. Car accident when I was five. I was raised by a family friend." I choked back another gulp of lukewarm beer.

"Tragic." Chris grabbed my hand as if to comfort me. I let him linger there for a moment before I retracted my hand. Something wasn't right. He was trying way too hard.

The door to the bar opened, and in stormed Scott. I waved to him as he came barreling through the bar, a little too buzzed to care about the storming part. Hatred was plastered across his face, and his lips were pressed into a thin, angry line. He pushed a chair out of his way, sending it into the wall with a loud thud. Ah, shit.

"Maddie, what the hell are you doing here?" he asked, leaning over the table.

"I just wanted to get out with the girls, let off a little steam. That's all." I batted my eyelashes at him. I'd seen my old roommates, Missy and Jenna, do that before, and it seemed to work for them. The frustration on Scott's face let me know I wasn't so lucky.

"Chris. Should have known you'd be here."

"You two know each other?" I questioned. Scott didn't sit down. He just stood over me like a protective caveman. I pictured him with a club over his head, dragging me off to the cave to have his way with me. I giggled. He glared at me. Shit, I was tipsy. When Scott looked over at me, though, I immediately sobered up.

"Oh, yes. I know Chris. Chris is a scumbag reporter for the Washington Herald."

"A reporter?" I looked between the two men. "Oh. My. God. I was talking to a reporter?"

"Yep. I often do stories on FBI cases and such." He was grabbing his suit jacket and getting ready to stand up.

"Then why are you here talking to me and my friends? We're still in the Academy. No stories here!" I was frustrated. I hated being used.

"I was interested in the daughter of Michael Walsh." Chris's eyes locked on mine. He knew. He knew who I was.

"Motherfucker!" I wound up and punched him square in the face, knocking him off the chair.

Ouch! That had hurt. I shook out my hand. It was just a dull throb, and the alcohol helped mask the rest of the pain.

I guess I'd gotten to show him my hand-to-hand combat skills after all.

Scott started laughing next to me. He'd been hot defending my honor with the reporter a minute ago, but the laughter… I loved Scott's laughter.

"That's my girl," he said as he picked Chris up off the floor and dragged him toward the entrance. I was furious. Not just with Chris, but also with myself.

I looked around the bar, and everyone was staring at me.

"Show's over, guys," I yelled as I picked up the tipped-over chair.

"Ugh! I can't believe I let that happen. Some guy comes in, buys us drinks, and listens for a minute, and I get diarrhea of the mouth," I told Garcia, Grant, and Marshall. When I looked up, they were staring at me with different degrees of shock on their faces.

"You're Walsh's daughter?" Grant asked. She didn't have the normal, annoyed twang in her voice. She sounded almost concerned.

"Yeah. Guess the cat's out of the bag now." I shrugged. I grabbed my clutch and was about to walk out.

"Oh, hell no!" Grant said, grabbing my arm. "You can't drop a bomb like that on us and then leave. More drinks! More dancing! You've had a fucked-up life, but don't run away! Face the doubters and the gossips head-on. For now, though, let's drink it all away!" She took a shot and started dancing again. I was surprised they weren't disgusted or upset. Instead, they had rallied around me, and were trying to lift me up. I'd never really had friends. I guess that was what it felt like.

"Don't let that fucktard reporter ruin your night, sweetie. Let's do this!" Marshall said.

"Scott's here," I replied, looking back at him as he reentered the bar.

"So, let him join us. Scott needs to loosen up too!" Grant screamed over the music.

When Scott reached me, I coiled myself in his arms and took him out on the dance floor. He didn't look happy, but I didn't care. I handed him a beer, and whispered in his ear that Grant had told me he needed to lighten up. He laughed.

Scott grabbed me around the waist and pulled me in close. I swayed my hips to the music, grinding against him. His eyes locked on mine and we danced. Our bodies fit so well together, flowed together. The sweat beaded down our faces and our backs, but as Scott's body met mine with each thump of the beat and each chord that was played, our bodies became one.

As the song ended, we stopped and he kissed me. He grabbed my face in his hands and licked at the seam of my lips. My entire body reacted. I wanted to undress him right there. The DJ stopped the music and interrupted our moment. I groaned into his mouth, and Scott smiled.

"Seems we have a volunteer for karaoke tonight," the DJ said to the crowd. "Would Madison please come take the mic?" I froze. What the hell had he just said? I did not sing in front of people.

Garcia, Marshall, and Grant started chanting my name. Those ladies! I would get them for this.

Scott clapped his hands and egged me on. Screw it! I grabbed my drink from the table and took a swig. Liquid courage. I went up to the stage and the lights dimmed. Sweat streamed down my face and into my eyes. I couldn't see the audience. A spotlight shone down on me, and only me. Everyone else was invisible.

"What song do you want to sing, pretty lady?" The DJ asked. I didn't need to think about the question. I knew.

"'Little Do You Know' by Alex and Sierra, please," I requested, and took the mic. It was heavy, solid, and cool in my hands.

"Um… Hi!" The mic was shaking in my hands, and I closed my eyes and listened to the melody of the song as it played.

"I want to dedicate this song to my boyfriend. Thanks for protecting and loving all of me. Even the messed up parts."

I cleared my throat and let go of my worries, let myself feel every word. The words were a part of me. The song was one I knew well. It was mine.

The melody played on, and suddenly an eerily familiar voice from behind me joined in. The raspy tones, mixed with the singer's raw emotion caused tears to form in my eyes. I looked back, hoping to catch a glimpse of the person who felt this song as deeply as I did, but the darkness of the stage prevented me from seeing him.

My heart clenched in my chest, pounding with every word the stranger sang. This was our song. Whoever he was, this song had been meant for us. We sang in perfect harmony. His raspy, soulful voice coupled with my tones were a great contrast. Like night and day. Like dark and light.

When I stopped and opened my eyes the lights were on and everyone was looking at me. I looked quickly back to where the mystery man had stood. But he was gone.

"Wow. Let's hear it for Madison one more time, guys. She sure has a set of lungs on her." The DJ led the crowd in applause.

I got off the stage and headed toward the door. I needed air. I needed to come down from the emotional high I was on. Before I could make it, Scott grabbed me and kissed me hard on the mouth. Hooting and hollering came from the bar patrons, and I tried to compose myself and breathe through my shock.

"You. Are. Amazing. I never knew you could sing," Scott said, his breathing staggered and uneven. He was turned on, and I thought of getting him in bed again. I wanted to feel his face between my legs. I imagined him doing that magical movement with his tongue, and heat rushed to my face.

"Thanks." I hugged him tightly.

"Harper!" My friends screamed as they raced over and pushed their way through the crowd. "You're so talented!" They hugged me. Even Grant.

"Thanks, guys," I said, giving them a huge smile, and then placing my hands on my hips. "But I have a bone to pick with you. Why did you sign me up?" I questioned.

"We didn't sign you up, Harper," Grant replied,

mimicking my stance but looking thoughtful.

"Hmmm," I said, confused. "Okay. A mystery..." I paused. I still needed to recuperate from the song. I'd deal with everything else later. "Well, I'm going to step outside for some air, but I'll be right back." I kissed Scott on the lips again, this time slipping in some tongue for good measure.

"I'm going with you," Scott said as he smiled against my mouth. I nodded. I knew he was trying to protect me but I just wanted a moment to myself, to clear my head. Scott's cell phone rang and he held up his finger as he stepped aside to answer the phone. I snuck away, taking my chance to be alone for some much-needed fresh air.

As the fresh air brushed against my warm skin, my turmoil, all my haunted memories swarmed me. I'd shared all of these with Scott. He knew my past. He knew my struggles. He knew everything about me. And yet, he'd waited. He'd told me he'd always wondered where I was, who I had become. I felt it all now. That song. Those lyrics. They had helped me realize how much I truly cared about Scott. He loved all the fucked-up parts of me. He embraced the good and the bad, and good God, how could I not love a man who saw the light amongst all of my darkness?

Chapter Seven

SCOTT

I should have been angry as I watched Maddie sneak out of the bar but she was exquisite. There wasn't anything that woman couldn't do. I motioned to Grant to get her attention, hoping she'd go out after Maddie. She scrunched her brow as I made hand gestures, trying to indicate for her to go outside. I shook my head because she started talking again, ignoring my efforts. I hoped this conversation with Director Stone would be quick so I could go out after Maddie myself. One of my buddies at the Quantico personnel office told me a custodian stopped showing up for work. I had to make sure Director Stone knew. I had to be sure it wasn't connected in some way to Walsh.

"Reynolds, this better be damn good to interrupt my Saturday night." Director Stone growled into the phone. He was request for a call back.

"A custodian didn't show up for work today again, sir," I said.

"Reynolds, I told you to let me handle things here.

I'm capable of doing my job."

"I understand that but don't you think it's suspicious?" I paused. "Working in any capacity for the FBI is a good job. Just to stop coming to work? What if Walsh—"

"Enough!" Director Stone's loud voice pierced my ears.

"I will look into it Reynolds, but this isn't the first time a custodian was a no call, no show. It isn't the most glorious job. At least you don't have to hire someone new." He sighed.

"Yes, sir." He hung up the phone and the silence seemed deafening. I had a pit in my stomach. Something just didn't seem right.

My mind shifted back to Maddie. I was captivated by her voice. It had resonated deep within me, making me feel each and every emotion she couldn't form into words. She cared. She loved. She had just proven with one song that she was capable of all the things she wanted. I couldn't wait to be the one to embrace those parts of her, help those parts of her emerge. No matter how slow the process, no matter how much the effort, I wanted to be that guy. I wanted to be the one who showed her how to love.

As I made my way to the door, Grant grabbed my arm and pulled me aside.

"Hey, Reynolds, who signed her up for the karaoke if it wasn't any of us?" she questioned.

"That's a good question. Anyone could have, I suppose." I shrugged. I was still thinking about Maddie's voice and how I needed to check on her.

"Earth to Reynolds?" Grant waved her hand in front of

my face. "Snap out of it, dude. I get it's great and all that you love her, but seriously, don't you think it's odd she was signed up and no one else was? And who the hell was that guy singing with her?"

"I guess." I'd give it to Grant; she would be a good agent. She was always thinking offensively, aware of her surroundings. She would be an asset to the FBI. "Wait, why didn't you go out after her? I motioned for you."

"Those hand movements were my clue to go out after her?" She snickered. "Reynolds, it looked like you were signaling me to throw a fastball." Grant rolled her eyes.

"O'Leary's here," Garcia said as she came up behind us. "I just saw him step outside. He looked very drunk. He was stumbling, mumbling something about Madison and singing." Garcia apparently didn't think there was any danger because she laughed drunkenly, grabbed Grant, and headed back out onto the dance floor. Grant gave me a concerned look as she was dragged away. She pointed to the door indicating I should head out.

She didn't have to, though. Before the words had even left Garcia's mouth, I had been ready to chase after Maddie. Fucking Liam. I had to hurry before he did something incredibly stupid.

Chapter Eight

MADISON

The cool air felt amazing on my skin. I propped myself against the brick wall and shut my eyes to take it in.

"Not quite the song I wanted you to sing, but I guess that's what I get, huh?" I looked over to see Liam mimicking my stance.

"Liam, what are you doing here?" I placed my hands behind me on the wall and propelled myself to a standing position. He staggered toward me. He was drunk. Go figure.

"This is my spot. I saw you come in. Thought I'd help you get rid of some of that stage fright. You really do have a beautiful voice." He moved closer, his hands coming to rest against the wall on either side of my body, cornering me.

"Liam, you're drunk. Let me pass." I tried to get through, but he grabbed both of my arms.

"We sound good together, don't we?" He looked me in the eyes, and I saw total darkness.

"That was you singing with me?" He gripped me tighter,

shaking me like a doll. I should have tried to break free of his grasp, but I didn't. Liam was the one who had sung with me? I searched his face for the man who had been on that stage, singing with me in such perfect harmony, but all I saw was evil. He was slipping slowly into hell, and I couldn't help him. He had made a deal with the devil, and the cost was his soul.

"I wanted you to sing for me, but instead, you sang for Reynolds." He hissed Scott's name. His eyes scorched me with a feral possessiveness. "What does he have that I don't, Madison? I found you first, remember?"

I eyed him curiously. That was what this was about? He'd wanted me, but I'd chosen Scott. Liam and I could never be whatever it was he wanted us to be. He and I were similar in many ways. Conflicted. Shaped by our screwed-up pasts. But I wanted to stand in the sunlight. I wanted to let the light radiate all over my body, to let light fuel me, to let light surround me. With Liam, it was a complete blank, an endless abyss of nothingness. He couldn't see beyond his pain, his heartache. I wanted to grab him and pull him into the light, but I couldn't reach... and he was slipping.

His fingers dug into my skin, causing me to wince in pain. I had to tell him. I had to let him know once and for all I'd chosen Scott.

"Liam, Scott found me first. He saved me, Liam." I looked at him with compassion and sadness. "You're... you're scary." I stumbled on those last words, but maybe if I told him he was scaring me, he would stop and come back to me. Maybe he'd be that guy I'd met running again. That guy who, for just a moment, had made me forget about everything that had gone wrong in my life. My eyes met his, and for a brief moment, his features softened. I held my breath, hoping I had gotten through to him.

He gripped my arms harder, his jagged fingernails tearing into my skin, and I felt blood trickle down my arm.

"Liam, you're hurting me." I tried to wiggle free, my arms burning.

"Good. Just like you're hurting me." He pressed himself against me and rammed his lips against mine. His kiss was rough, and my stomach dropped at the unwanted intrusion as fear skated through my mind. I was no longer a victim, though, and Liam should have known that about me. Breaking free of his grasp, I slapped him hard. The grin that formed on his face startled me, and my breath caught in my chest. He ran his finger down my arm, capturing some of my blood on the tip, and slowly brought it to his mouth. He closed his eyes as droplets fell on his tongue.

"I always knew you'd taste delicious." I smacked him much harder this time, the force of my hand causing his face to turn. He laughed—a deep psychotic laugh that had every hair on my body standing on end. My mind was telling me to run, to get the hell out of there, but I stood my ground and stared into the darkness that had overtaken this man. He could fight it—I knew he could.

"Don't you *ever* force yourself on me again. I love Scott, Liam, and I'm *not* sorry for that. Plenty of women here could be another conquest for you. You only like me because you can't have me. Because I'm not throwing myself at your feet like every other woman in there. I'm sorry this didn't turn out how you planned, but it will never happen. *We* will never happen." I turned on my heel, fear and anger pounding in my chest, and walked away, looking back just as he slammed his fist into the brick wall. A young woman in a short dress and six-inch heels came up behind him and rubbed his back. Without ceremony, he grabbed her and headed into the alley.

"Everything okay?" Scott asked, coming up behind me. "You've been gone a while." He kissed me on the forehead.

"Yeah, just ran into Liam. That's all," I said, my voice cracking.

"Oh yeah?" He looked around for him, trying to catch a glimpse, then pulled me in protectively, shielding me with his body.

"Yep. He just found some woman, and they went off in the alley. I'm sure he's preoccupied at the moment," I said as I took his hand in mine. I had to get out of there.

"Speaking of being preoccupied, we got some rooms down the street at the hotel. Responsible drinkers and all. I'd hate to have to sleep alone." I pulled away from him just enough to see his face.

"Well, I can definitely save you from sleeping alone." He smiled down at me and kissed my forehead.

"Let's go." I led the way. He caught up to me and put his arms around my shoulders. He knew. Scott always knew. The tension left my body as I relaxed into him.

As we walked to the hotel and passed the alley, we heard the passionate moaning and soft screams of the young woman Liam was fucking. Listening to her scream in pleasure or pain should have alarmed me, but instead I was relieved. Relieved Liam was letting off steam, and relieved it wasn't me.

Chapter Nine

LIAM

I woke up to the sun blazing through my hotel window. My head was pounding, and my fist was swollen.

Fuck. I was such a dumbass. Those Fireball shots had been a bad call. I'd made an ass of myself with Madison, fucked some broad in the alley, and I'd still woken up with a hard-on? I was some breed of screwed up, that was for sure. Grabbing the remote for the TV, I turned on the local news station.

"Miranda Keiger here with a breaking story. News reporter Christopher Singleton was found murdered outside a local bar. Singleton was covering a story on the notorious serial killer, Michael Walsh. Sources say he had located the serial killer's daughter, Aimee Walsh, who was adopted after her father was arrested twenty years ago. With Walsh's recent escape from prison, one must question whether Walsh was behind this brutal attack. Stay tuned for more details."

I flew out of bed. My head was spinning and last night's

drinks were threatening to surface. I pushed the feelings aside and rushed to get dressed and head back to the FBI training facility. Even though it was the weekend, this would require immediate attention. Fucking Chris, man—always up our asses—but he hadn't deserved to die.

When I arrived, I could hear Assistant Director Harper screaming from where I stood outside the office. He must have rushed right over to Quantico as soon as he'd heard about Chris's death. He had much more experience with Walsh than Director Stone, and even though Assistant Director Harper was supposed to be retiring, he was still an FBI legend. In short, even though he could be a hard-ass, he knew his shit.

"What the hell were you thinking, Madison? Going out and talking to a reporter? You know how this looks, right?"

I entered the room and tried to interject on Madison's behalf. "With all due respect, sir—"

"Don't give me 'with all due respect,' O'Leary. That's your way of saying I'm wrong—and I'm not. She wasn't supposed to be out. Now we have a dead reporter, three agents who know her true identity, and it's only a matter of time before the whole world knows she's here."

I stood there in the middle of the room as everyone looked me over. I probably looked like shit warmed over after the night I'd had. Reynolds and Assistant Director Harper's eyes bored into me like I was a goddamn fool. Madison looked at me with such disgust I couldn't help but bow my head in shame. She didn't have that look of concern or care in her eyes for me anymore; she looked at me like the repulsive man I was. I'd messed everything up.

"Assistant Director?" The director's secretary interrupted his tirade by knocking on the door and popping her head in. Thank God. Everyone's stare switched to her, and I moved to a chair to sit down. "The news just reported Harper's true identity. They say it was an anonymous source who sent in the picture." She turned on the projector screen and we all saw a picture of Madison on stage from the night before.

"Goddammit," Assistant Director Harper growled.

"Jesus," Reynolds said, pacing the floor. Madison sat in the chair across from her uncle, shoulders pushed back and chin held high. She was stronger than before—she was becoming an agent in every sense of the word.

"To get ahead on this, we must announce it to the team here. Madison has a few qualifications to complete today, as do some of the other agents-in-training. Let's call an assembly after the qualifications and let those at the Academy know what's going on in the outside world. Walsh isn't hiding anymore, folks. He's closer than we thought." Assistant Direct Harper gave the orders, and the secretary scurried out to make the arrangements.

"Yes, sir," we all said in unison. I got up from my chair and walked up to Madison. I had to talk to her. I had to apologize for what had happened the night before. I had to make it right.

"Madison, can we talk?" I placed my hand gently on her arm to get her attention. She recoiled under my touch, her face constricting in fear.

"Get your hands off her, you asshole." Reynolds barreled in between us, his eyes flaming with hatred. His hands gathered into fists at his sides, and his jaw twitched. It was taking everything for him not to punch me squarely in the face, but I wanted him to hit me. I wanted to feel anything. I was so void of emotion. Maybe a good punch in the face would do me good.

"Scott, baby." Madison moved to him and placed her hand on his shoulder. "It's okay. Let me talk to him." Reynolds took a deep breath and his eyes softened at the sound of her voice. I looked away quickly, not wanting to bear witness to the love I saw between them.

"If you lay one hand on her, O'Leary… so help me God…" His eyes weren't as wild and rage-filled as they had been, but I knew he was serious. I had thought I would never hurt Madison, but the visible marks on her arms revealed how much I'd lied to myself about how far I had fallen. That thought made me lose my breath. I was a monster.

"Scout's honor." I didn't look at him, but I glanced at Madison, trying to get her to see I could be a decent man. That no matter what haunted me, I would never intentionally hurt her. My demons were much larger than me now, though, and I felt them taking over more and more each day. She nodded at me and gave Scott a reassuring kiss. Before heading out with me, she also went over and spoke quietly with her uncle. She gave him a kiss and a long hug. Scott and Assistant Director Harper's eyes never left us as we headed into the file office next door.

"I just wanted to say I'm sorry for last night. I had a few too many and—"

She placed her hand up to stop me. "A few too many? You've got to be kidding me!" The low vibrato she spoke in made the hair on my arms stand on end. She wasn't yelling, but she was pissed off. Fuck. This was going to be harder than I had thought.

"I didn't mean to hurt you." I leaned toward her, reaching for her hand. She ripped it away, the grinding of her teeth filling the quiet room. I cringed at the sound, and her disgust at my touch almost broke me.

"See these, Liam?" She lifted up the sleeves of her FBI-issued T-shirt so I could see the welts and bruises covering her arms. "These are from you. You hurt me, Liam." Her eyes filled with sadness, and a sigh fell from her lips. "I never thought you would hurt me. I thought I was the one person who could get through to you. I know you have demons in your past that haunt you, but we all do." She dropped into a chair with a loud thud. "Hell, if anyone knows about demons, it's me. But that doesn't give you an excuse to become an alcoholic, sex-crazed maniac." I stood there, staring at her intently. I did not once take my eyes off hers. She was right, but I felt so lost. Alcohol and sex were the only things that had fixed me—until her. Now, I wasn't even sure she could stop the voices in my head.

She sat up straight in the chair, and her eyes fixed on mine. I caught a hint of compassion in her gaze, and my heart clenched. She still cared. "I know it's hard to see beyond your own pain, to realize there is hope, to realize there is love and compassion in the world. But there is, Liam, and even though I really care for Scott, please know that I care about you, too. I just want to make sure you're okay and you get the help you need to fight these demons. Without help, Liam, you will fall deeper and deeper into the darkness dragging you down, and no one will be able to save you." Her voice quivered, and her eyes glistened with tears.

"What do you mean?" I asked, moving closer to her. I wanted to feel something, anything. Her words were nice, but my body wanted her to touch me—all of me. My eyes must have shown my intentions because she looked away quickly, shifting awkwardly in the chair.

"The way you were with me and that young woman last night? Forcing yourself on me? Licking my blood?" Madison stopped and shuddered at the memory. She wrapped her arms around herself, trying to find comfort in her own embrace. "I should have said something then. I should have stopped you with that young woman. But to be honest, I was just happy someone was there for you. You really need to talk to someone and get some help. Whatever happened in your past, you can fight it. We can fight it." The way she said we made my heart jump. No matter what, Madison would be there for me. Just not in the capacity I wanted her to be.

"Sex and booze help me deal. The pain in the sex, well—in some way, I always pay for it, so they don't care much." I sat down in the chair across from her.

"That isn't healthy at all. Inflicting pain on someone

for your pleasure is no different than what any of these people do." She motioned to the file boxes of criminals that were surrounding us. "You aren't like them." She got up and crouched down in front of me, her face filled with such sadness.

"I *am* like them, Madison. More than you know." I got up, kissed her on the cheek, and walked out of the room.

It was better she didn't know I'd started hearing voices. It was also better she didn't know the taste of her blood had made me want to fuck her even more. She cared too much about everyone. She should have told me to go fuck myself after what I'd done to her last night, but she hadn't. She'd been pissed, but she'd also felt bad she wasn't kinder to me. Those moments were why I loved her. She was so different from me. She felt things I could never feel.

I headed off to the track for a run. I could feel my pulse racing—those feelings were boiling again, and I needed to release them somehow, someway.

Chapter Ten

MADISON

My mind kept wandering during the day, drifting back to what had happened between Liam and me last night. I knew there was something wrong with him. His anger, his drinking, his addiction to rough sex—but last night, his aggression had caused him to lash out at me. At times, I saw glimpses of the good man I knew he could be, but lately I saw more of his hate.

Walsh hadn't shown his face or tried anything in weeks, so there was no action, no fire Liam had to put out. The fire was within him, and it was blazing, threatening to take over. Maybe if I could convince him to seek psychiatric help, whatever terrible things he had gone through during his childhood could be worked out. I hoped some help would be enough. It *would have* to be enough. He deserved a second chance, a chance to redeem himself. He thought I could save him, but it wasn't anyone else's job to save a person. A person needed to protect and save themselves.

Grant had taught me that. She had taught me many

things over the past month. Like that mean right hook that had taken Chris down. And about cars. I know, *weird*. She didn't look like the car-loving type, but her 1967 Firebird was her baby, and well, she talked about him—yes, him— like he was a boyfriend. What she probably needed was a *real* boyfriend, but she distanced herself from men. I suspected it had to do with her dad leaving her to be raised by her aunts when her mother had committed suicide. She had been just eight years old, and instead of love and comfort, she'd been cast aside by her father, so he could climb the ranks of the FBI. We had that in common—losing our mothers. We didn't talk about it, but the knowledge of it made us that much closer. She was a kindred spirit, a sister of my soul.

Despite everything that had happened last night, I still had to qualify with my Glock. Again. This time, I had to do it with some random guy. Without Liam there to distract me, the weapons qualification was actually easier than before. Who knew zero sexual tension would make me a better shooter? I shot a nearly perfect score, which put me in second, behind—you guessed it—Grant, whose score was perfect with a 60/60.

After finishing at the range, I had to do hand-to-hand combat. As I switched into my workout gear—including the shorts that didn't quite cover my ass—an announcement played over the intercom system: "All recruits, immediately head to the auditorium for an emergency briefing."

I quickly finished dressing and headed toward the large mass of people. It didn't matter how long I had been at

Quantico; I still got terribly lost.

"Wait up!" Scott yelled, running to catch up with me. "I heard you kicked ass at the range today." He pulled me in for a quick hug. The adrenaline from the range still coursed through me, and the closeness of Scott's body made me ache for him.

"I suppose. I would have liked a perfect score." I shrugged. "My mind is still preoccupied."

"Fifty-eight is amazing. You'll easily be in for top recruit." He gave me a quick smile, and I melted a little more inside.

"Don't let Grant hear you say that. Pretty sure she'd want to gouge my eyes out no matter how close we've gotten."

"I wouldn't say 'gouge your eyes out'—maybe just slightly maim you," Grant said, coming up behind us. I shook my head. She was such a drama queen.

"Yeah, you go easy on my girl there, Grant. She has a mean right hook." He winked at me.

We made it to the auditorium and we all sat together on the bleachers with the other recruits and instructors. I sat in the middle with Scott and Grant on either side of me. Garcia and Marshall arrived not long after, and they climbed over everyone and sat in the row in front of us.

"Way to kick ass today!" Marshall exclaimed. Garcia nodded in agreement next to her.

"Thanks. Word here sure does get around fast," I whispered.

"Ahem," Director Stone, the director of the Academy,

said loudly into the microphone. The room went silent. "Good afternoon, everyone. I am terribly sorry to interrupt your daily training and lessons. Unfortunately, news that will impact the Agency has come to my attention. Michael Walsh, as you all are certainly now aware, escaped prison about a month and a half ago." He paused. I was sure he did it for dramatic effect because the entire room's worried chatter filled the air.

He demanded the attention of the room again by clearing his throat loudly. "As many of you might have been told, Walsh murdered Macey Winslow a month back, and just last night, a reporter by the name of Christopher Singleton was found brutally beaten and murdered as well."

He turned on the projector to show pictures of the crime scenes. Poor Macey. Poor Chris. Macey looked unrecognizable. Her entire body was exposed to the room. The pictures showed everything. She had no secrets in death. It really hadn't hit me until that moment what had happened that night with Macey. Because I had been drugged, many of the memories were distant and foggy. I stared at her now, and I had almost too clear a view of the circumstances and the crime that had been committed against her.

A few murmurs went through the crowd, and I tried to keep my composure. It was useless, though, as the only comfort I found was in biting my nails. Scott sensed my tension and rubbed my shoulders. It wasn't just Macey's photos, though. Looking at Chris's pictures made me want to throw up as well. His eyes were missing, gouged from their sockets. There were black holes where his once shockingly green eyes had been. His previously nicely tailored suit was ripped and bloodstained. His throat was cut, a distinctive thin red line.

"Walsh has been looking for his daughter, Aimee, who was seven years old at the time of his capture." A picture of me at the age of seven popped up on the projector. I immediately panicked. I looked a bit different now, but the eyes, the structure of my face, were the same. It was definitely a younger me in the picture, and in the image, I was so small, so fragile. My hair was wild, and I was wearing a black shirt and a red-and-black tutu. I smiled, remembering one of the few good memories I had of my childhood. That had been the day my mom had given me my doll. I felt a tug at my chest. I wished silently I still had her.

I looked around. There was no hiding anymore. The girl on the screen was me; and as more heads turned in my direction, the auditorium became a rowdy mess.

"Enough!" Director Stone yelled, slamming his fists on the podium. "Cadet Harper, please come forward." I gulped. Trying not to bust my ass on the bleachers, I headed down to the front.

"As you all know, Harper transferred in about a month back. Clearly, the resemblance to Aimee Walsh isn't a coincidence. They are one and the same." He placed his hand squarely on my shoulder. It was probably meant for reassurance, but it felt staged, purposeful. I cringed.

"Harper recently graduated with her PhD in Forensic

Psychology and would have started the Academy in a few months with a new recruit class. However, due to the happenings surrounding her father, we needed her immediate assistance to recapture him. He will absolutely come after her; he already has tried. This resulted in the death of Macey Winslow." Guilt clenched at my chest and I gasped. Scott had followed me down to the stage area, and he placed his hand at my elbow to comfort me, but all comfort was lost. The fact that I had been the cause of someone else's death had just been made abundantly clear—and it was fucking eating away at me, just like all the other deaths.

"We wanted her here to keep her safe, but also to train her. She is one of you. I do not want her treated any differently. In light of recent events, we must be more observant and conscious of what is going on around us. As of now, all recruits will be issued their own personal firearm to carry at all times." He glanced down at the paper. "A buddy system will also remain in effect until further notice. You will go nowhere without your buddy."

He frowned, flipping through his papers to make sure he hadn't missed anything.

"One more thing. We also have two of our best agents here helping in this investigation. O'Leary and Reynolds, please make yourselves known."

Scott was already on stage with me. He nodded. Liam stood and gave a quick nod as well, exposing both of them. Our plan had failed. Walsh sure had a way of ruining things and getting me exactly where he wanted me.

"That's all for now. If you have any more immediate concerns that need to be addressed, please discuss them with your team leaders." He started to walk off.

"Help! Please! Please, help me!"

A woman ran into the room, crying hysterically. I immediately recognized her. She was a new recruit who'd just started her training. Her collared shirt was torn in pieces, exposing her black bra. She wore one sneaker, and was wobbling on her left leg to compensate for her other missing shoe. Her face was beaten and her nose was broken and hanging at an odd angle. She had one of those faces where you knew she had once been beautiful. Now, she'd be scarred for life.

"He's here. Walsh is here." I shook uncontrollably, barely able to stand. Liam rushed to my side and caught me before I fell to the ground.

"Code Red. I repeat, Code Red," a voice stated over the intercom. I was shifted into Scott's arms, and I noticed the recruits heading out to get their weapons. Walsh was here. Walsh was here. My brain turned into a foggy mess, and I froze in place.

"Snap out of it, Harper!" Grant screamed, shaking my shoulders. I blinked, focusing on her. "Let's go. We'll head over to the armory and grab our weapons. Now isn't the time to clam up. We protect ourselves. We've got to protect ourselves." She grabbed my hand and pulled. She was right. He was here for me. Not them. I had brought him here. I was who he wanted. These people had nothing to do with this.

"You're right," I replied. I collected myself, stepped away from Scott's protective hold, and ran in the other direction. They screamed after me, but I ignored their cries. I glanced back to see Scott and Grant trying to push through the massive crowd of people who had gathered in the halls. There was no way they were getting to me, at least anytime soon. If Walsh wanted me, he could have me. *Now, come and fucking get me,* I thought. I ran and ran and ran down what seemed like an endless hallway. I didn't make it as far as I'd hoped, though, and about halfway to my exit, I barreled into a large body.

"Ugh!" I looked up as I rubbed my head. Liam stood in front of me.

"Where the hell are you going? Other way." He pointed down the hall.

"I just want to find him. Get this over with!" I pushed forward. Liam gripped my arms, trying to keep me from moving. I twisted his arm behind him, putting him in an arm bar, and catching him off guard. A snicker vibrated from his mouth.

"Harper, now's not the time. Let's get back to everyone else, and we can come up with a plan."

I laughed. Just go back to everyone else? Fat chance.

"No. I won't keep hiding from him. I'm ready to have my life back." I took my head and slammed it against his. I had caught him off guard and he fell to the ground with a loud thud. He was knocked out. He had taught me well. I smiled to myself.

"Oh, Aimee, how I missed you." I looked back and saw

GEN RYAN

Walsh standing there in a custodian uniform, dragging a large trash barrel. It was large enough for two bodies. He removed his hat so I could see his malicious smile that stretched across his face. I looked around the area. It was deserted. No more crowds of people shuffling for safety. I gulped loudly. *This is it for me. For us,* I corrected myself as I looked down at a still unconscious Liam. Walsh's lips were curved into a crazy smile, and small wrinkles fanned out at the sides. He had aged a lot since I'd last seen him almost twenty years ago. The years had not been kind to him. His hair was curly, graying, and longer than before, hitting just past his ears. When I looked at him, I saw so much of myself that I cringed. I glanced down, and in his hand was a knife covered in copious amounts of blood.

As I turned to run away, I felt my hair being ripped from my scalp, and I let out a bloodcurdling scream.

"I've waited so long to hear you scream again. It's music to my ears."

"Leave me the fuck alone!" I tried my best to fight back, but he had me by the hair, and the knife was to my neck. There was nowhere for me to go. "Just kill me already. Anything would be better than a life of looking over my shoulder." I was willing to die to save the lives of innocent people. I was sure of it, but my mind couldn't help but wander to Scott—to the love of my life. I just hoped he would understand the choice I had made was not because I didn't love him, but because I cared so much for him. Scott didn't deserve a life with someone so scarred by her past, or someone who could bring so much pain to his doorstep.

"My dear, I have bigger plans. This isn't just about you. I want you miserable. I want you in pain. I am a part of you. I made you. You can never escape me." With that, he hit me hard with the butt of the knife. The last thing I remembered was seeing his smiling face standing over me.

Chapter Eleven

LIAM

Panic set in. I couldn't move. My hands were tied behind my back, and my legs were tied together in front of me. Looking around the room, nothing was familiar until my eyes set on hers.

"Liam," Madison managed to croak out. Her left eye was swollen shut and her lip was bleeding. She had a large contusion on her head, and her face was riddled with bruises. I saw red.

"What the hell happened? Where are we?" I asked, pulling on the rope.

"Walsh showed up. I tried so hard to get away for everyone's sake. I didn't want this to happen. I wanted him to take just me. I wanted this to be over. I'm so sorry." She cried silently.

"Shhh... Madison. Why would you think getting yourself captured would be the best solution? Now look where we are." I tried to reach out to her, but the frayed edges of the ropes dug into my skin. "Fuck!" I screamed, and shook in the chair. I had to get us out of there. The ropes seemed to be loosening, but I felt so weak. It was even hard to move.

"It's no use trying to get free. Even if you did, there's no way out. I know Walsh, and he's not stupid." She closed her eyes, and let her head fall to her shoulders in defeat.

"Stay with me, Madison."

"My face hurts so bad. I just want to sleep," she whimpered.

"No. We're going to get a plan together, and we are going to stay alive until the FBI comes for us. Do you hear me?" She nodded.

I heard the creak of a door and footsteps on the stairs. I froze. He was here.

"Well, good morning, Liam. Aimee," Walsh said, tilting his chin toward each of us in greeting. "Glad to see you're awake." His eyes found Madison, and the look he gave her was mixed with rage and need. Bile crept up in my throat. He was out of his goddamn mind. I watched as Walsh moved toward her, his gaze never wavering. Madison's horrified eyes found mine. She looked like she was pleading with me to help her. I felt so useless, so helpless, bound by the ropes that held me. His movements held no finesse, no mercy; he was on a mission, and I felt fear enter me as he ripped Madison off the chair by her hair. She yelped, and trickles of blood trailed down her face. Then he pinched a nipple, and I saw a new terror enter Madison's eyes. I fought against the bonds that held me, but they were steadfast. I wanted to kill that fucking bastard.

"LEAVE HER ALONE!" I yelled. Walsh laughed a maniacal, crazy laugh. He dragged Madison across the floor by the hair and up the stairs. I frantically struggled in my chair, trying to break free. All I could hear were her screams and the bumps of her body across the steps of the stairwell. As I continued to try to free myself, I heard Walsh descending the stairs again.

"What did you do to her?" I croaked, as he entered the room again. She was quiet, and I was afraid. *Please don't let her be dead,* I pleaded silently.

"She's alive, for now." He moved toward me, placing the knife under my chin, tilting it up so I was looking at him. "Whether that remains the case depends on you. I need you to do some things for me. If you oblige, I will let you guys go."

"I won't help you," I said calmly. He smiled at my response, removing the knife from my chin. Speckles of blood hit my shirt. He didn't ask me anything further. He just walked right back up the stairs... to Madison. His heavy footsteps sounded through the basement, and soon after he made his way upstairs, I heard Madison's screams.

"What do you think, Liam? Should I push my dick deep inside of her first? I never did get the chance." Madison whimpered loudly.

"No. No. There is an order to things. Cutting first," he said. "So, Liam. Should I cut her arms or her legs?" He asked from the room above. "Hmmm... Let's start with the legs..." The clanking of chains broke up the sounds of her screams. I flinched, closing my eyes. He cut her again and again as Fleetwood Mac's "Songbird" played in the background—the soundtrack to his torture.

I started yelling as Madison's screams filled my head and the room, and the more I yelled, the more he laughed. The voices were pushing through, and with each slice of his knife, their muffled cries got louder. I couldn't take it. I was stuck, trapped, and unable to help her even as she cried out. Even as she begged him to stop. Finally, the screaming subsided, and the voices in my head dissipated as I heard Walsh's booming voice again.

"I will cut every inch of her body, slowly, until you agree to do as I say." He stood in the basement doorway, a crazed but calm look on his face. His gray hair clung to his dark, sweaty face in wet tendrils. His eyes were wild and excited, and in his hands was a knife dripping with blood— Madison's blood.

"I'll never agree," I spat. I would not be used as a pawn in the sick, twisted game he was playing. I would hold my ground.

"Then you'll kill her." The door shut, and I was left alone in the dark, dank basement. I had to figure a way out of here—and fast.

I continued to try to remove the ropes for hours until the ones around my legs were loosened. My body was sore and aching, but I knew it was nothing in comparison to the pain Madison must be experiencing. I thought of her—her sweet voice, her bright smile—as I stood and continuously slammed the chair on the hard cement ground below me. With each blow, the chair creaked and splintered. Finally, it gave out, breaking in two. My arms were still tied behind my back, and I desperately needed to free my hands. I needed to help Madison. I walked around the room and noticed there were knives on an old table in the corner. I managed to place myself near one, and I removed the ties that bound my hands. Blood trickled from the cuts I had just created, but I didn't care. I was free. I would be able to save Madison.

Chapter Twelve

MADISON

I forced my eyes open. My face was caked in dried blood, which made it difficult to see. I was hanging by my arms, and I could feel the socket of my arm pop every time I tried to move, as though the arm were threatening to give way. I wanted to cry out, scream and fuss, but there was no use. No one would hear me. "Songbird" was playing on repeat. Tears flowed from my eyes. I had shared that song with my mother. The song that had given me music. The song that helped heal the scarred parts of me. The comfort the music gave me was gone. I'd never sing again. My father, Michael Walsh, had taken everything from me. He'd taken my music. He'd taken my mother. He'd taken my voice.

The pain hit me like a ton of bricks. I shifted, trying to relieve some of the pressure and see what had been done to my legs. I looked down. Each leg was covered in gashes, some long, some smaller, but each wept with blood. A few of the cuts had begun to clot, creating what Walsh would have called a beautiful masterpiece.

The cuts did sort of look like an abstract painting. You know? One of those paintings you have to squint to see? Unsure of whether it's dark or light, you squint as hard as you can to try to make out the shapes, the faces, the feelings being revealed through the paint. I cringed. So, that was why he called every victim his masterpiece? That's what he saw when he was cutting? I was now one of those girls: a beautiful fucked-up masterpiece.

I felt the constant tug of my hands and arms against the ropes—gravity was attempting to pull me to the floor. I felt like I was dying, slowly, the life being taken from me with each tug. I tried so hard to stay awake, but the brutal spear-like pain swept through me. My mind wandered to Scott and the moments we had shared the night before at the hotel. I had been so upset about what had happened with Liam, but being in Scott's arms had taken that anger and fear away. We'd made love last night. He had been slow and gentle, and I'd felt every ounce of the love he had for me. I had cried in his arms afterward. He didn't speak. He'd just held me, and he'd let me work out my emotions. God, I just wished I had told him how much he meant to me—that I loved him too. I looked more closely at my surroundings. I had to find a way out.

I shouldn't have given up on happiness, on friendship, on standing in the light. Grant had told me to fight for myself, to protect myself. I glanced around the room. I was certain I was in a small cabin. The wood beams were thick, and held the old structure up, but the place was in disrepair. Just a table was visible on the other side of the room, and on the table was a knife with my blood caked on the hilt. Large lamps shone down at me from each corner of the room. Fabulous. He had set the room up like a viewing, so he could see his masterpiece being made. I shook my head in disgust. Directly across from me was another set of shackles and another table. This table had a much greater variety of tools. A hammer, nails, a drill, knives of varying sizes, whips, and a blow torch. The stereo sat on that table, playing the same song repeatedly. The song that had helped me find comfort in some of my darkest days. The song that made me feel only hatred now. Just empty and lost. I averted my eyes, only to see the bloodstains covering the floor. I couldn't hold my frustration and fear in, and my tears started to fall quietly.

After some time, my eyes felt heavy, and the pain began to hammer away at my body. What I wouldn't give just to lie down. I couldn't fight the tiredness that overwhelmed me, and I had started to drift off when I felt a tug at my arms.

"Madison? Madison? Maddie?" I heard a faint whisper.

I pried my eyes open and breathed a sigh of relief when I saw Liam. His right eye was swollen from where I had head butted him, but otherwise he looked unscathed.

"Jesus, what did he do to you?" he asked me, gently caressing my face. I winced and pulled back, trying to break free of the agony that had overtaken my body. I stretched out my legs as far as I could, so he could see, and forced a small smile. "Made me into a masterpiece. See?" My vision turned white as crippling pain battered me. My head bobbed to the side as consciousness faded in and out.

"Goddammit." Liam frantically began to untie my arms. I tried to fight back the pain, but each touch sent sharp needles down my arms. I yelped.

"Shhh… Maddie. We have to stay quiet." He worked a little longer until finally I fell into his arms. He gently brushed my hair out of my face, kissing me on the forehead. It made me think of Scott. Scott was always kissing me on the forehead, and I wanted nothing more than to be in his arms. Everything hurt. My legs and arms throbbed. My face felt like it was one big bruise. Searing pain enveloped me. My only comfort was Walsh had a method, and he hadn't raped me.

Liam knew that we didn't have time to waste, but he also knew I needed a minute to catch my breath. He took my hand in his and we stood in silence for a moment. I could feel each cut and each bruise. We were both so incredibly tired, but slowly, we began to move.

"Wait." I let go of Liam and hobbled over to the table and took out the CD. I smashed it on the ground, shattering it to pieces. I then grabbed the knife—the knife Walsh had cut me with. It was smeared with my blood. I cleaned it off on my PT shorts and stuck it in my pocket. The next time Walsh laid his hands on me, I would be prepared. Liam grinned.

"That's my girl."

We had no clue where we were, how to get out, or where Walsh was but we headed toward the front door. Liam positioned himself in front of me and quietly turned the knob. There was a loud creak as the door opened. God, did this house have to be so loud? I closed my eyes, hoping Walsh wasn't outside. Liam cautiously looked around the corner. He left for a minute to search the perimeter, and apparently seeing nothing dangerous, he motioned as if to say the coast was clear. He ventured out in front of me, and I followed.

Each step I took sent pain up my legs. I winced but kept going. I knew Liam was in pain as well, but he didn't make a sound. He just looked at me and held me as we walked. His eyes were different. They were less dark. They were softer. Lighter. It was the Liam I had been fighting to bring to the surface, the one I always knew he could be. I leaned against him, placing my head on his shoulder as we moved around the outside of the house. I was worried it had been too easy. How had Walsh not heard my painful moans? Why hadn't he stopped us as we'd stepped outside the front door? I had a nagging sense something wasn't right.

Liam looked back at the cabin and stopped suddenly.

"This is the cabin," he stated matter-of-factly.

"What cabin?" I asked.

"The one he buried all the bodies at. Where everyone was found after your own house was raided."

I looked back. The large wooden cabin seemed so gloomy and run-down. A single light shone on the cabin, illuminating its decrepit state. Some windows were busted out, and glass covered the browning grass. The wood was splintering and full of holes. Termites must have taken their fill. Liam was right. Walsh had brought us back to one of his favorite torture chambers. Even under the mask of darkness, the cabin was ominous. It had been one of the places where his masterpieces had been created, where girls had been destroyed to make his twisted art; I couldn't afford to think of my childhood home—the place where other masterpieces had been made. The place where my mother had died.

But even though I couldn't afford the thoughts, they came unbidden. I remembered Walsh's other torture chamber at my childhood home, in our basement. I remembered waiting at the top of the stairs for my mom to come up and play with me. I stopped that train of thought. The memory beat and clawed at me. No, that couldn't be right. Why had my mom been in the basement? I shook my head. No, I must have remembered wrong.

Liam interrupted my thoughts. "We've got to move. No time to think now. Come on. Stay close," he said. "I don't want to lose you." He looked at me with such devotion, my breathing stuttered. He grabbed my hand, and I squeezed his in return, trying to let him know that I cared, too.

The sound of a car engine roared down the driveway, and the headlights shined on our badly beaten bodies.

"Oh no. He's back." I backed up and let go of Liam's hand. I wasn't sure where I was going, but anywhere away from Walsh was where I wanted to be. Liam grabbed my shoulders and looked me square in the eyes. As the car picked up speed, Liam yelled, "Run!"

He took off in front of me, grabbing my hand as he left. I tried to keep up. My legs screamed with each step. I lost my grip on Liam's hand but I kept moving and eventually caught back up to him. He took my hand again as we weaved in and out of the trees. With no shoes, it was hard to run at full speed. Each step sent branches and twigs right into the soles of my feet. I felt so slow, and I wanted to give up, but I tried. I tried with all my might to keep going.

"Come out, come out, wherever you are…" Walsh sang from the woods. I cowered at the sound of his voice, and then I cringed, remembering the feeling of the knife slicing into my skin, and his intent to rape me. I couldn't go back there.

It was dark, and we couldn't see very well, but I knew Walsh was close. I could hear him whistling, and I could hear the sound of the gun being loaded.

The shot just barely missed my head, instead hitting a nearby tree.

"We've got to find a place to hide," Liam said.

"Okay," I squeaked. We trekked through the woods, getting deeper and deeper with each step. I became increasingly unsure if hiding was the best idea. Walsh knew these woods like the back of his hand. Every inch. Every nook. Every crevice. Liam starting climbing a tree—going up was smart. When he had climbed up, he reached out his hand.

"Here. Let me help you up." He started to guide me up the tree. I placed my foot on its large base, and with Liam's help, I was able to start my ascent. Liam gasped, and I felt a sharp pain in my leg. Looking down, I came face-to-face with Michael Walsh. Without hesitation, Walsh started slicing and pulling at my legs in an attempt to force me out of Liam's grip. The skin opened on my calf, and searing pain radiated up my spine.

"Fuck!" I screamed.

Frantically, I reached for the knife I had hidden away in my pocket and began to wield it, catching Walsh in the hand with a jab. The flesh ripped from his hand with ease.

"Goddammit," he yelled, shaking the pain out of his hand. I had just made him angrier. He propped himself up on the tree and pulled my hair, forcing me to the ground. I clawed the ground, trying to gain some sort of leverage and momentum to run. Liam jumped from the tree, landing directly on Walsh. They began to wrestle.

"Run, Madison. Run!" Liam screamed at me. I took a second and looked at what was going on a few feet away. Liam had just risked himself to save me. I wanted to stay and fight... to help him, to protect him.

"Don't even think about it, Madison. Just go. I can take him." The look in his eyes said differently. He was tired. He was beaten. He was bruised beyond recognition, but his eyes. His eyes said it all. He was ready to die. To die for me.

I fought back the tears and managed to get upright, and I ran. As I got further away, the need to look back overwhelmed me. Despite the constant coaching and telling myself to move forward, I had to know. Looking back, all I saw was Walsh dragging Liam's limp body by the feet. A thin red line of blood trailed behind them and glistened in the moonlight. As if he knew I was looking, Walsh stopped briefly and turned around. He waved, and I ducked behind the nearest tree. I was a survivor, and I wasn't going to let Liam's sacrifice be in vain.

My feet were swollen, and blood caked my entire body. I wanted to give up and drop to the ground, but my instincts wouldn't let me. My stupid beliefs and ideals. I had thought I could prevent this from happening. I couldn't believe I had gone after Walsh at Quantico. If it hadn't been for my selfish act, one of the only men I had ever cared about would still be alive.

Chapter Thirteen

SCOTT

The last thirty-six hours had been absolute hell. After finding another of Walsh's victims, we'd come up empty-handed. Our last resort was Walsh's cabin. We had scoped it out beforehand and there was no sign of anyone. Honestly, we hadn't thought he was brazen enough to go there.

There was no direct access to the cabin, except a long driveway from the north, but to have the element of surprise, we parked near the south woods entrance. The hounds were sniffing out the scene, the sirens were blaring, and before the car had even stopped moving, I was jumping out. I heard a scream as I ran into the woods. *Oh God, please let me not be too late,* I thought. Assistant Director Harper yelled for me to stop. The crunch of leaves filled the silence, and the branches swung at my face as I ran toward Maddie.

The woods were brutal and vast, and they stretched out like eternity before me. I had to get to her. I had to find her. I could barely see where I was running. The dark silhouettes of the trees gave me some landmarks to avoid, but I tripped and fell more times than I could count.

As I ran, I saw a shadow in the woods, each step dragging. I squinted and made out the curly hair and the curves of Maddie's body even in the darkness. I ran harder, my legs pumping out their last bit of steam.

As I got closer, I whispered her name, "Maddie. Maddie." Her wild eyes found mine, and I sucked in a sharp breath at the sight of her. Her face was swollen and beaten, and her legs dripped with blood, but she was alive. Thank God she was alive.

"Come on, baby," I said as I reached for her arm. "Let's go." She snatched her arm away from me. Her eyes were red rimmed from crying, and all of her fears, all of her worries were reflected on her face. She crumpled to the ground, her body shuddering as she wept. She held herself, her eyes vast and empty as she stared out into the woods. She never once looked at me. She just kept saying, "Liam, I'm so sorry. Liam, I'm so sorry."

"Maddie, sweetheart, it's going to be okay." I knelt beside her, taking her into my arms. She stopped crying, and I breathed a sigh of relief. She looked at me, the emptiness consuming her. She stood up slowly, and as she started to walk with me, her body trembled.

"I can't leave him. I just can't." I grabbed her around the shoulders, pinning her arms at her side and picking her up off the ground in a fireman's hold. I wanted to let her go, to let her end this, but I couldn't bear the thought of her getting hurt—of losing her again.

"Please Maddie, we have to go."

"You don't understand!" She kicked, and one of her legs connected with my stomach. I hated taking her against her will. With each kick of her legs, each pound of her fists, I tried to take some of the pain away from her. Because Lord knew, I'd take all of her pain onto myself if I could.

"Shhh… Maddie. Shhh… calm down," I whispered as I carried her away. "I won't hurt you. I'd never hurt you. All I want is to save you." I hoped my words would reach her. I had to keep her safe.

"You can't save me, Scott."

Chapter Fourteen

MADISON

Scott let me down as we reached the end of the woods, but he didn't let me go. I was tucked into his side when I saw Uncle Tom. Uncle Tom had seen a lot, but whatever he saw on my face and on my body had him swearing and turning around to punch the hood of his car. Uncle Tom never lost control. He was the most levelheaded person I knew. All of the adrenaline left my body, and I felt tired and broken. Scott and I walked to him and my uncle took me in his arms. I was finally able to look at Scott, and I saw in his eyes the pain I had caused. I had wanted to punch him in the face, but now all I wanted to do was wrap my arms around his neck and bury my head against his shoulder and tell him I loved him. Suddenly, waves of emotional and physical pain overcame me. I had been trying so hard to keep it in, but everything hurt now. I felt every scrape, every cut, and every bruise. Even my teeth hurt. And right there, in the middle of a mess of emergency vehicles, with Scott looking for a way to help me, I broke down. I couldn't help it; I started to cry hysterically.

"It's okay, Maddie. It's over. You're safe now." Scott took me into his arms again. They were strong and warm. A bandage for my emotions. His words of comfort only made me cry harder. I cried for all the girls Walsh had murdered. I cried for myself, and my newly scarred body. But I cried most of all for Liam.

After my breakdown, I was put in the back of the ambulance. Agents moved around the area. The hustle and urgency of them made me uneasy, and I felt the need to help—to be doing something other than sitting on my ass, weak and fragile. I was far from weak. I was strong and capable. My constant breakdowns sort of belied that fact, but I was ready now. I was filled with a new resolve. I knew I was capable of doing my job and catching Walsh. No one believed me, though. They cradled me like the fragile little girl who had been taken from the house that day so long ago. I wasn't fragile. Not anymore.

The paramedics applied some disinfectant and bandages to my wounds. The strong smell stung my nostrils and made me want to gag. Their fussing agitated me and they insisted that I go to the hospital overnight for observation. I was fine. At least I was alive—unlike Liam.

"We can't find O'Leary. All we found was his phone and his badge a few yards back," my uncle said, motioning to the woods behind us. Scott looked at me. He knew something had happened to Liam, but he didn't know what. "I sent some men to the cabin." Uncle Tom sighed. "Other than the copious amounts of blood, there wasn't much else."

"You aren't going to find Liam," I said calmly, preparing myself for what I had to come to terms with. "Liam is gone. My f-f-f- W-Walsh—" I took a breath attempting to stop my stutter.

Uncle Tom looked at me with concern in his soft brown eyes. The same concern-filled eyes I had seen the day I was accepted into my adoptive family. He had always been there for me, protecting me, helping me through the nightmares and the struggles of trying to live my life after my mother's death. Uncle Tom had never once made me feel bad for my feelings or my thoughts. He'd understood me. He'd known I'd needed to heal on my own terms, in my own time.

I took a breath. "We managed to escape the cabin, but Walsh started coming up the driveway. We ran into the woods, but because my wounds were so raw, I could barely keep up with Liam," I shared, and a tear rolled down my cheek. "Liam tried to help me, but I was too weak. Walsh caught up to us, and Liam saved me. Walsh would have killed me—or worse—if it hadn't been for Liam," I said, and my voice croaked a bit. "When I looked back, Liam's dead body was being dragged off by Walsh. And I had to keep running." I felt the sadness of his loss deep in my bones as I remembered Walsh dragging Liam's limp body through the woods.

"Jesus, Madison." Uncle Tom's eyes were filled with tears. I couldn't look at Scott just yet.

The anger had built up in me as I spoke, and I couldn't sit any longer. Not after talking about Liam's death, his sacrifice. I stood up, and the entire world spun. I stayed standing, though. I was hurt, but I wasn't going to be treated like some invalid. Liam had sacrificed himself for me. I was almost an FBI agent. I knew this case. And I had to step up. I had to be the one to stop Walsh. I had to be the one to stop my father.

"It's okay, sweetie," Uncle Tom said, squeezing my shoulders. "It's all over now."

It wasn't over. It wouldn't be over. Not until I was standing over Walsh's dead body.

Chapter Fifteen

LIAM

I opened my eyes and was blinded by the lights beaming from overhead. *Nope. Not dead yet,* I thought bitterly. My wrists were raw from the ties that held my hands, and my legs were cramping from sitting for so long. I tried to move, but searing pain made me immediately close my eyes. Walsh turned and faced me, exposing a young woman on the table. She was completely naked. I would have thought her a victim, except she lay unconscious, her lips turned up as if she were dreaming peacefully.

"Lovely, isn't she?" Walsh asked.

She was. She was magnificent.

"Fuck you," I spat as I fought against the restraints. Thoughts clouded my brain. I had hoped that by saving Madison, I could fight off the malevolence a bit longer. It was there, though, hovering. I had tried to ignore it, but as I looked at the young woman on the table, the need to protect her was quickly replaced by the need to satisfy the hunger inside of me. The glint of the knife caught my attention as

Walsh slowly moved the weapon along the curves of her body. Need. Want. Anger. The voices started whispering their seduction, and those wicked emotions swelled within me as blood slowly pulsed into my throbbing cock.

"It's okay to be intrigued by her, Liam. She's a beautiful masterpiece, isn't she? Not my usual type, but I wanted someone older, someone you'd be more willing to take." Walsh roughly stroked her pussy, forcing a pleasured moan from her ripe, red, fuckable lips. She pressed herself against his calloused hands, begging for more. Every stroke of his hand across her vulnerable flesh sent me higher into the chaos of my mind. I wanted to be him. I wanted those to be my hands pulling out her tortured yet pleasured cries.

Even as he used one hand to pull pleasure from the woman, he took his mouth and placed it against her breast. He looked directly at me as he ripped the ring from her hardened nipple with his teeth. Blood flowed from her breast like warm molasses, and she screamed in unadulterated ecstasy. There was no hiding my interest. I was fully hard and bulging from my pants.

Walsh turned his head, and I heard the clang of the ring as it fell to the bloody cement floor. The silence was deafening, and Walsh used the magnitude of the moment to move slowly toward me. He forced me to my feet.

"Your turn, Liam." Walsh smiled as he brought me to the woman on the table. He flicked the other nipple ring with his hand, and I knew what he wanted me to do.

"No pussy business here, Liam. Mouth to breast. Now," Walsh ordered, pushing my head closer to her breasts. I jerked away, trying to gain my composure and to distance myself from him. Hell, I needed to distance myself from her. She looked at me with lustful eyes, and her unnatural wants crept into my blood. The sinful desires and the voices flowed more freely in the face of her pain. She wanted this. I wanted this. The only thought holding me back was that Walsh *also* wanted this. Our victim was ravenous, and every time I looked at her, my defenses slowly diminished.

My cock ached to be inside this woman. To release the anger and tension I was feeling—release it deep inside of her—but I couldn't. I wasn't supposed to be this. Hadn't I just saved Madison? Hadn't I sworn to protect those who couldn't protect themselves? I'd chosen this life to avoid my past, but looking at the woman on the table, I knew I couldn't *really* escape my past. I was one loose screw away from becoming Walsh.

"I won't. I can't." But my statement lacked conviction.

He pulled out a steel pipe from the drawers next to the table where the woman lay.

"I think you need a little motivation."

"Fuck! Just do it. I won't hurt her. I'm not like you, Walsh." The voices laughed at me. The voices knew I had little sense of self. *Just do it,* they whispered. *Free yourself. Embrace the wickedness.*

Walsh laughed, joining the voices. "You wouldn't be here if you weren't like me. You want her." He pointed to my still erect penis. "You aren't really in control. Now rip the goddamn ring off." He pounded the steel bar into my shoulders. I roared with rage and threw my body into his, but the movement was weak, and Walsh barely felt it. The next thing I knew, his firm right hook had sent me spiraling to the floor. He gave me a minute to catch my breath, but not much more.

"Up," he yelled as he kicked me in the ribs.

I got myself up, but my legs felt weak underneath me.

"I won't do it," I said. I spit a mouthful of blood on the floor, but I stood my ground as he swung again. He rammed me with the pipe, and he didn't hold back. I didn't feel the hits. I willed my mind elsewhere, protecting my body from the physical pain he was inflicting. In my mind, Madison and I were together. We were happy, and far away from her father. Far away from the murder and the destruction. In my mind, I felt no pain. I was free of Walsh. She was free of Walsh, and we had each other.

Chapter Sixteen

MADISON

The hospital stay was uneventful. I got no sleep as they checked on me every hour. The incessant buzzing of the machines and blaring overhead light only added to my already building frustration. Scott and Uncle Tom each took turns staying by my side. I was thankful to have them, but I just wanted this to be over. It was all like a bad dream.

The next evening, when they finally released me into Scott's care, I didn't want to go home... wherever home was. Scott got us a room at the Holiday Inn. When we pulled up, Scott and I walked in silence. He carried the bags, and I let him. I wasn't even sure I could make it to the room without collapsing from exhaustion.

Scott checked us in quickly, and we entered the elevator to go to the eighth floor. As we stood in the corner of the elevator, our shoulders touched and my body responded. I wanted to be closer to him. I needed to be. My mind drifted to that day I had first seen Scott again after almost twenty years. I remembered the immediate feelings I had had for him, and how badly I had wanted him to be near me in the elevator. The ride that sent us to hear the news that would set the next month of our lives spinning out of control. It didn't matter how much time had passed, I still felt the same way about Scott even to this day. Just being close to him wasn't enough. Scott glanced down at me and smiled. I couldn't help but want him in every sense of the word. The elevator door opened and Scott shifted the bags to one hand so he could take mine in the other. We walked in silence to our room. I let go of Scott's hand and put the key card in, my heart thumping loudly against my chest. The last time I'd stood in front of a hotel door—besides the night before my capture—Liam had been there. The door felt heavy in my hands as I opened it. I couldn't help but hope Liam would jump out in front of me, his sarcasm and dark humor pulling me out of the guilt washing over me. I knew that wasn't going to happen, though, and it just further solidified my need to kill Walsh.

I took the bags from Scott as we entered the room. "I have a plan, Scott, but you aren't going to like it," I said as I placed the bags on the bench that lined part of the wall across from the two double beds.

"So, what's this plan?" Scott asked me as he sat on the bed. I moved apprehensively toward him, my muscles crying out with each step. Scott pulled me gently down on the bed, propping a pillow behind me so I could stretch my legs out.

"I want to go after him. Just you and me." I placed my hand up, halting the objection I knew was on the tip of his tongue. "And before you interrupt me to tell me how awful that sounds, hear me out." Putting my hand down, I let it all out. All the thoughts roaming through my mind, all my fears.

"I can barely focus on the Academy right now with Walsh out there trying to kill me and everyone I love. He killed Liam; and regardless of how much of an asshole Liam could be at times, he was Liam, and I cared about him." Tears began to stream down my face. Every muscle in Scott's body seemed to constrict with those words, and he stiffened with jealousy. I moved closer to him. He had no reason to be jealous. I hurt for Liam. I felt guilty about Liam. But I loved Scott. I smoothed his hair back as I faced him, and his deep blue eyes locked on me. Scott's body responded to my touch, and he slowly released the balled-up tension. After a few moments, I laid my head in his lap and my curls fell frecly.

He stroked my hair and each curl sprang back to life as it was released. The loss of life was something I'd experienced too often. I knew how much it hurt to have those you loved taken away from you. Scott and I stayed like that for what seemed like forever. I needed Scott to know how much he meant to me. I couldn't say the words, but I could show him.

"You have your whole life ahead of you, Maddie. A life of fighting crime and catching criminals. Isn't that enough?" Scott asked, breaking the silence.

I got up from the bed and picked up my black shoulder bag. I needed clean, comfortable clothes. The EMTs had cleaned me up with alcohol, but I still wore the same dirty clothes from before. I felt responsible for what Walsh had done to his victims—and to Liam. I didn't ignore Scott's question, I just took my time answering as I rummaged through my bag.

"I thought it would be enough, Scott. I really did. But now, after Liam—"

My voice trailed off. Every time I mentioned Liam's name, it was like a dagger to my heart. Scott's eyes softened as I stammered over my words. "After Liam, that need to protect and serve became second. I need to make this right. Otherwise, I don't think I can move on." I pulled out my black yoga pants and a pink T-shirt.

"You can move on. You're surrounded by people who care about you. Your uncle loves you and would do anything for you. I'd do anything for you. You have Garcia, Marshall, and Grant. You are surrounded by so much love. We can help you through it. Going off on some vendetta isn't going to make the emotional scars go away, Maddie. They will always be there." He sighed. His words made sense, but part of me knew even if he offered me the world on a platter, I would still have to do this.

"Maddie, listen. You haven't finished training yet—you want to go in just the two of us? Against him? That's a death wish, and I won't let you get yourself killed. And your uncle? Jesus. He'd kill me before Walsh even could." The fact that he could die was like a smack in the face. I winced. I couldn't let my mind go there. Scott was right about one thing: I needed to focus on myself, and I needed this—for me. He rubbed his face in frustration. "Hell, we don't even know where he is."

I knew where they were. I could feel it with every fiber of my being. There was no other place this could have ended. "I know," I said with certainty. "They're at the house. My house." The house where my father, Walsh, had committed all those murders, where he'd tortured those girls, where he'd killed my mother. Our house in Connecticut had been left to me, but I hadn't been able to go back. I hadn't been able to face my past. I looked at Scott, the weight of the situation and my grief written on my face.

"Scott, I am doing this with or without you, but when I said I wanted to be with you, I meant it. I lo— I care a lot about you. I wanted to be honest about my plans. I'm not asking you for permission to do this. I'm asking you for your help." I lifted my arm to remove my shirt, and my face contorted in pain. I was so incredibly sore. Each muscle in my body stretched and ached. Scott moved in front of me and put his hands at the seam of my shirt. His fingers lightly brushed against my bruised skin. I didn't feel the pain, though—just the sensual coolness of his touch. The unexpected pleasure masked the pain that had overtaken my body. I melted into his hands. He removed my shirt with such care I didn't feel a single muscle strain. I lifted my head and our eyes connected.

His blazing eyes were full of sex and comfort, and I wanted what they offered. As he touched my cheek, my body curled in to him.

"You almost said you loved me." His eyes were lustful as

they wandered down the length of my body. They stopped at my center as he licked his lips in anticipation. I clenched my thighs together for fear that the wetness that had formed there would seep through. I felt vulnerable. Exposed. I also felt amazing. No barriers were between us, no walls that needed to be torn down—just pure unadulterated love.

Scott grabbed my ass and lifted me off the ground. I gasped. No man had ever lifted me before, but Scott never had any issues. His muscles bulged under his shirt, and I wrapped my arms around his neck, taking some of the weight. Our crotches were aligned, and I could feel his erect penis through my pants. I moaned at the feeling.

"Am I hurting you?" He searched my face for pain, but was only met with pleasure.

"No, Scott. Please, make it go away. Make all the pain go away." Tears streamed down my face and my lips crashed down on his.

"Shhh… I'll take care of you." Scott kissed me softly and carried me to the bathroom.

He set me down gently. I watched him under hooded eyes when he took off his shirt, his bare chest igniting my sexual thirst. Each time I saw him naked was better than the last. Sweat glistened on his chest as it slowly streamed down the most deliciously defined abs I had ever had the pleasure of touching. He removed his pants without taking his eyes from mine, his erection finally breaking free of his boxers. I squirmed and tightened in anticipation. I placed my hands behind me as I leaned against the counter. His eyes were possessive, and with a quick move, he joined me. In no time at all, he had removed my pants and bra with ease.

"Hmm," he growled. "Loving the no underwear." His domineering need sent shivers up my body. Scott was taking control. I was right there with him, and his excitement ignited every part of me. Scott loved my stomach, and as his hands plucked at my nipples, he gently kissed every inch of my slightly rounded belly. I tried to keep still, but each touch sent me further and further over the edge, and I was sure I would come undone from his touch alone. I needed him inside me, immediately. I wanted to feel love. I wanted to feel something other than the guilt eating away at me.

Scott took a washcloth and filled up the sink with water. I didn't need stitches but due to my wounds, I was told not to shower until the next day. A sponge bath was just what the doctor ordered. The warm water against my skin burned at first, but Scott's gentle touch allowed me to focus on the comfort instead of the pain. He washed me, slowly soothing my aches. His languorous movements soon became sensual, though, and I couldn't stop my response.

I wanted this. I needed this. I leaned myself against the wall, reached down and swirled a finger inside my wet folds. Scott didn't let me get far. He grabbed my hand and I groaned as he slowly lifted it to his lips and sucked away the juices. "You taste so amazing, Maddie. I could taste you all day." I gasped at his words, and trickles of moisture between my legs dripped free. Scott sucked on my bottom lip, leaving it swollen and me wanting so much more. He stopped kissing me, and his eyes burned with possession.

"You're mine, Maddie." That was it. Those three words undid me. Scott seemed to sense the moment. I smiled as he guided himself inside of me, and I moaned as I stretched to meet his needs. My hips lifted to greet his thrusts, and I allowed him to take control. Each time he pushed into me, my body quaked. The movement was hypnotic, entrancing. He took me completely.

"God, Maddie, you're so tight." I pushed against him, my nails digging into his back and willing him to go deeper, harder. His eyes became more primitive, and I whimpered as he picked up speed. I was close, and by the way his fingers dug into my side, I knew he was too.

"Scott, please... I'm right there... harder..." I reached down between our intertwined legs and kneaded his balls gently. He grunted, taking my breast in his mouth. That was all it took for both of us. I released onto his cock.

Leaving our clothes in the bathroom, Scott and I made our way to the bed, fully naked. Scott's arm came to rest across my body. The weight of it was comforting and warm. My breaths were deep, and I felt fulfilled.

"Shit!" I sat up in bed.

"What?" Scott sat up as well, looking confused and on alert.

"We didn't use a condom." I bit on my bottom lip nervously.

"I'm clean, Maddie. It's okay." Scott took me in his arms, laying us back in the bed.

"I'm clean too, Scott, but there is this thing called

pregnancy." I sighed into his chest. I looked over at him and he shrugged, seeming unfazed by the thought of me being pregnant. That was all I would need: a pregnancy amongst the chaos that was my life.

Time passed, but we didn't move. Exhaustion eventually took us both, but Scott succumbed first. I heard the faint sound of his snoring, and I stroked his damp back. When I knew he was asleep, I whispered, "I love you, Scott Allen Reynolds," and then drifted off to sleep as well.

Chapter Seventeen

LIAM

Waking up was painful. There wasn't an inch of my body that wasn't wrenched and twisted. Just breathing hurt, and as I pried my eyes open, I realized I wasn't in the same room as before. The moonlight crept through the yellow curtains, and I glanced around. The white walls were stenciled in sunflowers. It was a child's bedroom. I sat on a double bed covered in a yellow comforter. Nightstands were on either side of the bed and each held a white lamp. Cobwebs hid a small picture frame. I looked closer at the framed image and found I was staring straight into the eyes of a young Madison. Her face was round and happy, and she was holding on tightly to her mother's hand. My stomach sank. This had been Madison's childhood bedroom. I was in her home. I was on her bed. My heart ached to see her again, just one last time before I slid too far into the abyss. A single chair sat alone in the corner, a doll perched on the worn fabric of the seat. The doll had no eyes, and yet she looked like she was staring into the innermost, soulless part of me. Her once-porcelain skin was caked with dirt and blood, and the right side of her face was cracked. I cringed. What the ever loving fuck?

Shaking off the eerie feeling, I forced myself into an upright position. I held my injured ribs, but I was too battered to avoid the seething pain entirely. I sensed movement and glanced next to me, catching the eyes of the woman who had not that long ago lain on the surgical table in the basement. She was curled up in the fetal position trying to keep warm, so I took the blanket off myself, dragged my body over a few inches, and draped the thin wool over her small frame.

"Thanks," she said, snuggling into its warmth.

"No problem. You okay?" I asked, looking intently at her face. She was so beautiful. Her body was lean and her legs were long and toned. My dick twitched against my pants thinking about her longs legs wrapped around my waist as I plowed into her.

"I guess. I'm a little sore, but I suppose it could be worse." She stretched, her naked breasts peeking over the top of the blanket.

My groin clenched. "What's your name?"

"My name's Samantha. What's yours?"

"Liam."

"Nice to meet you, Liam." She gave me a big smile. I couldn't help but smile back. The woman was happy despite her circumstances. "So, what are you here for, Liam? You seem like a big, strong man. How did Michael get a hold of you?" she asked, seemingly puzzled.

"Shouldn't I be asking you the same question?"

"Right place, right time, I suppose." She shrugged.

"Guess it's the same for me. I let Madison go. Otherwise, we'd both be here. No worse fate than watching and listening to the one you love get tortured. Walsh is fucked-up."

Samantha sat straight up and the blanket fell to her waist, exposing her breasts to me. One nipple ring still clung to her left breast. The other nipple was visibly swollen and irritated from where the ring had been ripped out.

"Don't talk about him like that. He's just misunderstood." Samantha gave me an angry look. Her body softened when she talked about Walsh. It was clear she cared about him. Wow. That was some twisted case of Stockholm syndrome.

"Misunderstood? You've got to be fucking kidding me! He's a serial killer, Samantha—not some teenager experimenting with his identity. Don't think for one second that he's a good guy." I got up from the bed and leaned over her. She leaned in closer to me as well, anger burning in her eyes.

"He *is* a good guy. He's taken care of me. He clothed me. Put a roof over my head. I wouldn't be alive if it wasn't for him." She'd started yelling.

"You won't be alive for much longer," I sarcastically replied, disgusted she was defending a man like Walsh.

I didn't see it coming. I should have.

She slapped me.

I rubbed my cheek. "Tell me this—if he cared about you, why did he kidnap you? Beat you and shove you in this room with me? Is that because he loves you and wants to protect you? No. You are just another pawn in his game." I stomped over to the door. "These fucked-up games he likes to play with people's lives…" I paused.

"DO YOU FUCKING HEAR ME, WALSH? I'M DONE PLAYING GAMES. TELL ME WHAT YOU WANT FROM ME!"

I banged on the door over and over and over again. I wanted to get his attention. I wanted some acknowledgement. I wanted to understand what he wanted from me. I flipped over the nightstand, and the picture fell to the floor, leaving Madison and her mother's faces looking shattered. The rage in me rose swiftly, and I needed a release. Breaking stuff felt like my only option. Grabbing one of the white lamps, I swung it against the wall. I heard faint laughter as the lamp shattered into tiny pieces.

"He was right about you. You'll be perfect." Slowly, the woman who had introduced herself as Samantha removed the blanket. It was like she was unwrapping herself. She was a gift. My gift. The heat radiating from my groin increased as I watched her intently. She lay back on the bed, and it creaked under her weight. She opened her legs, placing her fingers directly between her folds. As she went deeper in, wet noises filled the room. Her fingers slipped in and out gracefully. I smiled when I realized the ease with which her fingers went in and out. She was no stranger to the art of pleasuring herself. The smell of her sweetness permeated my nostrils, causing my dick to roar to life.

"You need this, Liam. This is what helps calm you down,

isn't it?" She continued to play with herself, withdrawing her fingers and bringing them to her mouth. As she sucked off the wetness, she made the most delicate and subtle sounds. "Join me. I'm nice and wet. Come on… don't be shy." She opened her legs wider, her breasts fell to the side, and her nipples were perfectly showcased.

She was breathtaking. So raw. So natural. Her smell continued to surround me. No matter how much I tried to tell myself to stay away from her, my cock and the anger that was fueling my desires would not subside. She started caressing her pussy faster, harder, with more purpose. Arching her back and moaning louder and louder, she called to me. "Liam, please…"

Moving toward her, I grabbed her legs, unzipped my pants, and whipped out my cock. I positioned myself at her entrance and rammed it inside of her. Her cry was loud and need filled, and it spurred me on.

"Fuck me harder, Liam!" she screamed.

Thrusting in and out, I rammed into her with fierce intensity. She grabbed me and raked her nails down my back, drawing blood. She laughed, pushing herself harder into me, making me plunge deeper into her slick, wanton heat. Crying out in ecstasy, she yelled over the wet noises. "Choke me. Choke me while you fuck me!"

"What?" I looked down at her. I stopped mid thrust and withdrew from her needy heat.

"Choke me." She grabbed my hands and wrapped them around her neck. "Do it." A treacherous grin formed at her lips. My hands were on her neck, and I couldn't help it. I caressed the neck she offered, subtly at first. Her skin was so soft and pliant under my calloused hands. With each stroke of my hand on her neck, she moaned louder and louder, fueling my aggression and my need for more.

Adrenaline surged through my body. My dick throbbed as it reentered her. No matter how many times I buried my cock within her wetness, I ached for more. I needed more. My hands remained on her neck, but my grasp got tighter and tighter with each slap of my balls against her ass as I continued to fuck her. The voices, once a faint whisper, taunted me, encouraged me. The voices were roaring, and I had no control of my hands as I succumbed to their call. Letting go felt goddamn amazing.

The grip on her neck wasn't gentle anymore. My grip was cruel, malicious, murderous. I squeezed hard. I felt the muscles of her neck collapsing beneath the hard grip of my hands, and her eyes lit up as she gasped for air. I rammed into her repeatedly, while the pressure on her neck got more and more intense. She grabbed at my hands, scratching my skin, but the pain fueled my anger, my lust, making me go faster and harder. Her legs jerked wildly, like an animal's, and I looked into her eyes. They were no longer glistening and lively, but accepting. The voices in my head laughed as I watched the life I held in my hands slip away.

My release approached, and I knew I couldn't let go of her fragile neck. I was so close. Too close to stop this...

I came inside her, finally complete. Looking down at her lifeless body, I no longer felt the anger welling up inside of me. I felt different. I felt alive.

Chapter Eighteen

MADISON

A knock at the door startled me awake, and I jumped. Scott reluctantly got up, kissing me on the lips as he put on his pants. I jumped out of bed, grabbed my clothes, and headed to the bathroom. I heard the creak of the door and voices filled the room. I quickly dressed, my sore muscles protesting with each movement. I didn't care, though. The pain was welcome. The sex had been amazing and well worth the added strain. I opened the bathroom door and was greeted by Garcia, Marshall, and Grant. They ran over and hugged me tightly. Their apologetic gazes met mine when I grimaced in pain.

"We thought you were dead. What were you thinking? Why did you give yourself up?" I moved away from the barrage of questions, overwhelmed.

"You don't want to hear her newest scheme, then?" Scott asked, folding his arms over his bare chest. He sat down in the corner chair.

"Really, Scott?" I sat on the bed, agitation spewing from

my mouth. That plan wasn't for him to tell.

"No, Madison." He sat up in the chair. "I won't let you bully me around with this. Maybe they can talk some sense into you, because I sure as hell can't." He ran his fingers through his hair, determination and concern firing within his eyes.

I wanted to be angry with him, but he only wanted me to be safe. I was so happy to see the girls, the anger faded, and I knew I had to share. I wanted them to know why I felt such a need to avenge Liam's death. I wanted them to know why I had to end this for good.

"Liam's dead." Marshall and Garcia gasped. Grant's eyes were the only thing that gave away her true feelings. They were soft and full of compassion. "He sacrificed himself to save me." My voice broke. No matter how many times I said the words, they still stung like the first time. "Uncle Tom searched the woods and the cabin, but Walsh is gone and for some twisted reason, he took Liam's dead body with him. Probably to torment me even more." I took a deep breath. "I have a feeling he went back to my house. The house I grew up in. I need to end this. I need to close this chapter of my life." I waited for them to yell and scream, and to try to talk me out of my plan.

"Let's do it," Grant said, sitting down next to me on the bed.

"Jesus," Scott said, shocked. He stood up and paced the floor.

"Reynolds, can it, okay? You love her, and you can't see beyond keeping her safe," Grant said as she patted my leg.

"She has a point. She knows where he is, and maybe with a smaller team we have a better chance. Only thing is, we all go." She looked at Marshall and Garcia, and they nodded in agreement.

"Done," I replied. I looked at Scott and waited for his protests. Instead, he threw up his hands and walked out of the room, slamming the door behind him. He didn't have a say-so in this, and he knew it.

"We'll need weapons, though. Not like I can just go and sign out guns."

"I've got that covered." Grant stood up. "My dad pretty much has a mini arsenal at his house."

"Well then." I let out a small laugh. "Looks like we're in business."

The girls got a room right next to ours and left to get the weapons from Grant's dad's house. By the time they got back, it was late in the evening. We planned to leave the next night, under the cover of the darkness. Scott wouldn't talk to us, but he still left to go get us all dinner. I knew he didn't think going after Walsh was a good idea, but I also knew it was the right thing to do. Regardless of what he thought, though, Scott was standing beside me, and for that, I loved him even more.

Chapter Nineteen

LIAM

The sun rose on Samantha's dead body. I'd killed her. I looked down at the woman I had murdered, and although a hint of sadness rumbled within me, I felt calm, relieved. The feelings, the voices, the headaches—they were all gone.

I heard the door to the bedroom creak open, and I glanced over to see Walsh carrying a heavy-duty luggage bag and balancing a plate of food.

"Well, this is unfortunate," he said as he looked down at Samantha's dead body. He placed the food on the remaining nightstand and started dragging Samantha off the bed and placing her in the bag. "She was one of my favorites. So easy to train. She really would have done anything I wanted. Just like Aimee's mom." He sighed as if disposing of her body was an inconvenience.

"Don't say that, you piece of shit. She was—"

"Was what, Liam? A good friend? You didn't know her. She was exactly what I needed her to be. She made you realize what you truly are: a killer. Aimee's mom was obedient, too, but only because of her little brat. She wanted to protect the girl from this life. She would have done anything I'd asked. She *did* do anything I asked." Walsh kicked Samantha as he zipped the bag. "A mother's love." Walsh sighed again. "She died saving that worthless kid." He dragged Samantha to the door, and her body bumped against the floor.

I started pacing again. Walsh was right. I was a killer. I'd always known I was violent, an alcoholic, and fucked-up in the head. The voices had come back and were getting progressively louder now. Nothing I did made them truly stop. Not the pacing. Not the killing. Not the sex. Not the alcohol. The voices kept hammering away at me—relentless and unforgiving.

"This, Liam." He motioned to Madison's childhood room. "This is all for you. Not Aimee. I wanted her dead, but when I escaped and found her again, I noticed you, and from that moment, I knew you were something special. Like me, you had that look in your eyes, the clench in your fists. I knew if presented with the opportunity, you could and would reach your full potential. Watching you struggle with your inner demons has been so enlightening. I had to help set you free." He grabbed half of the sandwich from the nightstand and sat on the bed.

"I don't understand. You were after *me*? Not Madison?" I stopped in front of him. That made no sense. He hated Madison for taking his wife away from him. He'd just ranted about that fact not a minute ago.

"Yes and no. I want Aimee for you. You love her. She loves someone else. Such an interesting dynamic. I'd be curious to see what masterpiece you could make her into." His lips curved into the most malicious smile.

"Masterpiece? I wouldn't do anything to Madison, you piece of shit!" I pushed him down on the bed, wrapping my hands around his neck.

"Do it, Liam. Prove me right yet again. You are a volatile human being… Just. Like. Me." Walsh snickered. His eyes were crazed, and he looked as though he were ready to welcome death.

I closed my eyes, took a steadying breath, and Madison's smiling face loomed in front of me. Rays of light shone down and warmed me from the inside. I released my grip and quickly stepped away from Walsh. My blood boiled and my fists twitched at my sides as I let him up.

Walsh looked at me with such disgust and disappointment. "Fuck, Liam! Why won't you just fucking be who you truly are? Aimee has blinded your ability to see what you were destined to be. You just need more. That's all." His eyes sparkled as he looked me up and down. My jaw scized, teeth grinding. "Don't worry. I have just the thing," he told me, placing his partially eaten sandwich on the plate.

He dragged Samantha out of the room and down the stairs. I heard the thumping of her body against the wooden staircase. He returned a few minutes later with another young woman. She was scared. She was shaking. And underneath the restraints, there were welts on her wrists. She wept freely, but again, I couldn't look away. Madison's face shone down on me each time I closed my eyes, but the voices—they were constant. Their insistence masked the light I was so desperately trying to hold on to. In that moment, I couldn't fight it. When I closed my eyes to distance myself from the young woman who stood in front of me, I reached out for Madison, but there was nothing but a void.

The young woman wore a college cheerleading uniform with the word TITANS embroidered across her perky chest. Her skirt was short, and as Walsh let her go, she fell to the floor, revealing a tight bottom covered by white compression shorts. I wondered what her firm ass would feel like. I wanted her youth. I wanted her grace to surround me as I moved inside her tight, young body. I watched as she cried, but the tears didn't awaken my protective instincts. Her sobs only caused her body to rock more, and her ponytail—and certain parts of her anatomy—swayed with her scared and pained movements. She was perfection.

"I'll just leave Alice here for you, Liam. Do what you want with her, she's proven to be useless anyway." And with that, the door shut behind him.

"I'm sorry. He made me do those things. Get that girl to follow him and find you. Pay that waiter to drug that poor girl." Her sob broke free from her mouth. "Please don't hurt me. I'm sorry."

The reality of what Walsh had made her do should have fueled more anger within me, but it didn't. I was once again left alone with a woman and all I wanted to do was fuck her. My body slid down the far wall to the floor. Who had

I become that I would consider taking this young woman against her will? *What* had I become that I would consider letting loose my demons on someone I should protect?

Chapter Twenty

MADISON

The next day came much quicker than expected. Scott remained apprehensive about the entire plan, and I knew he wished I would change my mind. When afternoon came, he sat on the hotel bed and watched me silently as I got ready. I was decked out in my black outfit and weapons from Grant. The black leggings hugged the lower part of my body just right, comfort and flexibility all in one. The shirt was loose around me—at least a size too large—but it didn't brush against my already bruised body. I felt good. I was prepared for what was to come.

"Don't you think this is a bit much, Maddie? It's just one guy." I placed another gun into my right ankle holster and Scott looked at me with concern.

"I know it's just one guy, Scott. He also has a house of horrors that we are walking into. Who knows what he's done to it?"

"I know what he's capable of. I saw your wounds." He sighed as he rubbed his hands over his face. I sat down next to him and took his hand in mine. He looked up at me. "This is just all so crazy, Maddie. I don't want to lose you."

I leaned in and kissed him, long and hard on the lips. He pulled away and looked at me, his eyes filling with concern. It all felt so final.

He kissed my forehead before getting up from the bed. "It's almost noon so finish up. We have a six-hour drive ahead of us and I'd like to get there right after dark." Scott took his revolver and put it in his holster.

As we piled into the truck and began our journey toward the house I had once called home, I couldn't help but allow little slivers of fear to inch in. I didn't know what we were walking into, and the unknown frightened me. Grant, Marshall, and Garcia filled the backseat, and my heart welled with friendship, but also with respect at their selflessness. No matter what the consequences, those women were there for me.

About a half a mile from my childhood home, Scott pulled over to the side of the road. He turned off the truck and we found ourselves encased in darkness.

"This is where we start trekking it on foot. No sense in letting him know we're here any earlier than we have to," Scott said, opening the truck door.

We all walked in silence. The dark surrounded us, keeping us safe and hidden. Marshall started humming. Her soft sounds broke the silence without being loud enough to give away our location.

Each step mixed with Marshall's sweet humming. I wanted to join her, to sing my heart out as I went to meet the man who had once been my father, but Walsh had taken singing from me—just as he had taken everything else I loved. My mind drifted to my mom; to the horrific day I had watched Walsh murder her. I had been so little. I knew that the lives of many future victims had been saved, but the loss of my mother still stung. I had lost so much and I couldn't help but feel I was close to losing Scott as well. I glanced over at him as he walked. His head hung low, and his lips were pressed tightly together. He was there for me, but I feared each decision I made was pushing him further away.

"Guys, over here. I see the house," Scott whispered. We all gathered behind him. Trees surrounded the house, and the natural cover allowed us time to plan our strategy.

"Looks like there are two entrances... the front door..." Grant pointed in the direction of the house.

"And a little side door there. Maddie and I can go through the front if you"—Scott looked at Grant—"and Marshall want to go in the side. Garcia, I'll have you keep watch here. Let us know via the walkies if anything out of the ordinary happens." He handed everyone a walkie-talkie, and we all nodded in agreement.

I fought back the tears as I looked at the house that held all of my terrible childhood memories. It had once been such a beautiful brick house. The front had been covered in large white windows, and pillars had once stood tall, welcoming, and inviting. Now it was so run-down, the windows barely hung on. The once solid white pillars were crumbling, and it appeared that at any moment they would collapse under the weight of the secrets and the murders they had been holding all of these years.

"He's in there," I whispered, leaning in to Scott.

"What?" Scott asked, pulling me closer.

"He is in there. Right now." The words fell heavy on my heart. Tonight, it would all end.

Scott kissed my forehead.

"That's why we came, isn't it? So he would be here, and we would be able to catch him?" Grant asked. "Don't back down, Harper. You are strong, and we are going to help you end this so you can move on and live your life." She patted my shoulder and gave it a reassuring squeeze.

"Yes, it's just… I guess it's real now." I shivered. I wasn't feeling brave anymore. I was scared. Scared about what I was going to find inside that house and scared for what might happen to my friends.

"We've all got your back, Harper. Don't worry. He can't outsmart us all." Marshall gave me a quick hug. Their reassurances fell on deaf ears. I smiled and shook my head, trying to convince myself they were right. Five against one. This had to work, right?

We started toward the house, careful to conceal ourselves. It was now or never. May the best man win.

Chapter Twenty-One

LIAM

"What are you going to do to me?" Alice asked, shaking uncontrollably. She'd been quiet all day, and her silence had allowed me some respite from the voices—at least the more persistent ones.

"Shut up." I rubbed my temples hard. I needed to relieve some of the pressure welling up in my head. The voices were coming more frequently, their whispers now agitating screams clinging to the pathways in my brain. I tried not to look at her, but she was magnificent. Her smooth, creamy skin was glistening with sweat. Her warm, supple lips longed to be kissed. My cock sprang to life, and my head pounded even more. Screams. All I heard were screams.

"Fuck." I paced, my heavy steps threatening to break the floor beneath me. She started weeping again, her cries getting progressively louder. I didn't know what to do. I knew what I wanted to do, though. I headed over to the nightstand, hoping there was something in there to offer the cheerleader that would make her shut up. I needed her to shut up so I could deal with the screaming inside my head. I rummaged through the nightstand, and instead of a useful tool I found knives, rope, and nipple clamps. The paraphernalia in the nightstand only set the voices up for more screaming. They wanted me to complete the task Walsh had set out for me. When I pulled out the nipple clamps, she started crying louder. She scooted herself as far into the corner as possible, as if she thought hiding would protect her from the monster.

As I took out each new toy, the whimpers behind me increased, and I couldn't stop the excitement from coursing through my body. All of my defenses began to diminish. The voices took over, and as I surrendered to them, I felt my eyes turn dark and my soul follow. The darkness finally took hold, and energy thrummed through me.

A slightly maniacal smile formed on my face, and the cheerleader looked at me with trepidation. Her whimpers increased, and I twirled the clamps in my hands. God, they felt fantastic—heavy, smooth, and cold against my fingers. Her face showed fear, and that fear spurred me on. I took the knife and the nipple clamps, and I stalked toward her. My hands twitched, and I ached to carve into her body. I needed to release my pain into her. I ripped off her shirt, and placing the knife on her breast, I carefully carved a straight line down to her belly button. As I carved, she writhed in pain. She tried to move, but I used my body to hold her down. I pushed my covered cock against her, imagining what it would feel like to take everything from her. *Soon,* the voices said. Blood seeped from the gash, and I watched as thin red lines diverged down her body, covering her stomach, her breasts, and her clean white cheerleading skirt. The sight had me spellbound, and I smiled serenely. This time, I would not hold back. This time, I would take everything from her.

As I placed the knife on her cheek to cut her again, I heard a voice in my head. My savior. My salvation was here to drag me from the abyss and back into the light. She was here to save me.

"Liam? Liam, what are you doing?" The words were barely a whisper. My savior was frantic, confused, scared. Looking up at the doorway, I saw her. My Madison. The woman I loved—the woman I would do anything for. The only one who could save me. I dropped my tools, and the clang of metal sounded like a crash to my oversensitive ears. I went to Madison, my heart thumping loudly against my chest. I just wanted to feel her, touch her, to have her make all of the anguish disappear. She looked at me with such disgust, with such horror, and put her hand out in front of her, not allowing me any closer. I gasped. I wanted her. I needed her so badly.

I backed away until I hit the wall, and then crouched down in the fetal position. She didn't move toward me, and I knew the little bit of her I'd had—I had lost.

Chapter Twenty-Two

MADISON

He was alive. Relief coursed through my veins, followed by despair. I had seen the look in his eyes as he had cut into the young woman, and I was shattered by the memory of that look. Liam had finally broken, and I was afraid I was too late to save him.

"Don't you dare move, Liam," I hissed at him. I rushed over to help the young woman, who was lying there bleeding, crying, and in shock. Her body convulsed with fear and she just looked at me, wide-eyed and scared. When I tried to assess her and ask her questions, she wouldn't talk.

Liam was still crouched down. He wouldn't take his eyes off me, and I wasn't sure what had come over him. Had Walsh made him do this? That was the only explanation. I covered the young woman in a blanket and whispered soothingly that it would all be okay.

Scott entered the room moments later with a look of horror.

"What the hell happened?" he asked, rushing over to me and the young woman.

"I d-d-don't know," I stuttered. I shook my head. There was a lot to process. I assumed from Scott's shocked look that the young woman wasn't his only surprise. He'd assessed the scene when he'd come in.

"I found her like this, and Liam was sitting like that," I lied, pointing to Liam. I didn't want to lie to Scott, but Liam needed help. Mentally, he was unstable, and he deserved proper care. I knew people who were mentally ill, and individuals like him often didn't receive the needed treatment. I had failed Liam. Failed to see the signs until it was too late. If I could just get him help, he could get better.

"Let me get her out of here. I'll take her downstairs." He had accepted my lie. He took the young woman from me, protecting her, shielding her with his body.

"There are no signs of Walsh," he said as I watched him carry her away. I wondered if she'd be okay. I hoped I'd gotten here in time. I hoped she would recover.

I glanced over at Liam. He looked troubled, confused, and even a little bit mad. I walked slowly over to him. He stared at me, but it felt as if he weren't really looking at me. His eyes were distant. I shuddered and goose bumps formed on my arms.

"Liam..." I whispered cautiously. I crouched down in front of him and reached out to touch his knee in comfort.

He jerked away, as if fearful of my touch. After a moment, he blinked, almost deliberately, and then looked directly at me. His eyes blazed, and not a hint of the goodness I knew Liam had in him peeked through. I reached for him again, hoping I wasn't too late.

"I did it, Madison. I did it all. I killed Samantha." Liam's eyes were crazed. "I cut that woman. I would have killed her, too, you know? I did it," he whispered. "I did it," he said again, his voice loud and tortured. "I did it!" Liam screamed. He started hitting his head as if trying to release something. "Go away!" he shouted. Clumps of hair came out as he pulled at his scalp.

"Shhh… It's okay. It's not your fault." I smoothed back his hair, showing him with my movements that he could trust me.

"No, you don't get it. It's my fault. I wanted to do it. I've always wanted to do it. This is who I am." He was frantic, and he apparently couldn't accept my comfort any longer, because he stood. Liam—the man who had saved me just a couple of days earlier—gazed at me with a look of hatred and desire, and I felt like ice, like the little bit of hope that I had was drained from me leaving me cold and numb.

I was afraid he had finally succumbed to his feelings, to the darkness that had been haunting him since his youth, yet I couldn't make sense of what he was saying. He'd wanted to do this? I turned away from him, and he started laughing, a maniacal full-bellied laugh. I needed him to snap out of it. This wasn't Liam.

I smacked him across the face and his eyes quickly shifted and cleared. There he was. "Come back to me,

Liam," I pleaded. Tears slid down my cheeks, and he closed his eyes. He moved closer to me, the deep breath he took fanning across my face.

"You always smell so wonderful." He opened his eyes and smiled at me. But his eyes weren't a deep brown. They were black, and the clarity I had just seen not a second before had quickly been replaced by darkness.

I averted my eyes. I couldn't look at him. The person in front of me wasn't Liam; it couldn't be. My eyes landed on the chair in the corner, the chair my mother had once sat in at night. She'd read me stories in that chair, sung me beautiful melodies. My breath caught in my chest, because my doll now sat there. I jumped up and ran over to her. She looked so different, so worn and broken. She'd been through a lot, the poor thing. I cradled her in my arms. She'd deserved better. She'd deserved so much better. Next to her was Walsh's journal.

I reached for the journal. I'd need to read it. I wanted to read it. Maybe then, I'd understand him; understand why he'd done it all. But looking at Liam—at his pain, at his psychotic rage—it became clear to me Walsh would never make sense. Liam would never make sense.

"Madison?" Liam whispered. I ignored his call. I placed the journal back on the chair, hugged my doll closer to me, and closed my eyes. Pieces of my mother enveloped me.

"Well, isn't this special?" I opened my eyes and saw Walsh hovering in the doorway. In his hands was a knife covered in blood. "I see you found your doll. Figured you missed her. That journal, too. It'd be such an enlightening read."

His laugh was low and deep and seemed to come from the very core of him. It rattled me, but I stood my ground, unwavering. Don't let him see your fear, I thought as I got to my feet. I put my doll behind my back, to protect her. I was fixated on the knife, and whose blood it might hold.

"Where's Scott?" My voice quivered. Whose blood was on the knife? Why hadn't Scott come back? I couldn't lose him, too. I just couldn't.

"He won't be interrupting us." Walsh smiled at me. A cunning, cool smile. His eyes were filled with so much darkness, but what frightened me more was the fact that Liam's were similar, just as dark, just as evil, just as diseased. Tears stung my eyes, and my breath caught. Had Walsh killed Scott? Had Walsh really killed the only man I had ever loved?

I didn't think; I acted on instinct. Dropping the doll, and pulling the gun from my hip holster, I pointed it at Walsh.

"Ah, so you came prepared, my sweet daughter? The question is can you do it? Can you pull the trigger?" He taunted me with his words, smiling again. He didn't try to fight me. He didn't try to convince me not to kill him. He just looked at me. He wasn't afraid of death. He relished it. He closed his eyes and lifted up his arms, willing death to come for him. I couldn't give him that satisfaction. I placed my gun next to me on the table, and I pulled out my cuffs. He deserved to rot in prison. I wasn't like him. I would never be like him.

I walked toward him, but before I could cuff him, there was a loud clap, and a whizz sounded from behind me.

Splinters of bone and mushy, warm parts of Walsh's brain sprayed all over my face and body.

Stunned, I turned around to find Liam holding the gun. Fury bubbled up inside of me. Liam had killed Walsh, murdered him without any hesitation. As soon as the anger hit, though, it dissipated, and I was soothed, my being cocooned as if in a warm blanket on a cold night. I welcomed it, allowing myself to be overcome by the feeling. Walsh was gone, and I was free.

"You'd never have been free, Madison. If he wasn't dead, you'd never have been free." Liam dropped the gun and sat down on the bed. He started shaking his head. He talked softly to himself, a mantra. "I had no choice. I had to save her. I had to protect her." He said it over and over again.

Scott, my mind screamed. Liam may have killed Walsh, but Scott—Oh God, please don't let him be dead. I grabbed my doll off the floor and ran down the stairs. Scott lay at the base, a large wound on his side. Blood had soaked his shirt, and he wasn't moving. Oh God, please don't be dead. Reaching out, I touched his wound.

"Ouch," he moaned. He pushed my hand away from the wound.

"You're alive!" I exclaimed, touching his face.

"Yes, I'm alive." He seized in pain, gritting his teeth. "What happened?" His voice rose in fear at the sight of me covered in blood.

"It's Walsh's blood. Liam killed him." My eyes met his. He shook his head and tried to sit up.

"Don't worry. I'll get you help." I grabbed my walkie-talkie and told Garcia to call in backup.

I heard the rough fall of footsteps right before Marshall and Grant appeared, wielding their weapons and ready to fight.

"We heard the gunshot. Is he okay?" Grant asked, looking to me for Scott's prognosis. Marshall covered the room, remaining vigilant of anything out of the ordinary.

"Walsh is dead." I smiled at Scott. Clutching his hand in mine, I stared at him, letting what could have happened—losing him—leave my mind. I didn't need to go there. Not now. He was here, and he was alive.

Marshall cleared the room and went to take care of the young woman Liam had hurt. She sat with her on the couch, and they waited for the paramedics to come. The young woman wasn't crying, and she seemed void of all emotion. She was damaged now. I just hoped she could heal.

"Are you okay?" Grant asked me as she looked Scott over. "Here, put pressure on the wound." She took his hand and placed it on the injury.

"He'll have to stay here. We shouldn't move him," Grant said as she sat down next to Scott.

"What's with the doll, Harper? She's super creepy." Grant asked, motioning to my side. I held on to the doll tighter, and Scott spoke up first.

"Wait. That's your doll. The one that was always with you when you were younger. She's uh—well, she's a little worse for wear, isn't she?" Scott glanced at the doll, and then at me.

"She helped me through some dark times." I looked at the doll's crushed, broken face. Her eyes were empty, her body broken. She no longer signified hope. She no longer held the few happy memories of my childhood. She reminded me of the bad times. She reminded me of my stolen youth. She reminded me of my mother's horrific death.

I stood up, walked into the kitchen, opened the trash, and tossed her away with the rotten garbage. That was where she belonged. She wasn't like me anymore. I had hope. I had love. I had light in a world filled with so much dark.

When I came back into the hall, Scott looked over at me, and he gave me a gentle, understanding nod.

I sat down on the other side of him, taking his hand in mine.

"I'm going to help Garcia and Marshall." Grant said as she got up. Scott looked at me as he whispered, "Maddie, what about Liam?"

Oh, shit. I jumped up, my mind going to the dreary, deep-seated thoughts I had buried inside of myself. I realized I had succeeded in killing Walsh, but I hadn't pulled the trigger. It didn't matter. Walsh was gone. He had been removed from the world he had once tormented. But Liam. I had left him again. Left him when he'd needed me the most. I ran back up the stairs.

Please Liam, I thought desperately, let me not be too late to lead you to the light.

Chapter Twenty-Three

LIAM

"Liam?" I saw Madison creep back into the room, but when she called my name her voice was hesitant. I clutched the journal in my hands as I crouched in the corner. The voices in my head were more persistent now that she had entered. I fought them with the little bit of myself that was left. I would never hurt Madison, and I would fight until my last breath to protect her, even from myself.

Madison's concerned eyes met mine, and they filled with confusion. I knew I looked like a monster. My eyes were wild, and I could feel the darkness swirling around inside me. Oh God, what had I become?

She crouched down, and her hands found mine. I closed my eyes, feeling her warmth pulse through me. She was my heart. She would always be my heart.

"It's okay. I'm going to help you, Liam." She took me in her arms, and I felt her tears on my cheek.

The darkness pulled me in and out of consciousness. "Liam, stay with me." She cupped my face in her hands, staring intently into my eyes.

"Don't let it take you. Fight, Liam. Fight," she pleaded. I didn't want her to see me like this. I didn't want her last memories to be of me embracing the darkness. I had killed Samantha, and if it hadn't been for Madison, I would have killed that other young woman as well.

I knew no matter how far I fell, Madison would try to protect me, to save me. I rested my head against hers, and her light surrounded me.

"Madison, take this." I placed the journal in her hand, and our fingers brushed. The same feeling I had felt that first day with Madison flowed through my veins. Madison was warmth. She was the sun. She was love.

"I should have told you about your mother, but all the answers will be in here. I promise." I gently caressed her cheek. She was so beautiful, so full of life.

"I wish it could have been different, Madison, but I can't fight it anymore. Since I was a child, I've been tormented. I watched my father and random men fuck my mother. He would sell her body to the highest bidder." She gasped at my words and reached for my hand.

I knew she had guessed at parts of my past, but neither she nor I had spoken the truth aloud. Her touch helped me finish.

"I was beaten and abused my entire life. Just like you, I thought by joining the FBI and fighting crime, I could fight off the evil I felt inside me and make amends for my fucked-up past. It doesn't work, Madison. No matter how many criminals you catch, or how many demons you slay, it doesn't mask the pain you feel. You have to fight it head-on. Pretending it doesn't exist just makes it worse. But I can't fight it like you. I'm not strong enough anymore. I'm not strong like you." I reached out with my free hand and caressed her cheek. She leaned into my touch and her eyes filled with tears. Madison had been my guiding light from the beginning. I had thought she was going to help me by giving me the strength to fight the darkness, but instead she was giving me something greater.

"I have to answer for the lives I took and for the lives I would have taken." I wiped away a tear that had fallen from her somber eyes. "You have shown me how to love, how to be a selfless person. My entire life was complete shit until I met you. You have given me the courage to fight the darkness and choose the light." I kissed her on the lips. It was subtle, yet it set my body on fire. She was hesitant. I knew she loved Scott, and Reynolds deserved her love, but she let me have that moment. She didn't pull away. She relaxed against me, and she let me feel that a part of her did love me. Maybe not the love I had wanted from her, but she loved me nonetheless. I felt it in her kiss and smiled. All I had ever wanted was to be loved. "You and Scott deserve each other. You deserve so much happiness, and I know you can give each other that." I kissed her again, and I tasted her tears mingled with my own. She understood me.

I pulled out the gun from Madison's holster and put it against my head. It was cool and hard, but it was also everything I needed. "I love you, Madison." I briefly saw her reach for me, but then I was light. I was air.

I felt myself leaving my body, and there were no more voices. There was no more darkness. There was no more pain. I was surrounded by the most beautiful light as it welcomed me home.

Chapter Twenty-Four

MADISON

"Liam, no!" I screamed. I was too late. "Please God, don't take him, too." I shook Liam's body, bringing him into my arms. Blood soaked my shirt, but I didn't care. I brushed the hair and blood away from his face so I could see him more clearly, ignoring the gaping hole. He looked so peaceful, so free of his demons. I *wanted* him to be free from torment. I wanted him to be happy. I just didn't want him to leave us.

"Madison, come on, honey. You have to let him go." Grant pulled me away from Liam's lifeless body. I fell into her arms and wept against her. She held me, never once letting go.

I couldn't believe I had lost Liam, too. My entire life, I had fought to save people. I had thought if I could make amends for what had happened in my past, I wouldn't feel so pulled into the chaos and tragedy of my youth. But there I was, sitting in front of another dead person I had once cared for. And *also* again, he was dead because of me. People I loved tended to die because of me. I clung to the journal Liam had given me. He had said it would hold answers. Answers I needed. Answers I hoped would help heal my broken soul, and put the pieces of me back together.

"Grant." I placed the journal in her hands. "Please hide this for me."

She looked at me, hesitation apparent in her eyes. Grant did everything by the book and by asking her to hide evidence, she was directly going against the rules.

"I know this isn't protocol, but I need to know... I need to know what's in this." I sniffed.

"Of course. You don't even have to ask, Madison. I'll always be here for you." She smiled at me as she put the journal in her shirt and sat down next to me. They were the most sincere words I had ever heard from Grant.

We sat together until an agent named Peter Bailey came and took me downstairs into the living room. The living room I had once played in as a child. My hand held Liam's until the last minute, when Agent Bailey pulled me away and Liam's lifeless hand fell to the floor of my childhood bedroom. It felt surreal—like an out-of-body experience. Every time I closed my eyes, I saw Liam's face as he pulled the trigger.

After telling my side of the events, Agent Bailey made me repeat the story. I knew he was doing his job, but my anger resurfaced and I couldn't keep the frustration out of my voice. Uncle Tom stood in the doorway, looking so much older than when this whole mess had started. I told Bailey about what had happened, what I had seen. I let them know Liam had killed Samantha—the woman they had found in the bag. I told Bailey of Liam's confession—that Liam had raped Samantha and almost killed the other young woman—her name was Ava—as well. The young woman I had stopped him from killing. I felt like I was betraying him. Liam had reached out to me so many times, and I had pushed him away because of fear. Fear of his darkness.

Scott was whisked away in the ambulance. He'd lost a lot of blood, and the paramedics had hinted he might need surgery. Scott had wanted me to go with him, but my uncle was hell-bent on keeping me away. Paramedics fawned over me but physically I was okay. The wounds from the other day were still bandaged. Psychologically, I wasn't so sure. All I felt was numb. I asked to go to the hospital to be with Scott but my uncle said I needed to speak with the psychologist. I knew he wanted to keep an eye on me, to keep me close.

Scott had kissed me on the forehead, and before he'd left, he'd whispered words of comfort and told me he loved me. I saw the love in his eyes as he was taken away, but my heart dipped slightly as I tried not to notice the disappointment that flickered underneath. I wanted to be by his side, to talk to him about everything, but answering the procedural questions took precedence over any of my needs or wants.

Each question the psychologist asked created more chaos in my mind. I had lost Liam, and I had feared losing Scott when I'd seen him bleeding on the ground. I wouldn't have been able to handle losing Scott. There was no denying it anymore. I loved Scott. Who was I kidding? It was him, had always been him. From the day he had saved me, that blue-eyed little boy had been the love of my life.

My mind reeled with doubt as I thought about the lie I had told earlier. To protect Liam, I had said I'd found him on the floor, away from Ava, but Scott now knew that was a lie. I feared Scott didn't know that even though I'd protected Liam, Scott was who I loved. He was the one I wanted to spend the rest of my life with. I had been so indecisive, so confused about what I wanted in the beginning of our relationship. I wasn't sure if Scott knew how much I loved him, and I was afraid love wouldn't be enough. Was that lie going to push Scott away?

I was deep in thought as I was taken to a hotel in Connecticut. Until the crime scene was wrapped up and Scott's condition known, it was just me with my own thoughts. Uncle Tom wasn't happy with our vigilante vendetta, but Scott had given him a heads-up about our plan, and Uncle Tom and some agents had been right behind us. If only they had been a little bit earlier, Liam might still be alive. Because we had stopped Walsh, we were called heroes and gutsy by the seasoned agents. I didn't feel like a hero. I didn't feel gutsy. I felt lost, and without Scott, I felt alone. I didn't know where my cell phone was and all I wanted was to check up on Scott. Uncle Tom said that he'd have an agent outside my door if I needed anything and he'd get me an update on Scott as soon as he heard anything. I tried to get the agent that drove me to the hotel to take me to the hospital, but he refused. "Assistant Director Harper's orders," he said.

When I got to the hotel room, I went straight to the shower. The hot water ran down my body and my skin turned red in the heat. I rested my head against the cool tiles and sobbed. Deep uncontrollable sobs. My mind shifted between the loss of Liam, the loss of my mother, and the fear that I had lost Scott, too. I felt so alone, so fucking alone. I grabbed a towel from the rack and dried myself. The heat of the shower had loosened my sore muscles, and the pain had subsided a bit. I got into my pajamas and made my way to the bedroom.

A knock at the door made me jump. I had to remind myself that I shouldn't be scared anymore. That my father was gone.

"Yes?" I asked from the other side of the door.

"Sorry to disturb you but someone named Avery is here for you."

I opened the door and looked at the woman who had become my best friend.

"Thank you," I said to the agent as Grant entered the room. I shut the door behind us, but not before catching a glimpse of the sullen look in the agent's eyes.

"I won't stay long. But I wanted to give you this." She carried a small bag and gently took the journal out of it. I took it from her hands, holding it close to my chest.

"You don't understand how much this means to me." Tears threatened to break free from my eyes.

"Hey. Don't cry." She awkwardly put her arm around

me and gave me a side hug. I smiled. Physical affection wasn't exactly Grant's thing. "Remember, I said I'd do anything to help you. Even break the rules." She laughed.

"I owe you. Big time," I said as I pulled away from the hug.

"You don't owe me anything. That's what friends are for," Grant said as she opened the door to leave. "Call me if you need anything." And with that, she was gone.

I felt comfortable and at ease with Grant here. I thought about asking her to stay but I wanted to read the journal, to close the door of uncertainty that had followed me my entire life.

I went into the bedroom and lay on the bed. The down comforter was cool against me. I propped up the feathered pillows and grabbed the journal. It was heavy in my hands, as if it carried so much weight in its small frame. I opened the first page, and my heart stopped beating.

Audrey Valentina Walsh.

I stared at the penned name. I traced the letters with my finger. This hadn't been Walsh's journal; it had been my mother's. I felt a new connection to her in that moment. Her laugh came into my mind, and I shut my eyes as I remembered her smiling face.

This was it. I was finally going to get some answers.

April 16, 1989
She's here. Aimee Marie Walsh. She's beautiful. Like a little doll.
Michael hasn't held her. He won't even look at her. He scowls at her, a permanent look of disgust plastered on his face. He's changed so much in just the few short hours she's been here. I'm actually frightened to go home and be alone with him. Maybe I should take Aimee and go stay with my mother for a

while, just until he gets used to the idea of being a father. Yes, that might be for the best. I'd never let anything happen to this precious gift. She is the best thing that has ever happened to me.

April 23, 1989

I tried to leave. I tried to explain to Michael that maybe space would help him process his new responsibilities. He took her, holding her so tightly in his arms I thought she'd pop. I tried to shield her from his wrath, but when I went to grab her, he twisted my arm. I don't know what has happened to him. He has always been such a troubled man, struggling with his own monsters. But I felt the goodness in him when I first met him. I thought I could keep those monsters at bay. I was wrong.

Oh God, his eyes now. They're filled with such hatred when he looks at her. I can't leave her alone for a second, for fear of what he might do to her. I sleep in the chair in the nursery, and I watch her always.

I've caught him standing in the doorway at night, holding a knife in his hands. I think he wants to kill her.

May 2, 1989

The man I once loved is gone. He took me into the basement today, telling me he had a surprise that would make me fall for him all over again. He's been distant lately, but hasn't tried to hurt Aimee again, so for that I am thankful. I followed him down there, hope filling my heart. Then I saw her, a young girl of about seven or eight, lying on his workbench. Her lips were powder blue, her eyes wide and lifeless. I didn't scream. I couldn't form any words at all. Michael hugged me from behind, his penis hard against my back. He said this was for us; this new adventure would be our little secret. He handed me a knife, telling me to carve her into a beautiful masterpiece. A masterpiece permanently fixed in our imaginations. A memory we could share together, always.

I refused, throwing the knife on the ground, and he actually smiled at me. I get sick to my stomach just remembering that smile. He picked the knife up calmly, placing it back into the palm of my hand. He said if I didn't do this with him, he'd kill Aimee.

He hates her.

Hates her so much.

He said this would bring us back together. It would bring back the love Aimee had taken from him.

...I should have run. I should have taken my Aimee and left. But I couldn't. The look in his eyes was pure determination and murderous rage. So I took it. I took that knife, and I sliced into that beautiful young girl. Oh, God. That poor baby. No matter how many times I washed my hands today, I couldn't get the feeling of her blood off me.

It's worth it, though. It's so worth it. Looking into Aimee's face, the softness of her skin and the light that shines in her eyes... I'd do anything to keep that light. I'd kill for her.

Tears stung my eyes as the words my mother had written reached into my soul. She had been my constant, my love, and my light during the hardest times of my childhood. She had given so much of herself for me, to protect me from my father. I flipped to the end of the journal, to the last entry.

June 1, 1996

I can't do it anymore. The past days have been filled with so much torment, blood, and death. I tried to let one of the girls go yesterday, but Michael stood in the doorway, holding Aimee in his arms with a knife to her throat. Even at seven years old, she seemed so fragile in his arms.

His eyes were wild and hate filled as they bored into me, letting me know he could crush her at any time he wanted. I knew from the moment I brought that sweet girl into the world, he would hurt her. But seeing him with a knife to his own daughter's throat made it real—made my worries come to life, and I knew no matter what I did, no matter how many girls I cut, no matter how many times I made him believe I loved him, Aimee would never be safe.

He brought home another girl about a month ago. Her name is Macey. She's eight years old, just one year older than Aimee. I tried to comfort her, sing to her as I do to my Aimee when she is scared of the dark, scared of her father's rage. We talked about Aimee, about God, about love. Macey cried and I soothed her, but it was useless. Michael knew I was becoming more undone each day. He threatened to withhold Aimee from me until I did it. Until I cut into Macey's flesh. So, I did it.

I felt pieces of myself dying with each slice of the knife. I felt my soul leaving my body. Each time I cut poor Macey, her eyes stared into mine. She knew I did this to protect Aimee. I sang to her as I cut into her, but when Michael came to take his turn, he wasn't as kind. All I can remember is Macey's little voice telling me, "Don't look, Ms. Audrey."

As she hung there, blood seeping from her fresh wounds, I knew this was it. I couldn't do it anymore. It's only a matter of time before Aimee realizes what's going on, and then it will be too late. Michael will take her from me, forever.

Chapter Twenty-Five

MADISON

My tears hit the paper. I had forgotten about the time my father had held a knife to my neck. He had seemed distant for most of my life, spending most of his time in our basement or at his cabin, but that night he had felt my mother slipping away.

My mother had done those horrible things to protect me. I was angry she had been put in the position of having to do that to a little girl. I was disappointed she had felt the desire to protect me so much she had hurt another for me, but I wasn't angry or disappointed *with* her. In fact, I loved her more.

She had always promised to protect me, but the true meaning behind those words filled me. They allowed me a semblance peace for the first time. I wiped the tears from my face. She had been such a strong woman. She'd known Walsh would have hunted us—would have killed us—but she'd done what she'd had to, to protect her daughter. Understanding filled my chest and determination coursed through my veins. I was her daughter. Strong and steadfast, she had given me the drive I had needed to overcome the losses that plagued me throughout life. I could beat this. I refused to let the darkness overcome me.

She had tried to help Walsh, hopeful he would come around, just like I had been with Liam. No matter how hard I had tried, I could never have fixed him. Liam had known I would have tried to keep saving him; and instead, he had given me parts of myself back. Although I had had a troubled youth, I had the answers at my fingertips. I had peace.

I felt a comforting touch on my shoulder; but as quickly as it had come, it was gone.

The struggles from the past few days—my kidnapping and torture and tonight's events—had left my body aching. The shower had worn off along with the earlier adrenaline, and I felt completely bruised and broken. I closed the journal and placed it on the nightstand beside the bed. I threw on some clothes, turned out the light, and got under the covers.

My eyes adjusted to the darkness, and finally settled on the outline of the room. The pitch black made me panic. I didn't recognize my surroundings, and a tightness formed in my chest. I rolled over onto my side and faced the open window. The moonlight shined brightly, casting a shadow across my face. I was anxious, and it wasn't just the dark. There was something else. Something I couldn't put my finger on. I grasped at my chest, unsure of what feeling was welling up inside of me. Tears came to my eyes, and I stopped struggling against the thought forming in my mind.

Scott. I love Scott. I was void of all feeling without him lying beside me. My soul was incomplete. My heart ached for him. Scott wasn't just my protector anymore. Scott was the man I loved, my partner. The man I wanted to spend the rest of my life with. And in that moment, I couldn't just lie in the dark, anxious and afraid. I needed to tell him. I needed to let him know how much he meant to me. Tomorrow was never promised.

I wiped away the tears and put on my shoes. Lacing them was painful, and my legs and back screamed. I pushed away the pain, willing myself to fight. I had to see him.

Pure willpower fueled my every move, and I headed to the door.

"Harper, do you need something?" the agent at the door said. I stared daggers at the agent in the fancy suit, and he shifted uncomfortably under my glare. Now that I could really look at him, I noticed that he was a little shorter than Scott, with mocha skin like mine, but his eyes were a rich caramel color. His hair was cut short to his head, and his scalp peeked through. He looked tough as nails, but the way he shifted under my glare let me know I had him just where I wanted him.

"What's your name?" I asked, still standing in the doorway.

"Agent Torres," he answered, and his brows arched in curiosity.

"Agent Torres, please take me to Middlesex Hospital. I need to see Special Agent Reynolds, now."

"Ma'am, I have specific orders from your uncle. I mean Assistant Director Harper."

I walked closer to him, stopping only inches from his face. "I will leave with or without you, Agent Torres, so I suggest you take me or I will drop kick your ass right here!" I folded my arms across my chest, giving him the most dramatic look I could muster. I would not stand down.

He sighed as he gave it some thought.

"All right. Let's go." His shoulders slumped in defeat. I grinned with satisfaction and started walking to the car.

The ride to Middlesex Hospital took fifteen minutes. Impatience and yearning radiated from my very being. Torres tried to break the tension that floated in the car with music. I was surprised when he put on a Norah Jones CD, and "Those Sweet Words" came through the speakers. I looked at him. He smiled at me.

"Her voice calms me" was all he said. I laid my head on the seat, and listened to her sweet words. They were like a melody of my feelings.

Torres parked the car and I jumped out before the engine had even stopped. I ran to the entrance, my legs pumping beneath my sore body, ignoring his yells as I rushed ahead. I went through the automatic door, breathlessly walking to the receptionist's desk.

"Hello, how may I help you?" A young woman stared back at me. Her green eyes were lost in the atrocious purple eye shadow covering her eyelids, and her shirt did nothing to hide her youthful, perky breasts.

"Hi. I'm looking for a patient here. Scott Allen

Reynolds." I drummed my fingers against the counter, waiting for his room information.

"One moment, please."

I waited anxiously. Her bubblegum-pink manicured nails furiously typed on the keyboard, and the plinking sounds of the keys filled the quiet reception area. It was *too* quiet. I looked back. A single man sat in the corner, looking more like he was in need of a good bath than medical care.

"I'm sorry, ma'am, but I can't give you that information. Immediate family only." She looked at me without sadness or concern. She was unfazed by my pain.

I wanted to cry. I wanted to make her take those little pink nails and type on that computer again.

Torres came up behind me, out of breath and pissed off. I glanced at him, and he frowned at me, propping himself next to me at the counter.

"I'm his wife. Madison Reynolds." Those three simple words made my body roar to life. Gosh, that had sounded good. Madison Reynolds.

"Right, and I own the hospital." She rolled her eyes at me. "I can't give you the information."

"You bitch—" I lunged over the counter. Torres grabbed my arm and yanked me back.

"Ma'am, please give her the room number." Agent Torres flashed his badge. She shifted awkwardly in her chair.

"He's in room 503. Take the elevator to the fifth floor. Once you get off, take a right. Third door on the left."

The ride up on the elevator seemed like an eternity.

Torres rode with me in silence, respecting my need to reflect. I thought about the past month and a half. I thought about how much Scott and I had been through. We had agreed to be together, but I was worried now. I had lied to him. I had covered up Liam's horrific crime. Although I'd felt the need to protect Liam, to help him because of Walsh's involvement, I hadn't loved Liam the way I loved Scott. I loved Scott more than I had ever loved anybody. Reading my mother's journal and discovering her role in the crimes Walsh had committed had hurt, but the journal had also filled me with a sense of knowledge, of closure, for which I would always be grateful.

My mother had loved me. That had not changed. If anything, she had loved me more because of what she had been willing to endure. Liam had been so much like her, willing to do anything to protect himself and to protect me. But Scott—he held the key to my happiness. The key to a life I had always wanted.

I shot off the elevator and followed the perky young receptionist's directions to Scott's room. My feet felt heavy, and my heart beat wildly in my chest.

Room 503. I stopped. The door was shut, and instead of walking right in, or even knocking, I stood there, panic-stricken. Torres cleared his throat from behind me, and I turned to face him.

"None of my business, Harper, but it seems to me you should just go in there and tell him how you feel." I nodded.

"I'll stay out here." He stood right outside the door and turned around. I placed my hand on the doorknob and turned it slowly.

The sounds of beeping equipment stifled the sound of my beating heart. I looked at Scott, hooked up to all of those monitors, and my heart twisted in my chest. I walked quietly over to his bed and looked at him, taking all of him in. His chest gently rose and fell, his breathing strong.

"Are you just going to keep staring at me?" He opened his eyes.

"I had planned on it." I sat down at the edge of the bed, and smiled cautiously. I wanted to wrap myself up in his arms, but I didn't know if *he* wanted that, so I didn't get too close—not yet.

"Why are you here, Maddie?"

"I'm here—I'm here b-b-b-because—" I stuttered, unable to form words. Goddammit. *Please, just this once, let me get this out.* "I'm here because I can't live without you, Scott." I took his hand in mine, and I moved closer to him.

"I lied to you." I paused, and I felt his hand twitch. "I hope you can forgive me for that, but I need to tell you first why I lied, and also how I feel." Scott nodded gravely, and I continued. "I've always felt something was wrong with me. I'm sure you can guess why. But Liam... I felt that *if* I could save Liam, I would be okay. But that didn't matter. I never could have saved him. Despite Liam's mental health, his troubles, he helped me see you are my light and my happiness in this fucked-up world of darkness that surrounds me. I-I love you. With every ounce of my being, I love you." I couldn't look at him. My eyes bored into the floor and I tried to focus on the tiles.

"Maddie, look at me." I shook my head.

"I can't," I whispered. Tears threatened to break free.

"Why?" he questioned.

"I'm scared." I let go of his hand and grabbed on to one of my curls for comfort.

"Scared of what, Maddie?" He adjusted his position and winced in pain as he sat further up on the hospital bed.

"I'm afraid you don't love me anymore. That I pushed you away." I glanced at him from the corner of my eye. He reached out and caressed my cheek.

"Madison Sky Harper, look at me, *now*." I turned to him, and our eyes connected.

"You could never push me away. It was hard for me to watch you hold such loyalty and concern for Liam, but I never stopped loving you. I get it now, though. You had to work through your past on your own. Accept the things you couldn't change."

"I know, Scott," I said solemnly. "I read the journal that my mother kept. That Liam gave to me to help me understand. My mother did those things. She helped my father." I gulped loudly.

"I know, Maddie. Liam and I both knew she had a hand in the crimes your father committed." He brushed his hair away from his face. "We didn't want to tell you for fear it would put you over the edge. There was a right time for you to find out, and I guess tonight was that time. She did those things for you, you know? To protect you." He took my hand in his. Each time he opened his mouth, my heart beat louder against my chest. I wasn't mad he had known about my mother. He was right. I would have spiraled out of control if I had found out sooner. Scott and Liam had protected me. I could no longer fight the tears.

"Liam killed himself to end his life on his terms. He wanted to stand in the light and the goodness you helped create for him. He loved you." He looked away briefly. I knew it hurt him to admit Liam had loved me, but Scott *did* admit that truth. *For me.* "But you did help save him. Even in the end, when he was so far gone, you gave him the courage to set himself free."

A small whimper came from my lips as Scott said those words. "I love you, Scott."

"I have always loved you, Maddie. From the very first day we met." He leaned in to kiss me, and as his lips met mine, I felt such devotion, such tenderness. I ached with the sensations he was stirring in me.

"Marry me, Maddie." His statement shocked me. I looked at him with wide eyes, and his eyes were filled with sincerity. "Go over to my bag. There is a box on top. Bring it to me, baby."

I couldn't speak, my voice lost to the overwhelming emotions that surrounded me. I walked over to his bag, and my knees wobbled with each step I took. I reached in and pulled out a black box. My palms were sweaty, and I felt like I was going to faint. Marriage? With Scott? For the past month and a half, that was all I had dreamt about. Could I really have all of that happiness?

I handed him the box.

"Hell, Maddie, I wish I could give you the romantic proposal I had built up in my head, but I can't wait anymore. From that first day I saw you again, I knew I was going to marry you. Please, do me the honor of allowing me to spend the rest of my life proving to you just how much I truly love you."

He opened the box and my hand flew to my mouth. The gold ring had the most beautiful sunflower-shaped yellow diamond in the center. "I know how much you love sunflowers, and I wanted you to have something that reminded you of the good times, Maddie. I promise you I will give you a lifetime of happiness, of good times. Just say yes."

He placed the ring on my finger, and it fit perfectly. I remembered my dream of walking down the aisle surrounded by sunflowers. This dream. It had become my reality, and I couldn't picture my life with anyone else.

I thought about Liam, and how his last wish had been for me to be happy—for me to be with Scott. Because of Liam and his sacrifice, I now could embrace my happiness. Liam had been my savior. Liam had given me the strength to be happy, and to stand in the light. There was always light in the darkness, and one could not exist without the other. I had lived in the darkness for so long, I had teetered on the edge of life.

"Yes, Scott. Yes, I will marry you." The longing and the need inside me finally broke free, and my lips met his in a passionate kiss. I was his, and he was mine. It would take some time for us to heal, but we were going to get through this mess, together.

Acknowledgements

To my husband, for putting up with my crap for the past eleven years and loving me, despite all my craziness. I wouldn't want to be on this journey called life with anyone else.

To my mother: You are my rock, my savior, my voice of reason when I need it most… and my babysitter. You have given me the guidance, love, and most of all, you have given me all of yourself to help me become the best person I could be.

To my daughter: You have watched me struggle, get frustrated, be overwhelmed, and spend way too much time glued to my computer. This is for you, baby girl. Don't ever doubt how much I love you. You are, and always will be, my greatest creation.

To my students: Each and every one of you have touched my heart. Keep striving, guys! The sky's the limit.

To Theresa: You have provided me with something so invaluable—friendship. You have helped me grow as a teacher, a writer, and as a person. Thank you!

Lastly, to the entire Hot Tree Publishing Team. You rock!

Liv, thanks for reading my story and thinking it was worthy of publishing. Oh, and for loving Liam as much as I do!

Becky, thank you for taking a chance on a newbie like me. You are doing amazing things for writers and I look forward to watching the company you have built continue to grow and prosper and become even more kick-ass than it already is.

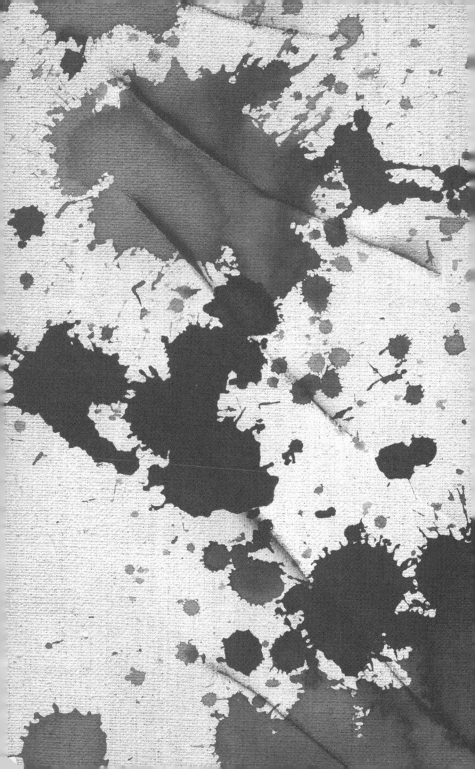

About the Author

You can find Gen curled up reading paranormal romance and romantic thrillers, or frantically typing her stories on her laptop.

Psychology is her trade by day, teaching and molding the minds of college students. Her interest in psychology can be seen in her books, each including many psychological undertones. Although she loves teaching, her passion, her true love, lays in the stories that roam around her in head. Yes, they all come from her mind-the good, the bad, and the totally insane.

She lives in Massachusetts-no not Boston-with her husband, daughter, and American Eskimo dog. With each story she shares, she hopes her love for writing and storytelling seeps through, encompassing the reader and leaving them wanting more.

Follow Gen:

Facebook: www.facebook.com/genryanauthor

Website: www.genryanbooks.com

Twitter: twitter.com/genryan15

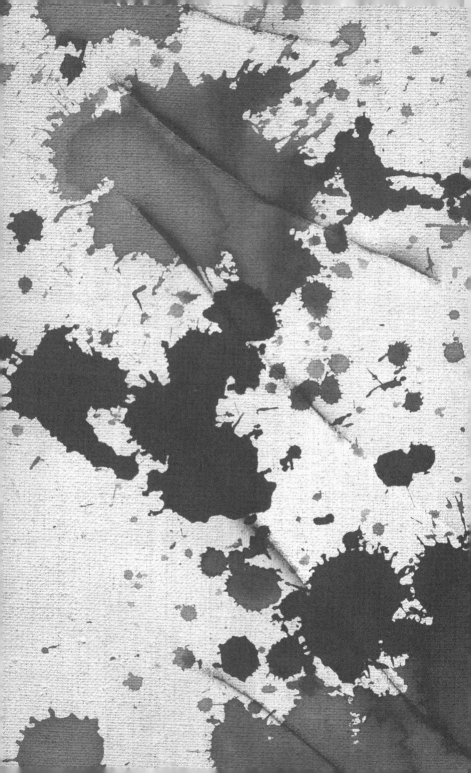

About the Publisher

Hot Tree Publishing opened its doors in 2015 with an aspiration to bring quality fiction to the world of readers. With the initial focus on romance and a wide spread of romance sub-genres, we envision opening up to alternative genres in the near future.

Firmly seated in the industry as a leading editing provider to independent authors and small publishing houses, Hot Tree Publishing is the sister company to Hot Tree Editing founded in 2012. Having established in-house editing and promotions, plus having a well-respected market presence, Hot Tree Publishing endeavors to be a leader in bringing quality stories to the world of readers.

Interested in discover more amazing reads brought to you by Hot Tree Publishing or perhaps you're interesting in submitting a manuscript and joining the HTPubs family? Either way, head over to the website for information:

www.HotTreePublishing.com